D0385892

CAROLINE TUNG RICHMOND

THE DARKEST HOUR

SCHOLASTIC PRESS/NEW YORK

Library of Congress Control Number: 2015048823

ISBN 978-0-545-80127-0

10 9 8 7 6 5 4 3 2 1   16 17 18 19 20

Printed in the U.S.A.   23

First edition, August 2016
Book design by Carol Ly

To my sister, Kristy—
one day we'll make it to France together

France

1943

ONE

My good Catholic mother taught me to never lie, cheat, or steal.

I pray she can forgive me, then, for what I've agreed to do—for this sin will be far worse.

I hurry down the cramped streets of the Marais district, leaping over the fresh rain puddles and smoothing the creases of my habit. The black skirt drags at my feet, and I hope I don't look like too much of a fraud—because I certainly feel like one.

It has been months since I've knelt for Communion and even longer since I was elbowed into a confessional booth. Yet here I am, rosary in hand, dressed like sour-faced Sister McDougal, who'd rap my knuckles in Latin class whenever she caught me reading Nancy Drew. But getting my knuckles bruised is small change compared to what I've been up to these last six months. If my mother could see me now, if she discovered what I've been training for, I'm sure she'd weep for my poor blackened soul.

But I'll tarnish my soul if that means smashing the Nazis under my boot. I owe that much to Theo, don't I?

I make a sharp right onto rue Charlemagne, a narrow wisp of a road that's crammed full of apartments with their curtains drawn.

Behind me, the sun sinks below the crumbling gray rooftops, tired after another day of this three-year war. I'm tempted to take off my veil and mop the sweat from my forehead, but you never know who's watching you these days. The old man peddling newspapers? The sweet girl playing a game of *escargot*? Almost anyone can turn into a Nazi collaborator for a few francs in their pocket. That's life in wartime Paris for you.

A church bell clangs, and I quicken my stride. My target, Monsieur Travert, won't arrive at Saint-Paul-Saint-Louis for another fifteen minutes, but I can't be late. Not this night. I've worked too hard to let Major Harken down again.

"This is your last chance, Miss Blaise," he told me an hour ago, just before he handed me the loaded pistol. "You know what to do. Stay sharp. Stay low. Don't let anyone catch a whiff that you're an American, and above all else don't get caught. There won't be anyone coming to rescue you this time. Understood?"

I'd given him a crisp "Yes, sir." Tonight won't be like the last time, when I made that one mistake and we ended up with a Class 3 crisis on our hands. I'll prove to Major Harken once and for all that I belong in Covert Operations, and that I deserve this promotion. If all goes well tonight, then he and the other girls—even Sabine—will have to call me "agent."

Agent Lucie Blaise, I think with a small smile. Theo would've gotten a kick out of that.

The smile slips promptly off my lips, however, when I hear the hum of a truck engine rumbling down the street. I don't have to turn around to know who's behind the steering wheel. There are few people left these days who can afford to drive, due to the gasoline shortage strangling France. It can only be Nazis.

The truck whines to a stop at an intersection ahead of me, and a cluster of soldiers spill out from the doors, all dressed in their crisp gray uniforms. At the sight of them, the whole block holds its breath. A wrinkled woman pedals her bicycle in the opposite direction, and a young mother snatches her children from their third-floor balcony. Meanwhile, I watch the soldiers split off into a nearby apartment building. They're probably searching for a Jew who escaped from the Drancy detention camp or a Resistance member who wasn't careful enough with his radio. Whoever it is, there's nothing I can do for them aside from muttering a prayer that tastes bitter in my mouth. That's a lesson you learn quickly under Hitler's iron fist: You can't save everyone who deserves saving, so you do the next best thing— you take out the ones who don't.

Gathering my skirt, I move silently toward my rendezvous with Monsieur Travert, but one last soldier hops out of the truck and strides down the sidewalk toward me.

Merde.

I try to retreat down a side alley, but it has been barricaded, like many others across the city. My hand itches for my pistol, but Harken told me to use it as a last resort. I'll have to rely on my wits and knife this evening, silent and deadly. That's our general plan of attack at Covert Ops—never draw attention, never leave a mess. So I dip down my chin and allow my veil to fall over my shoulders, letting the soldier see nothing except for the pale cheeks and innocent eyes of Sister Marchand, the alias I've adopted for tonight.

The slick-haired soldier raises a hand to stop me. *"Arrête! Où allez-vous?"*

Calm and collected, I remind myself. I've been trained for a moment like this.

"I said, where are you going?" he says in broken French. He can't be much older than I am, and he's a few inches shorter than me, too, but he snaps his fingers in my face like he's Napoleon himself. "Speak quickly!"

"I'm heading to the Saint-Paul-Saint-Louis church, mein Herr," I reply without any accent at all. My fluency is the only useful thing that my Parisian father has given me. We spoke strictly French in our apartment back home in Baltimore. If Papa heard anything else, I'd get the buckle.

"Where were you coming from?"

"I've spent the day at the American hospital, over in Neuilly-sur-Seine," I lie.

"The *American* hospital, eh?"

"I tend to the wounded and sick there. It's a true privilege to serve the Lord's children." I give him a humble smile. "Forgive me. The abbess is expecting me, and if you wouldn't mind—"

"Turn out your pockets."

I swallow the sourness on my tongue and reach for my skirt pocket, but apparently I'm not quick enough.

"What are you hiding? Contraband?" He throws me against the brick wall behind us so forcefully that my veil slips an inch, revealing my ash-brown hair. I try to readjust the veil, but I freeze as the soldier's hands roam over my habit. They brush over the rosary that conceals my scalpel-sharp knife, and they grope toward the very illegal pistol that's strapped to my ankle. Without thinking, my training kicks in. I twist away from his grasp, using a move that I perfected back in Washington until I realize I've shown too much of my hand. His nostrils flare wide.

Stupid, I tell myself. I should've let his meaty hands search over me, but I wasn't thinking. *So stupid, Lucie.*

"You surprised me, mein Herr," I say, in hopes that he's dense enough to believe me. "My deepest apologies."

He slaps me hard, just as Papa used to do during one of his drunken outbursts. "What's your name?"

"S-Sister Marchand."

He's about to interrogate me further, but then another soldier comes marching toward us. By the colorful markings on his lapel, he must be the commanding officer. A captain, perhaps.

Suddenly it's becoming much more difficult to remain calm and collected.

"Who have you detained now, Lieutenant Schuster?" says the captain in German. I've picked up enough of their language to follow what they're saying.

"This *sister* tried to strike me, sir. We should take her in for questioning."

The older man wrinkles his nose and juts a rough hand toward me. "Your papers." It isn't a request.

Reluctantly, I give him every document that I carry: census card, ration card, residence ID, and so on. They're all forgeries that have been crafted by the Office of Strategic Services—the mother organization to Covert Ops, based in Washington, DC—and, just like my pistol, these papers are highly illegal, too.

The captain scrutinizes each card, and my neck grows hot under my stiff collar. If he even catches a *hint* that I'm not a nun . . . An idea flashes through my head, and I snatch it before it flits away.

"Hail Mary, full of grace. The Lord is with thee," I whisper. The words tumble out of me almost like a reflex thanks to all the times I heard my mother murmur them. "Blessed art thou amongst women."

The captain sighs noisily and thrusts the papers at me. "That's enough. Hurry along."

"But, sir!" Lieutenant Schuster straightens. "We should question her at the very least."

"This stringy thing?" The captain juts a thumb at me, and for once I'm glad to be called stringy. "We'd be wasting our time."

"She's too young to have taken her vows! Look at her." The lieutenant flicks a hand at my face. "How old are you?"

"Eighteen." Another lie. I'm sixteen just, and with the right clothes I can look younger still, but even Major Harken doesn't know my real age and I don't plan on telling him.

"Eighteen? You look barely old enough to attend *lycée*," says Schuster.

The colonel shakes his head. "I said release her, Lieutenant. That's an order."

Schuster's top lip curls like a slug, and he shoots me a poisonous glare. "Get out of my sight. And don't be out after curfew, *Sister Marchand*."

"May our Lord bless you," I say in my smallest voice, and hurry past them.

One step after another, I wait for Schuster to run after me for more questioning, but I hear nothing except for the chirp of a songbird who sings a tune so sweet that if I shut my eyes, I can almost forget that Hitler conquered half of Europe before the rest of the world could lace up their boots and do something about it. Back in Maryland, the only Nazis in my life were the ones I read about in the papers or in the uncensored bits of Theo's Victory mail letters. But once those letters ran dry, that's when everything changed. A week after New Year's, I skipped school and headed to the Women's Army Corps to ask for a secretarial job—or any job, really—but the recruiter got this excited look on his face when I mentioned that I spoke fluent French. Not even six months later, I was airdropped into a new country. And now here I am, standing in Paris in its darkest hour, sent to a kill a man I hardly know.

Soon Saint-Paul-Saint-Louis looms over my head, standing proudly like a regal French king. A handful of parishioners shuffle through the front doors for evening mass, but I sneak down an alley that separates the church from the abandoned building next door. The path brings me to the church's courtyard, a simple space decorated with a wooden bench and a potted citrus tree that sweetens the air. Here, the priests and nuns come to ponder the wonders of God in between their duties, but the courtyard is empty at this hour. I adjust my veil and knock on the side door three times.

The ancient door creaks open to reveal a sliver of Father Benoit's black robes and wrinkled face. He looks a lot like the priests at my family's parish back home—old and hunched and leathery—and he frowns at me just the same. I suppose I can't blame him for that. I've asked a lot of him. Maybe too much.

"I'm sorry I'm late, Father," I whisper. "May I come in?"

Hesitation brims in his dim eyes. "I'm afraid Monsieur Travert hasn't yet arrived. You may have to return next week."

"I'm sure he's on his way." I place a careful hand on the door, a small reminder of our agreement. Father Benoit can't back out of our plans now. After weeks of coaxing, he finally decided to help us catch René Travert, who has attended Saint-Paul-Saint-Louis for decades. Father Benoit didn't want to betray a loyal parishioner, but he came around when I told him what Travert had done: how pious René accepted a handsome bribe from the Nazis and turned over two British airmen who had been stranded in France after their plane was struck down north of the city. We entrusted their care to Travert, but he delivered them like lambs to the Germans—all for a new pair of shoes and a wallet fat with cash.

I think about those airmen now, both of them so young. They were fighting the Nazis just as Theo had done, and remembering that fact will make my job easier tonight.

There's movement across the street, and I find the middle-aged Travert walking past the alleyway. My pulse jumps at the sight of him.

"I'll be discreet like we discussed," I say to Father Benoit. "Can you see to it that no one enters this courtyard for the next half hour?"

He grimaces. "Very well."

"Thank you, Father. I truly am—"

"Have mercy on René, as our Lord is merciful with all His children."

I give him a tight smile because that's the best I can do. I told him that I'd only imprison Monsieur Travert. I don't like lying to a man of the cloth, but he never would've helped me if he knew the truth of what we do in Covert Ops.

As I turn to go, Father Benoit places a heavy hand on my shoulder. "I shall say a prayer for you, my child."

He slinks back into the church, and I keep my mouth shut because I doubt he'd like what I'd have to say. The truth is, despite the clamminess in my fingertips, I don't need Father Benoit to watch over me tonight. I don't need his kind thoughts, and I certainly don't need his prayers.

But I can't say the same for Monsieur Travert.

TWO

My hand curls around my rosary while I race to intercept Travert. I had planned to greet him at his usual pew inside, but bumping into him out in the open will work in my favor. The fewer people who see me, the better. Major Harken would surely approve of that.

Travert's brown suit hugs his portly frame while his thinning hair resembles an abandoned bird's nest atop his shiny scalp. I've gotten well acquainted with Travert's balding head. For over a month now, I've been tailing him, watching him meet with his Nazi liaison in the perfumed shadows of the Tuileries Garden and seeing him smile at the leather shoes that his bribe money has afforded. I even know what he eats for breakfast—a hot cup of beef broth, thanks to the citywide coffee rations. I've learned quite a lot about Monsieur Travert, perhaps more than even his own mother.

Right before he reaches the church doors, I stumble into him and say, "I'm so sorry, monsieur!"

He jerks his elbow away but then catches sight of my face. "Sister Marchand?"

I nod; he has no clue of my true identity. To hide in plain sight, the girls of Covert Ops will dress as students or secretaries or humble sisters of the cloth, and our targets rarely give us a second glance. Little do they know that we're the blades they never see coming. For instance, Travert and "Sister Marchand" have exchanged pleasantries for weeks, ever since we discovered that he attends mass three times a week. Major Harken never thought that a traitor like Travert would be so pious, but even he can be wrong at times.

With our sights set, Harken had sent in Sabine first as usual. She had cozied up to Travert at his favorite brasserie, La Closerie des Lilas, dressed to the nines in her Clarinda alias—red lips, blond wig, and a black dress that made use of every one of her curves. But even with her Veronica Lake good looks, Travert had spent his entire meal admiring the restaurant's lilac garden instead of Sabine's carefully displayed cleavage. Afterward, Sabine had scoffed and told Harken that Travert must have been nearsighted or preferred the company of other men, but I'd seen the annoyance behind her rouge. It was the first time I had seen the unflappable Sabine look so very *flapped*, and I'd hidden my grin at that. Maybe that's petty of me, but I couldn't help it, not when she tosses me a snooty glance whenever she gets the chance.

Tilly had tried her hand next, opting for her Laverne alias, a chatty bookseller who's far too friendly for her own good. On a warm day in May, she followed Travert onto a stuffy métro car and plopped herself into the seat next to him. She had chitchatted about the Nazi-sponsored rowing regatta on the Seine and how fun it would be. Then she leaned into Travert and whispered, "They're not so bad. The Germans, I mean. Wouldn't you agree?" But he didn't look up from his newspaper.

With our options running low, it was my idea to give Sister Marchand a try, but Major Harken wouldn't hear of it. Every time I brought up the idea he'd shoo me out of his tiny office to return to his folders stamped *Classified—Zerfall*, but Tilly helped me convince him in the end. We figured that Travert might open up to a nun. And just as we hoped, he has played right into our hands.

Travert takes me by the elbow. "Are you hurt, Sister?"

"I don't believe so," I say, but I flash him a stricken look when I straighten. "Oh, my ankle!"

"Is it broken?"

"No, no, but"—I wince—"I must have rolled it."

"You poor thing." He looks at me with such pity that I know I've played him like a Glenn Miller record so far. I wish that Harken were here to see me, but he'd likely huff that my job isn't even half done. So I focus on what comes next.

Set the trap.

I throw Travert a sheepish smile. "Forgive me for asking, but might you walk me to the courtyard? There's a bench where I can rest for a bit."

Travert hesitates. I don't think he would refuse a nun, or have I misjudged him? My worries soon vanish when he offers me his arm. "Lead the way, Sister."

I lean on him while I hobble upon my poor bruised ankle. We're standing so close that I can smell the sweat staining his jacket, and I think how easy it would be to slip my dagger into his side and up into his heart, but I need to question him first. My knife will have to be patient.

Travert helps me to the bench, and before he can turn away, I pull out a box of cigarettes from my pocket.

Dangle the bait.

The box's edges have creased after jostling in my habit, but Travert stares at it like it's a treasured church relic, which isn't surprising with the war rations in full force. "A small token for your troubles?" I ask.

"Why, thank you," he says, snatching the cigarette from my hand. I mask my smile. The cigarette I gave him has been lined with sodium pentothal, a special concoction sent to us by the OSS's Research and Development branch to relax its victims and coax the truth out of them.

"Please don't tell Father Benoit that I have these." I tuck down my chin, faking embarrassment. The Nazis have outlawed smoking for women—I suppose they don't see it as very ladylike—but many Frenchwomen have skirted around the law. I offer Travert a match, and he can't seem to light the cigarette fast enough before he takes in a long draw.

"I hope your *maman* is well?" I ask, waiting for the chemicals to seep into his bloodstream. "We've missed her at mass these last few weeks."

"Her health hasn't been the best, but I'll pass along your condolences." Travert takes a seat, and I'm pleased to find his eyelids wilting like thirsty flowers. That's the calming effect of the chemicals at play.

"How has your work been going at *Je suis partout*? Will I be reading more of your articles soon?"

"Perhaps next week. My old witch of an editor has been giving me trouble about deadlines."

The sodium pentothal must be working its way into his veins. Usually Travert tells me only pleasant things about his job at *Je suis partout*, a "newspaper" that shouldn't even be called that since its pages are full of German propaganda. As he drones on, I nod and pretend to be fascinated, all the while unscrewing the rosary to release the needle-thin dagger hidden inside of it.

I decide to take my questioning in another direction.

"Tell me, monsieur," I say, "how are things going at your other job?"

"My other job?"

"You know what I mean." I drop my sugar-sweet tone and grip the knife handle, ready to block his exit if he runs. "How you've been passing Allied secrets to the Nazis."

"How did . . . ? That isn't true! I've done no such thing!" He drops the cigarette and fumbles to his feet, but I'm faster. Grabbing him by the collar, I thrust a knee into his belly to keep him from crying out before I force him to the cold stones of the courtyard.

"Don't lie to me, Travert. We've been watching you." Our noses are inches apart as I thrust the blade at the underside of his chin.

"*We?*"

I don't elaborate. I should ask him about his Nazi handlers, but with him quaking like a frightened altar boy I want to scare him a little more. I want him to feel a sliver of the fear that those airmen felt when they discovered that Travert had duped them.

"Two men died at your hands," I spit at him. "We trusted you with their lives, but you turned them over to the Germans."

"I had no choice! Maman needed her medicine and I needed—"

"New shoes? A fat cut of beef at Le Boeuf sur le Toit?" I say. His face drains of color when he realizes that I have been watching him. "The entire city might be starving, but why should you care? You're sitting at the best table in the house, drinking your Burgundy wine and ordering more sauce for your steak."

"You're mistaken! I've never set foot inside that place!"

I press the knife closer, shaving off the tips of his stubble, and that's all it takes to break him open like a summer melon. "Are you calling me a liar?"

"I didn't know!" he heaves. "Truly, I didn't know that the Nazis would kill them. Please, Sister Marchand, or whoever you are!"

"Somehow I doubt that, monsieur. Tell me the names of your Nazi liaisons. What are their ranks?"

"They never told me any such thing. You must believe me!"

I thrust my elbow into his gut because he's squealing too loudly. Thick tears course down his pathetic face, and he's begging me to think of his mother, please oh please. But I'm not Father Benoit. I can't be soft-hearted like the old priest. The Nazis robbed me of that when they killed Theo. The pain of his passing still chafes at my heart, and I'll never stop regretting that I didn't make things right between us before he died.

Travert and I go back and forth, but his answer remains the same: He doesn't know his liaisons' names or ranks. My mouth forms a grim line because I doubt that he's lying. The chemicals should have drawn the truth out of him by now. With the interrogation finished, I need to be quick about what comes next. A slash across the throat, a simple flick of the handle, and that will be that. The mission complete.

Be done with it, Lucie.

I pull back my hand, but my fingers tremble and my palms fill with sweat. I nearly curse aloud. My instructors told me that this might happen, that the nerves always come before the first kill, but I was sure I wouldn't have any problems taking out Travert. He's a traitor. A coward. But the trembling worsens.

Merde. What's wrong with me?

Travert gasps out, "Zerfall! I have information about Operation Zerfall."

I snap back into the moment, blinking hard at him. *Zerfall.* For weeks, I've seen Harken's desk buried in files that are stamped with that word.

"I'll tell you all about it!" he continues. "It'll change the course of the war!"

For that, I decide to spare him a moment longer. "What do you know exactly?"

Hope shines on his face. "If I tell you, will you let me live?"

I can't allow that, but I say what he wants to hear. "Tell me everything you've heard, and I won't cut you like a prized pig."

"You promise—?"

I push the blade a hair deeper. "You're not the one doing the negotiations." For good measure, I slide the knife toward the spot of flesh right under his chin, soft as my mother's clafouti pudding. "Talk."

"It's a classified operation." He talks so quickly that his words knock into each other like bowling pins. "I heard the Nazis whispering about it right before one of our meetings."

"What else?"

"They said the Führer had devised the operation himself. It's led by . . . Oh, what was the name? Reinhard! Yes, that's it. A man named Reinhard is in charge of it."

"What exactly does this operation entail?"

"They didn't say but"—his voice registers an octave higher when I drive the blade deeper, breaking skin—"it's supposed to change the course of the war."

"How?"

"I don't know!" He releases a sob. "I don't know, I don't know."

His cries shake his whole body, and I doubt I'll get anything more out of him. *Finish him now*, I can hear Harken telling me.

"That's all I know," he wails. "You told me you'd spare me if I told you everything I knew. You promised!"

"I promised you nothing," I whisper. I grip the knife tighter but the trembling returns double-fold and I stare at my hand. What's wrong with me? I try to shove my nerves away, but just then a truck engine roars down the road. My head jerks up automatically, and that's all the time Travert needs to push me off.

"Hilfe!" he screams in frantic German. *"Hilfe!"*

I scramble to my feet, but my shoe catches on my skirt hem and my knees crash against the street stones. I swear even louder. Travert has seen my face. If I don't get to him soon, my skinny neck will be on the line with an arrest to follow soon after.

"She's going to kill me!" Travert says, mere strides from the street.

My fingers are still quivering as I pocket the dagger and reach for my gun. Subtlety won't be in the cards tonight. Murmuring an apology to Major Harken, I take aim and shoot the Welrod 9mm pistol, but something malfunctions. With my pulse pounding hard, I slap the magazine and fire again. This time the bullet strikes home.

Travert cries out and staggers across the street. He teeters at the edge of the Seine, the river that splits the city in half. Gravity wins out and he tumbles over the stone embankment. I hear a splash and nothing more.

Relief hits me first, followed by a queasy shaking in my gut. But before I can think about what I've done, the sound of muffled German shouts infiltrate my ears. Nazis. The patrols must have heard Travert's cries.

I need to run, but first I have to make sure that he's dead. Springing down the road, I peer into the river to find Travert floating in the black waters, his shirt ballooning around him. His broad chest has gone still, even though it was thick with breath a moment ago.

Target #53 has been eliminated.

The shouts close in on me, but I linger where I stand, frozen still. Tilly once told me about this moment. This first kill. I thought I was prepared, but . . .

Move. I need to move. Ignoring the nausea swishing in my stomach, I rush back through the alley just as the church's side door swings open. Whirling around, I aim the pistol one more time and find Father Benoit gaping at me. He stares at the gun barrel and holds up his liver-spotted hands.

"What have you done, my child?" he whispers. "Where is René?"

I keep the barrel pointed at him, even though I don't want to shoot it. "I need your silence, Father. Swear it to me."

He hesitates before making the sign of the cross. "I won't tell the Nazis what you've done."

"You swear on it?"

"You have my word."

I let the gun drop. "Go back inside."

"May God have mercy on your soul, Sister Marchand. Or whatever your true name may be." He shuts the door and locks it in place.

That's my cue to run. I fly through the maze of empty Parisian streets, the buildings around me blurring into one gray mass. With every step I take, Father Benoit's words ring in my ears: *Whatever your true name may be.*

My skirt whooshes around my ankles and I think, *My name is Lucienne Blaise.*

I'm sixteen years old. I'm Théodore Blaise's little sister. And I'm certainly not a nun.

What I am is the newest agent in Covert Ops.

THREE

I flee across the streets of the Marais like the mice hiding in my family's apartment back home, bolting from the Nazis' sharp claws. For the first time since I parachuted into France, I'm grateful for the blackouts that strangle the country. There are no streetlights, no lamplights, not even a beam of moonlight to guide the Germans on my back—and I'll need every shadow I can get to shake them off my trail.

I dart across rue de Rivoli, right under the enormous swastika banners that hang six stories tall, and I turn onto a side street, ducking behind a shuttered boulangerie. As I catch my breath, I notice the bread counters inside, long covered in dust. They remind me of the counters at Pascal's, the bakery where my family has worked for over ten years. Six days a week, my parents minded the storefront and cash register, while Theo and I prepared baguette dough in the back, kneading and folding to the satisfaction of Mr. Richards, the owner. That was our whole existence for years: homework, bread, and earning pennies that Papa would take from us to buy more wine. The girl I was then couldn't have fathomed what I've become now.

I peel off my veil and habit, revealing the street clothes I've worn underneath, and shove them both through a hole in the glass. All the while I keep my ears peeled for the soldiers, but it's another voice that catches up with me instead.

Please, Sister, have mercy on me!

Despite the summer warmth, my fingers grow cold. *Travert.*

Tilly warned me that this might happen, because the same thing happened to her. Sometimes she'll get a haunted look on her face, and I know that she's thinking about the bomb that she planted in her first target's pied-à-terre. This is something that Covert Ops hasn't trained us for. They may have taught us how to kill—and how to do it well—but they never told us how to forget about our victims' last words. But I can't let myself regret what I've done tonight, not after the crimes that Travert committed. What if Theo had been one of those airmen who he betrayed? This is the thought I cling to as I hurry homeward.

I follow the map of Paris that I've stored in my mind, crossing over Pont Saint-Michel and entering the city's 6th district, or *arrondissement*. A left here and a right there and it isn't long until I reach the bookshop Shakespeare and Company. I enter through the tucked-away side door and lock it fast behind me, stepping into the dusty air. The store has been closed for months, ever since its owner was arrested for handing out illegal leaflets, but the place still buzzes with activity—if you know where to look.

Tiptoeing into the Middle Ages section, my fingers nudge aside a book about medieval clothing (too dry a subject for Nazi tastes) and curl around a hidden latch, which allows me to swing the bookcase forward to reveal a tiny room that's lined with banned books. But that's not all this room is hiding. I kick aside a well-worn rug to reveal a wooden hatch underneath. Covert Ops' front door.

I knock against the hatch five times, our signal that I'm a friendly, and I wait a second before unlocking it and heaving it open. A face stares up at me in the darkness.

"Sabine!" I gasp. It's a good thing I'm not holding my pistol because I might've fired off a round. "What're you doing here?"

Sabine pops her head out but doesn't ask me if I'm all right. Candlelight trickles up from the hatch, illuminating her pretty heart-shaped face. Well, *pretty* is too mild a word for her. Sabine is beautiful through and through, with Hollywood looks and flawless bronze skin. Even though it's the end of the day, there isn't a single black hair askew on her head. She might as well have stepped off the cover of *Glamour* magazine.

"Major Harken asked me to wait for you," says Sabine in French. "I've been sitting for over half an hour."

"Don't flip your wig. I'm here now, aren't I?"

"Wig?" She frowns. "I'm not wearing a wig."

"Never mind. It's something we say back home."

"I see." She sniffs.

I despise when Sabine does that. When I slurp my water? *Sniff.* Or mispronounce French slang? *Sniff.* Or roll my eyes at Major Harken? *Sniff, sniff.* After what I've gone through tonight, I'm ready to elbow her in that perfectly pointed nose of hers, but Harken would be livid if I ruined the face of his most prized protégé. He tapped her to become one of the first agents of Covert Ops thanks to her exploits in Paris as part of the homegrown French Resistance. Covert Ops may be an American organization, but half of our agents are French-born. Sabine is one of them: half French, on her father's side; half Algerian, on her mother's—and a thorn in my side in her entirety.

As she always does, Sabine gets straight to the point. "Did you kill the traitor or not?"

"Give me some room so I can get down."

"You didn't answer the question."

"I don't have to. I don't report to you." I squeeze past Sabine and climb down the ladder into our cramped quarters. A flickering candle sconce greets me at the bottom rung, the sole light source in the musty hallway. An old mirror hangs next to the sconce, and I catch a glimpse of myself in it. My hair is a sweaty wreck, and my brown eyes still have a frantic look about them, but I can breathe a little easier now that I'm home.

You'd think that Covert Ops' agents would live in a glamorous Parisian penthouse with wood-paneled walls and antique rugs, but the Nazis claimed all of those for themselves. So when the bookstore's owner offered her unused basement space to Major Harken, he said yes and moved right in. This is where he has hung his shingle for over a year, right under the Nazis' noses and they don't even know it. Frankly most Americans haven't heard of us, either.

Covert Operations—and the entire OSS, for that matter—was secretly formed under President Roosevelt's orders not long after the breakout of the war. There are over ten branches within the OSS, from Counterespionage to Censorship to Covert Operations, and we all serve the same mission: beating the Nazis through subversion, propaganda, and espionage. Although Covert Ops is a little different from the others in that we employ solely female agents. Major Harken has handpicked every trainee, too, but not all have stuck around. Some washed out early on, while others got the boot for being too mouthy, but a few have made the cut, like Sabine and a French Jew named Delphine Bernard, who has an impeccable smile and even more impeccable aim. Then there's me, I suppose. I'm the first trainee that Major Harken has taken on in months—and I have no plans on washing out like the others.

Sabine leaps down from the ladder, nimble as a Siamese cat. "Matilda hasn't yet returned from her assignment."

I nod, wishing Tilly had been the one to greet me instead of Sabine. But Tilly is busy trailing our next target: a Madame Favreau, who's suspected of spying on the Resistance for her German lover.

"Where's Major Harken?" I say as Sabine leads me down the hall. Doors flank us on both sides. There's the wardrobe closet that houses our many disguises, and there's the gadget storeroom that contains our most clever weapons, like a gun hidden in a tube of lipstick and a bomb disguised as a hairy black rat. Down the way there are several bunkrooms as well, enough to accommodate all ten of our agents if they descend upon headquarters at the same time, but that hasn't happened since I've been in France. They're too busy bombing

Nazis' barracks, sniffing out collaborators, and taking out said collaborators before reapplying their rouge and sneaking away.

When we reach Harken's office, Sabine gives the door a knock. "I've brought Lucienne as you instructed, sir." She opens the door and adds softly to me, "A word of advice—"

I shut the door before she can finish. I'm not interested in any "advice" she has for me or anything else she has to say.

"You're late," says Major Harken, his voice as dry as the bottle of vermouth behind him. His desk is piled high with files and folders, obscuring half his face. Three candlesticks, already burned down halfway, shed a flickering light over his graying hair and his grayer eyes, which seem constantly fixed in a glare, at least where I'm concerned.

I decide to speak first. Maybe if I lead with an apology, he'll be in a better mood. "I'm sorry for my tardiness, sir."

"I don't need you to be sorry. I need you to be on time," he says, not looking up from his stack of classified files, each one marked with a different name: *Berlin*, *Propaganda*, *Wunderwaffe*, and so on. There isn't anything personal of his in sight, not a picture of a wife or any memento from home. I hardly know a thing about him aside from the fact that he speaks beautiful French and that he rose up the ranks in the US Army before he got tapped to lead Covert Ops. If he had a personal life before the war, he sure doesn't mention it.

"I accomplished the mission," I tell him. "I took out the target."

Major Harken doesn't even blink. "Did you use the knife?"

I could lie to him. I could tell him that I used the knife and that was that, but I owe Harken the truth. "There was a slight snag in the plans. I had to use the pistol to finish him off."

"How many shots did you use? One?"

"Well . . . two."

Finally, he looks up. "Two?"

"I had to, sir. As a last resort, like you said."

"Did anyone hear the shots?"

I draw in a sharp breath. He's not going to like this. "There were a few patrols out, but—"

Major Harken gets up from his chair so fast that it topples over behind him. "You've waited until now to tell me that? They could've followed you! You know that full well, Blaise."

"I made sure that I lost them!" I've witnessed Major Harken's wrath before, but his face is so purple that I think he might have an aneurism. All of a sudden, I wonder if he'll demote me instead of promote me, and that makes my stomach twist into a big knot. I can't go back to Baltimore. "That's why I was late. I doubled back a few times, like you taught me. I lost them long before I crossed the Seine."

"Where's Travert's body now?"

"In the river. He fell in after I shot him."

"He *drowned*?" He shakes his head and stares at the door. "Agent Chevalier!"

There's a slight pause before Sabine pokes her head into the room. "Sir?"

"Make sure that the building is secure. Go now. Understand?"

"Understood." She heads out the door but glances back at me before it closes behind her. Her eyes linger upon me with pity, as if I'm a spider that she's about to smash with one of her fancy shoes.

I look back at Major Harken and all of my frustration with Sabine gives way under his disappointed stare. "I'm sorry, but I took out Travert like you asked me. I might've gotten a little sloppy but—"

"Sloppy isn't the half of it! You had a simple mission: Interrogate the witness, then kill him."

"I did both!"

"Hardly. If he drowned, then the Seine killed him, not you."

"He's dead either way," I offer weakly.

"A dead body floating down the Seine is not what I had in mind when I sent you on this mission. What happened to discretion?" He kneads his fingers against his temple. "We've already dealt with a Class Three with your first mission a couple months back. I'd expected much more from you this time around."

"This isn't a Class Three, though." *Not even a Four or a Five*, I want to add, but I know better than to say that.

"I can't have this, Blaise. On paper, you should be one of the best agents that Covert Ops has to offer. You know the language back to front. You've passed your training with flying colors. But you're not pulling your weight compared to the others. Tilly has worked for six months without any mix-ups, and Sabine has had a perfectly clean record."

I want to tell him that he isn't being fair, that the three of us are so different, but the truth is that he's right. If Tilly and Sabine can

29

pull off their duties, then why can't I? Despite everything I've gone through to get here—even *bled* through—I don't measure up. Tears pool in my eyes. I can't get kicked out of Covert Ops. I can't stomach returning to my parents' apartment where Papa's drunken ramblings shudder through the walls each night and where Maman never says a word about it. I can't move back into the room that I shared with Theo, staring at his cold and empty bed. When I was little he'd whisper stories to me whenever our father's yelling grew too loud. Then when we were older he'd tell me about his plans to run away to California. We'd go together: him, me, and his girlfriend, Ruth. *Don't you worry, Luce,* he'd say. *We'll go somewhere where Papa will never find us.*

But those plans shriveled once Theo died. There will be no California without him. That's why I have to convince Harken to let me stay.

"I'll do better next time," I tell him. "I promise you that, sir."

He slams both fists on his desk. "We won't win this war on promises."

"Please—"

"I don't want to hear it."

"But Travert mentioned Operation Zerfall!"

Harken freezes at the mention of that last word, dumbfounded. "What did you say?"

"Travert started talking about an 'Operation Zerfall' tonight."

His eyes darken. "What do you know about Zerfall?"

"Nothing, sir. Nothing at all, but I've seen the word on one of your files." I gesture at the folder right on his desk. "I thought it must be important."

"What did Travert tell you exactly?"

"That he overheard his handlers talking about the operation, and . . . and that it's going to change the course of the war."

Harken does something I've never see him do before—he pales. "What else did he say?"

"He mentioned a name. Supposedly there's a man named Reinhard who's in charge of the whole thing."

In the dim light, Harken gropes for a pen and paper. "I need you to tell me, word for word, what both of you said tonight." He's about to settle down onto his chair when there's a knock on the door. Sabine slides inside and I toss her a frosty glare, but she doesn't notice me. She's focused wholly on Harken.

"Major," she starts.

"What is it?"

"It's Monsieur Bordelon. He's just arrived. He says he needs to speak with you."

Harken doesn't look up. "Tell Laurent to wait."

"He said that he brings news. About the mission in Reims."

My head darts up. A mission in Reims? I hadn't heard a thing about that. Reims is a city east of Paris, about halfway to the German border. Covert Ops has had a few missions there, mostly to collect downed Allied airmen and deliver them to safety, but by the look on

Harken's face I somehow doubt that Laurent has brought news of another retrieval mission.

"Send him in," he says to Sabine before his gaze rakes over me again. "We'll continue our conversation later, Blaise."

"But . . ." I pitch my voice lower so that Sabine won't hear me. "Please give me another chance. I can't go back home—"

He points at the door. "Out. Now."

With a shaky nod, I exit his office right as the grandfatherly Laurent enters it. He's one of our most trusted contacts within the French Resistance, and he usually has a smile for Sabine, Tilly, and me. *Les filles*, he calls us. *The girls*. But tonight his face is grim. Whatever update he has brought about Reims, it has to be important enough for him to break curfew.

In the hallway, Sabine shuts Harken's door while she holds a glowing candle. "You're quite lucky. I didn't see any trace of the Nazis around the store."

I know I should ignore her, but the words leap out of my mouth anyway. "I made sure to shake the Nazis before I arrived. I'm not completely useless, you know."

She tilts her head to one side. "That's not what I said."

"You sure did imply it."

"It surprises me how sensitive you Americans can be." She sniffs. "It's as if you're looking for possible offenses."

I'm about to brush past her when we hear a pounding at the hatch. Five crisp thumps. Footfalls descend from the ladder and soon Tilly steps toward us, dressed in a plain brown dress and even plainer brown shoes, an incredibly ordinary outfit that's perfect if you want to blend into a crowd. And when you're as tall as Tilly—over five foot nine—you need every ordinary detail to count. She's certainly a sight for my sore eyes. After Harken's tongue-lashing and Sabine's gloating, I didn't realize how much I needed to see a friendly face.

"What are you two gossiping about?" Tilly says with her usual grin. She pulls off her long mahogany wig to reveal her auburn hair beneath it. "Were you talking about how pretty I am?"

Sabine's lips twitch a little, the closest she'll give to a smile. "Why, of course, Matilda," she says, using Tilly's full name. Then her mouth tightens. "Laurent is here."

"Oh?" The cheer recedes from Tilly's face. "At this hour?"

"I wouldn't retire for the night, in case Major Harken wishes to brief us. I'll be in my room." Sabine hands us the candle and disappears into the darkness. She must have eyes like an owl because I don't know how she isn't bumping into the walls or tripping over her shoes.

Tilly hooks her arm through mine and leads us to our shared bunkroom in the opposite direction. "You better fill me in on everything," she whispers, right before she flops onto her creaky cot and sets her wig on the old milk crate she uses as her nightstand. "How was the mission? Do I need to start calling you Agent Blaise from here on out?"

I wish I had better news for her, but all I can remember is Harken's fury. "I don't know. It's up to Harken, I guess," I say, deflated. She gives me a puzzled look, so I tell her everything: about Travert, about the pistol, and about the Nazis who heard the shots. When I'm finished, Tilly sighs and moves over to my bed.

"Look at it this way: You took out the target," she says, gently patting my back. "You completed your mission, and you escaped. How can Harken kick you out when you did what he sent you to do?"

"You should've seen him, though, when I told him about the patrols."

She winces. "Did he blow a fuse?"

"More like he blew every fuse in Paris."

"Let's not jump to any conclusions. He could be in one of his moods again."

"Maybe," I say, but I doubt it. Tilly hadn't been there when Harken reprimanded me. Granted, he did tell me that I was the perfect agent on paper, but paper doesn't do much good in a war zone, now, does it?

After Tilly retreats to her cot, I let out a sigh of my own and open the lone drawer of my nightstand, where I keep my valuables. To anyone else they're not really "valuable," just a square of chocolate, a bar of lavender soap, an empty glass bottle, and the V-mail letters that Theo wrote before he was killed. I carried these letters with me when I parachuted into France, and I've read them so many times that the papers have gone soft. All except for the last one. It still hurts too much to read it, even six months later.

I let the letters rest and reach for the bottle lying on top of them. It's an old soda pop bottle that I found on the street one afternoon, but it reminded me of Theo. When we were little, we'd write letters to our grandparents and stuff them into glass bottles that we'd then throw into the city harbor. We'd never even met our grandparents—and they passed away long before I reached French soil—but Theo loved talking about where those bottles might go.

"Think about it, Luce," he told me years ago. We were standing on a dock at the time, and he was staring across the bay and chewing a piece of gum. He always had something in his mouth: gum or candy or a cigarette when he got older. "Those letters could make it to Greenland or Iceland or all the way to Maman's old place in Saint-Malo."

"That's awfully far," I said. I didn't know where Greenland or Iceland were, but I did know that our mother had grown up in Saint-Malo, a whole ocean away.

"Not *that* far. I'll go there one day."

"You better bring me, too."

"If you'll fit in my suitcase."

"Theo!"

"I'm joking." He winked at me, and I could see traces of the bruise around his jaw that Papa had given him. Those bruises had been meant for me. I was the one who had burned the bakery croissants, but Theo had taken the blame when Papa saw the blackened trays. "We'll buy a big fancy sailboat."

"Could we have a butler?"

He laughed. "A butler?"

"His name will be Sir Chive. That sounds fancy, doesn't it? He'd be British."

"You sure say some crazy things." When I blushed, he slung an arm around me. "We'll call him Sir Chive if that's what you want."

"Can we bring Maman with us, too?"

"We wouldn't leave without her." He didn't mention a word about Papa, and I didn't, either. There was nothing to be said that we didn't already know—that we'd happily pile into a sailboat and turn our backs on Baltimore if that meant never seeing our father again.

I place the bottle back into place and shut the drawer tight. Harken has forbidden us to have any personal items at headquarters in case we're ever compromised, but Tilly and I have been discreet. In her own nightstand, she has hidden a small bottle of champagne that was a gift from Delphine and a silk handkerchief of her mother's that reminds her of home. Although *home* is a loose term in her case.

Tilly's family has houses all over the world—and in places I've never even heard of, like Porto and Catania. Her grandfather made a fortune in the fireworks business, and now the Fairbanks family has some of the deepest pockets in all of America—plenty to buy a seat in Congress for one uncle and a governorship for another. That's how her parents can afford their multiple mansions, though Tilly considers only one place home: the Bouvier Academy for Girls. It's the boarding school in Paris where she has lived since she was seven. She can speak French like a native, and that's one of the reasons why Major Harken tapped her for Covert Ops, along with her first-hand knowledge of explosives. She's our bang-and-burn specialist. Demolitions and sabotage.

Before I can ask Tilly about what she was up to tonight, there's a rap on the door. I sigh because it has to be Sabine.

"We'll keep our voices down," I call out, but the door opens and Sabine is nowhere in sight. It's Major Harken. Both Tilly and I jump to our feet.

"Get to the meeting room now," Harken says.

Tilly hurries toward him, although I linger in place. Does he plan on giving me the sack in front of everyone?

"Come on." Harken jabs a finger at me, and I dart out of the bunkroom.

"Is everything all right, Major?" I ask slowly, but Harken throws his hand up.

"No, nothing is all right," he snaps. Then, in the chilly dimness of the hallway, he tells us something that makes my very bones shudder. "We have a Class One crisis on our hands."

FOUR

When I arrived at headquarters three months ago, all bright-eyed and green and ready to take down Adolf Hitler single-handedly, Major Harken had brought me into the meeting room and launched into our very first briefing. It was right down to business for him, no time for chitchat, and what was the first thing he drilled me on?

Covert Ops' level of crises.

There are five levels total, ranging from the lowest infraction, a Class 5, and up to the highest, a Class 1. The lower crises will land you on desk duty for a week. That happened to Tilly a while back. She got slapped with a Class 5 for getting tailed by the Nazis and not shaking them off within a few blocks, and Harken had her rearranging the weaponry and washing everyone's sheets for a week. In the grand scheme of things, though, a 4 or 5 aren't too bad. Now, a Class 2 or 3 are more severe. Let's say the Gestapo dragged you in for an interrogation. Even if you managed to get away, you'd have to retire an entire alias, not to mention getting quarantined at headquarters until Harken deemed it safe for you to work above ground again. That's what happened to me a month after I arrived. A Class 3.

As for a Class 1, Major Harken hadn't uttered a word about it except to tell me: *If that happens—and it hasn't yet—you might as well hand in your resignation and swim back to Baltimore.*

I'd shivered then, just as I'm doing now. Filled with dread, I follow Tilly into the meeting room, ducking my head to avoid the ancient ceiling beams, and take the seat next to her. Sabine is waiting for us there and lighting a tray of pillar candles that sit atop a monstrosity of a farm table with trunk-thick legs. A map of Europe hangs on the wall opposite us, dotted with pinheads to mark where our agents are located.

Major Harken strides into the room and ignores the abundance of chairs in front of him, opting to pace in front of the map. I drum my fingers on my knee. The silence is slowly choking me, and the question tumbles out of me before I can rein it back.

"What happened in Reims, sir?"

Major Harken grips the back of a chair, kneading the wood like baguette dough. When he speaks, I hear a tremor weaving through his voice.

"They're dead," he says finally.

Dead? The shiver multiplies across my arms. He must mean our Resistance contacts. We rely on them to act as our eyes and ears around town—certainly not easy jobs, and there's always a risk that one of them might be compromised. I wonder if that's why Laurent was here.

"Who's dead?" Sabine asks. "Is it Xavier? Thierry?"

"No, I'm not talking about the Resistance." Major Harken bows his head. "Two of our agents are gone. Possibly three."

There are sharp intakes of breath around the room. Two agents dead? Maybe three?

This is far beyond a Class 1.

"Which agents were killed?" Tilly whispers.

Major Harken grips the chair harder, the veins on his hands pulsing. "Margot and Agnes were fatally shot. Delphine has been arrested."

Tilly goes chalk white, and Sabine does the same. My mind goes dizzy, spinning like I've ridden the county fair Ferris wheel too many times. The three of us may have been trained to keep our emotions trapped tightly inside our hearts, but all of that training has abandoned us now.

When Tilly speaks again, she fights to steady her voice. "The Nazis took Delphine?" There's the smallest flicker of hope in her words. "She's alive?"

"For now, yes. That's the news that Laurent has relayed to me," Harken says.

Silence falls over the room again like a death shroud. Under the table I squeeze Tilly's hand, but her fingers go limp next to mine. Delphine is one of our most seasoned agents. She's stationed in Vichy, the new seat of the French puppet government, but she stops in at headquarters every month to deliver supplies that the OSS has parachuted into the countryside. My mind flies back to the last time I saw her, just two weeks ago. She had come to deliver our newest parcel: a pile of forged francs for bribe-making, a dozen pistol pens, and a sack of potatoes to supplement our rations. But that wasn't all. In her usual Delphine way, she had brought small gifts for us, too: a precious flask of cognac for Harken; a handkerchief full of summer berries for Sabine and me; and a Barbusse novel for Tilly. Despite their ten-year age gap, they had become fast friends at the boarding school that Tilly attended and where Delphine worked as a literature teacher.

"What happened to Delphine?" I say, asking the question burning on my tongue. On all of our tongues. "Why were the three of them even sent to Reims?"

"Because I sent them there, that's why!" Harken barks. His hands slam against the table so hard that the wood shudders.

My teeth sink into my bottom lip. "Should we give you a moment alone, sir?"

"Do I look like I need a moment alone?" he snaps. Just like that, he has wiped his face clean and replaced it with his usual mask. "I called this meeting for a reason. Now, listen here. Our agents were undertaking a special mission in Reims—a mission that Delphine had spearheaded under my direction. This is all highly classified, understood?"

The three of us bob our heads.

"Good," Harken goes on. "About six weeks ago, we received a message from the local Resistance group in Reims. They believed that the Nazis have a secret operation in the works, one that they've kept very hush-hush. The Resistance in Reims had tried for months to mine more information about it, but they kept coming up empty aside from one key piece of intelligence." His gaze flickers toward me. "The Nazi code name for it was 'Operation Zerfall.'"

A chill pinches my spine, and I hear Travert's cries echoing in my ears: *I'll tell you about Zerfall. It'll change the course of the war.*

"Zerfall," Sabine says, testing out the word. "That's the German word for *decay*, is it not?"

Harken nods. "It is."

"What does this operation entail?" Tilly asks.

"That's the question, isn't it?" Harken says with a drawn-out sigh. "Could Zerfall be an airstrike? A U-boat attack? We were working around the clock—Delphine and I—but not getting anywhere. Until Delphine made a discovery. She uncovered a very promising lead in the hotel room of a Nazi lieutenant general."

"How did she manage that?" I ask.

Harken strides to the corner table to pour himself some cognac, but at the last second he reaches for the wine, likely remembering who had brought him that cognac in the first place. He throws back a long sip. "Delphine had befriended this general."

Befriended. My mind quickly fills in the blanks.

Harken continues, "She found a coded telegram that was intended for the Führer himself. It took a few more weeks for us to decipher it, but we did so with OSS help. The message said: *Zerfall near completion. Launch in August.*"

"Did the telegram mention anything else?" says Sabine. She has scooted to the very edge of her seat, ready to process Harken's words as soon as he utters them. "Early August is a month and a half away."

"Our thoughts exactly. Delphine was convinced that she could discover more information if she went to Reims. That's where the Nazi lieutenant general she 'befriended' had an office." Another sip of wine. "She decided to break into it."

"She did *what*?" Tilly blurts out.

Harken ignores her. "I didn't like the idea, but hundreds of thousands of Allied lives could depend on this one lead, and Delphine was sure that she could sneak in and out without anyone noticing. I sent Margot and Agnes with her—Margot to keep watch and Agnes to distract the guards if necessary. It was supposed to be a simple black-bag job. Break in, grab the goods, and go. After it was all over, they would radio Laurent or me. That was two days ago. I thought maybe they had trouble getting to a safe house but . . ." He trails off and doesn't finish. He doesn't have to.

Tilly hiccups, and I squeeze her hand again, but I know that we're thinking the same thing. Delphine may be alive, but for how long? She could have days, maybe weeks. She might even survive a month if she can withstand the torture, but if she breaks before then, the Germans will easily put a bullet through her head. I want to tell Tilly that everything will be all right, but even I can't lie that well. Two agents are dead and Delphine might soon join them. Nothing has been "all right" since this war started.

Though maybe we can change that.

I look up at Harken. "We need to go to Reims, sir. I know it's against protocol, but we can't leave Delphine to the Nazis. She knows too much."

"Lucie's right," Tilly jumps in. I glance at her to find iron in her eyes instead of tears. "We can be ready to leave in half an hour."

Sabine crosses her arms. "If you go to Reims, you'll be walking into your own murder. The Germans will have dozens of soldiers guarding Delphine's cell."

"Then what do you propose?" I say. "That we sit here and do nothing?"

"That's not what I said. I was merely pointing out that we shouldn't act in haste, as you've done tonight with Monsieur Travert." Her gaze cuts me like the knife in my rosary, but it softens when she turns to Tilly. "I'm sorry, Matilda, but we must be realistic. I very much respect Delphine, but if the Nazis have captured her, then the question must be asked: What if she is already dead?"

I wish I could yank out Sabine's tongue. "We can't assume that!"

"And you shouldn't assume that she's alive," Sabine replies.

"Enough of this!" Harken roars, making all of us jump. "Are you two finished flapping your lips yet? Or shall I wait?"

The heat cools from Sabine's eyes, but not by much. "My apologies, Major."

"I'm sorry," I mumble through clenched teeth.

"What are we going to do about Delphine?" Tilly says at last. "Can we reach out to Betty and Virginia? How about Georgiana or Germaine?" she asks, referring to the other agents of Covert Ops. "We could recall them and have them help us."

"You could send them a coded radio message," I add, pointing at the Type 3 Mark II transceiver tucked in the corner that we use to contact our agents as well as our OSS colleagues stationed in London. Only Harken knows how to use the device, but he has been teaching Sabine how to operate it, too.

"They're all embedded too deeply," Major Harken mutters. "I need them in the field right now. Betty is making headway in Zurich, and Virginia is too valuable to take out of Brussels. The same with Georgiana and Germaine. It has taken months to get everyone in place, and I can't get most of them out without jeopardizing their covers." He takes in a long breath and slowly releases it. "That leaves it to us to find Delphine."

My head snaps to his, as do Tilly's and Sabine's.

"We'll be outnumbered—" Sabine starts, but Major Harken raises his hand to quiet her.

"Like Blaise said, Delphine knows too much. We can't risk the Germans finding out about OSS or Covert Ops. If she tells them what she knows, it would put everything we've done in danger. It's not only our lives on the line—it's the lives of thousands of Allied soldiers who need us to cut the Nazis' feet from under them."

"Delphine wouldn't break," says Tilly.

"Everyone can break," Major Harken says darkly. "That's the truth."

"There's the suicide pill, though," says Sabine.

"She would've used it by now. The Nazis must have found it and disposed of it," Harken replies. "So that's that. We're going to Reims. We have to determine if she gave up anything during interrogation and if we're now compromised. If we can rescue her, too, all the better."

"I'll get my things straightaway," Tilly says in a rush, but Harken raises his hand again.

"We're not leaving tonight. There aren't any trains running and we don't exactly have a car at our disposal. We'll leave in the morning. Once we reach the city, we'll ascertain the situation first. If there's an opening to free Delphine, we'll take it." He glances at Tilly. "If not, we'll bring enough powder to blow the jail entirely."

Tilly freezes. "Sir—"

"It'll be our last option. If it does come to that, I'll be the one to light the fuse."

The thought of taking out one of our own—even if it's mercy to give her a quick death instead of the one the Nazis have in store for her—sickens my stomach, but we joined Covert Ops knowing what we were signing up for. If we were in Delphine's shoes, we'd choose a bomb, too, over the Nazis' little games.

"When do we depart?" Sabine says.

"We'll take the noon train to Reims. Make sure you're packed well before then."

I sit up straight. He had said *we*, hadn't he? Or was that a slip of the tongue?

Major Harken seems to sense the question I want to ask him. "You won't be coming with us, Blaise. You'll stay here at headquarters to keep watch."

That's another punch to my gut. "But—"

"The decision is made, especially considering what happened

tonight. You may have topped your class, Blaise, but you're not living in a training exercise anymore."

My throat grows tight with shame, and I look down at my hands that failed me tonight with Travert. I don't reply to Harken. What would I say to him? One botched mission is forgivable, perhaps it's even expected, but two? This isn't something my instructors had prepared me for.

Tilly clears her throat. "Sir, we may want Lucie with us in Reims. It might not be a bad idea to have a lookout."

Major Harken waves her off. "The three of you are dismissed." When we don't move fast enough for his liking, he shouts, "That's an order."

We leap out of our seats, but when I reach the doorway, I have to turn back. How am I supposed to stay here at headquarters when Delphine is in prison? Even if I went as a lookout like Tilly said, I could offer something to their mission. "Sir—"

Major Harken elbows me out of the room and slams the door on me, just an inch from my nose. I stumble back, but Tilly is there to catch me.

"Are you all right?" she whispers.

I straighten my shirt, hold my chin high. *No tears*, I tell myself.

"I'm fine," I say.

But both she and I know that it's a lie.

August 3, 1942

Dear Luce,

It's been nearly a month since you saw me off at the train station, but it feels like ages. How've you been? Miss me yet?

Guess where I'm writing you from? Right smack dab in the middle of the ocean. We weren't at base for long before they packed us into a big sardine can of a boat. I sure do wish that you and Ruthie could keep me company. We could play rummy and Ruthie could win every hand. Truth be told, though, I'm glad the two of you are at home, where you'll be safe. Besides, it's beginning to stink like an armpit in our bunkroom, and I don't think you girls would appreciate the smell.

We've been at sea now for three days, and I wouldn't mind switching out bunkmates for our old friend Sir Chive right about now. The bunkmate I do have—Gordon Paul—snores like a foghorn, but he shared his chocolate ration with me, so I guess we're square.

Other than the chocolate, the food isn't much better than pig slop. If the Germans don't kill us first, then the baked mutton will. It would be downright patriotic if Maman mailed me one of her galettes au beurre, but none of the officers will tell us where we're headed. I'm guessing ▬▬. Abner thinks ▬▬. Gordo says ▬▬▬. Can you imagine that? Me, sleeping next to a camel?

Sergeant Stanton is telling us lights out, so I better make this quick. Could you do me a favor and swing by Ruthie's place? Give her a hug for me and a big old kiss on the lips. I'm ragging you about that last part, but tell her not to worry. I'll knock off a few Nazis and be home to the two of you before you know it. Love to you both.

Theo

FIVE

That night I lie awake on my cot. Hours have passed since the briefing and all of headquarters has gone quiet, but I can't sleep. The eyes of the dead won't give me any peace tonight.

Travert's eyes come to me first, all wide and watery and begging me for mercy. I try to swat the fresh memory of him away, but as soon as I chase it off, I see Margot and Agnes. I imagine them in Reims, their eyes grim as the Nazis close in on them. I wonder if they had gone out fighting, emptying their pistols until their chambers clicked hollow. Or maybe they took the suicide pills that every agent is given before a mission, marked *L* for *lethal*. One swallow and you're gone. Nobody wants to use an L pill, of course, but sometimes you don't have a choice.

I grind my teeth and try not to think about the two of them, and I especially don't want to think about Delphine and what the Germans might be doing to her right now. So I force myself to focus on something else, *anything* else, and that's when my thoughts turn to Theo, like they always do when sleep eludes me.

Sometimes I think I'm forgetting his face, so I try to remember every detail. Theo often had this glint in his eyes, like he was thinking about a joke that our parish priest would rap his knuckles for repeating. He also had a bump in his nose and long hair that hung past his earlobes, which Papa hated. When Theo did finally cut his hair, it wasn't for our father's benefit but to join the service.

The last time I saw him alive, he was sporting that freshly clipped hair along with a new army uniform that hung past his wrists. He had already spent weeks in basic training and had come home for three days before he had to ship out. Our family went to the train station to see him off. The memory of that day has stayed crisp in my mind, like a newly developed photograph.

Papa was hungover like always, and we reached the station late, just in time for the conductor to cup his hand to his mouth and shout down the platform: "Last call! All aboard!"

Papa shuffled forward to give the first good-bye, a rough pat on Theo's back and a quick *bon courage* with his wine-stained breath. Maman went next. She started weeping into her handkerchief while Theo gave her a peck and told her how much he'd miss her crepes. Ruthie hadn't come to the station. She and Theo had said their good-byes late the night before, but I saw him scanning the crowd for her anyway. Hoping.

There was no more time to search for Ruthie, though, not with the conductor motioning toward us. Theo threaded toward the nearest car, and I sprang after him, leaving our parents behind in the busy throng.

"You'll write to me, won't you?" Theo said, smacking his gum and tucking a knuckle under my chin.

" 'Course I will."

"I'll be back before you know it." Then he mussed my hair because he saw the tears brimming in my eyes. "Don't worry that little head of yours, either. I didn't forget about California."

I blinked at him.

"What do you think I plan on doing with the cash Uncle Sam is going to give me?" he said.

So he hadn't given up on our plan. "What about Ruthie?"

"Shh," he said, and jutted a thumb in our parents' direction. They didn't know that he had a girlfriend, much less a Jewish one who Papa would never approve of. Not that Theo cared much about pleasing our father those days. He had signed up for the war without mentioning a thing to our parents. "Ruthie will come with us, too. Oh, don't make that face. You like her. Admit it."

It was true. I did like Ruth Green. I was all prepared to hate her for stealing away Theo's heart, but she won me over when she made him study for his tests and single-handedly brought his C average up to a B+. She was nothing like Theo at all. She was serious while he was all jokes. She kept the books at her mother's sewing shop, and Theo couldn't save a nickel if he wanted to. But somehow they fell for each other, and they'd been glued at the hip for almost a year.

"When I get back," he said, "we'll all hop on a bus, the three of us. Just you wait."

"You promise?"

He grinned. "When have I ever broken a promise to you?"

The train started to move, and Theo gave me a fierce hug before he jumped onto the car, a smooth move straight out of the pictures. As the engine chugged and ushered him away from me, he winked and called out, "Say a Hail Mary for me every night, won't you, Luce?"

I shouted back to him that I would, and I did him one better. When I woke up every morning, I said a prayer for him. When I folded dough after school, I whispered another. Then late at night, when I tried to ignore Papa's drunken shouts, I said two Hail Marys for Theo just as I'd promised.

Until the telegram came.

I remember that day, too. January 14, 1943. Maman collapsed onto the kitchen floor, weeping; Papa left the house and didn't return for two days. All the while the telegram sat on our dining table like a shard of glass, untouched. A Western Union emblem was printed at the top, followed by the lines: *Dear Mr. and Mrs. Blaise, The Secretary of War expresses his deepest regret* . . .

After the funeral, I dreamed of Theo for weeks. It was always the same—of him lying on a sandy battlefield in North Africa with his mouth blue and his beloved uniform shredded. It was his eyes, though, open and lifeless, that would make me wake up screaming. Maman would rush into my room while Papa would yell at me to shut my mouth. Months passed before that nightmare went away, but tonight it comes back to haunt me. This time, though, instead of Maman waking me up, it's Sabine.

"What are you doing in here?" I say groggily. Sabine rarely sets foot in my room, which means she isn't here for chitchat. She's here for a reason. "Is there an air raid?"

"No," she says plainly, and I breathe out a sigh of relief. Ever since the Americans formally entered the war, the air raids have become a regular part of life. And while it might be comforting to know that our boys are so close, they don't always hit their marks.

"Then what do you want?"

"You were having a bad dream," she says, holding up a candle that drips wax onto my covers. Her tone is unreadable; I don't know if she's chiding me or comforting me. Knowing her, it's probably the former.

I clutch my covers tight to me, a tattered shield against her words. "Is having a bad dream a crime these days?"

"No, but you were thrashing about loud enough to alert every soldier in a two-block radius. Major Harken sent me to wake you."

"Well, I'm up now. You can give Harken my apologies."

"Tell him yourself. He wants to see us in the meeting room. Matilda is already there."

"Why? I'm not going to Reims." I expect Sabine to smile at that, but her mouth tightens into the shape of a prune.

"Those were his orders. Get dressed." Before she leaves, though, she lights the candle on my nightstand, and I notice that she's dressed in her Fifine alias. Fifine is a sweet-as-sugar dressmaker who whimpers at the sight of a gun, and her wardrobe matches her purity: a strawberry-blond wig that's braided down the back and a pale yellow dress that sings pastel innocence—although I'm sure Sabine has at least two daggers strapped to her thighs and a pen that doubles as a single-shot pistol in her pocket.

I should thank her for lighting the candle for me, but my gratitude sticks in my throat. Seeing her ready to go to Reims reminds me of how I've disappointed Major Harken again.

"Don't keep the major waiting," Sabine says, and then she's gone.

I drag myself out of bed and don't bother changing out of the clothes I'd fallen asleep in last night, but I do scrub my face clean from the bowl of water on my dresser. Running water has turned into something of a joke in Paris, so we fill up our cups and pitchers whenever the pipes are working. When I reach the meeting room, I find Tilly and Major Harken sitting at the table while Sabine slices a loaf of bread and disperses a knob of cheese. I find someone else with them, too. Laurent.

"Ah, Lucie!" He gives me a giant hug beneath the doorframe. His arms are warm and strong, and I feel like I'm embracing a bear. "I wish I could stay, but I'm afraid I must hurry back to the club."

I step back, puzzled at what has caused him to return to headquarters so soon. Laurent usually visits once every two weeks to bring us information that he has gleaned from the Nazis who visit the jazz club that he owns. The soldiers who frequent Le Grand Duc have no clue that Laurent speaks fluent German. They simply see what they want to see—a black Frenchman with a limp from the Great War—and that's how Laurent has mined his precious intelligence for us, like where the Nazis are manufacturing munitions and any news about the Pacific theater of the war. As much as I enjoy Laurent's drop-ins, however, two visits from him within two consecutive days can mean only one thing—he must've brought urgent news to Harken. I wonder if there has been an update about Delphine, but he's clearly eager to leave.

Before Laurent departs he whispers, "Safe travels to you while you're gone."

"Oh, I'm not going to Reims. I'll be staying here."

"In Paris? But aren't you going to Cherbourg?"

Cherbourg? Why would I go to the northern French coast? Laurent doesn't elaborate any further, though, simply waves good-bye and disappears down the hallway.

"Join us at the table, Blaise," Major Harken says sourly, and I take the chair next to Tilly. She has donned her Laverne alias, complete with a pair of horn-rimmed glasses. Despite the night that she has had, she gives me a tired smile.

"Did Laurent bring news about Delphine, sir?" I ask.

"No, he did not," replies Major Harken. He leaves his chair to pace in front of us, and I notice that he hasn't changed since last night, either. "I'll get right to the point. There has been a change of plans. Agent Chevalier, you'll no longer be traveling to Reims."

From the look on Sabine's face, he might as well have slapped her. "I beg your pardon?"

"You'll be heading to Cherbourg." Major Harken looks over to me. "And you, Blaise, will be going with her."

I'm not sure that I heard him right. "Me?"

"Yes, you. Who else is named Blaise in this room?"

"You cannot be serious, sir!" says Sabine, her face twisting from shock to suspicion. Meanwhile, my own face is stuck in plain shock. I wonder if Major Harken is pulling my leg, but he isn't the sort to do any leg-pulling.

"What about Delphine?" Sabine says. "Yesterday you were determined to rescue her, but today you've changed your mind?"

"Far from it, and do watch your tone. Agent Fairbanks and I will continue to Reims as we discussed last night," Harken replies, "but I'm sending the two of you on a different mission."

Sabine's eyes fill with daggers. "May I speak with you in private?"

"No, you may not."

"Then might I point out that Lucienne is a trainee?"

"I'm well aware of that, yes."

"With all due respect, she's simply not ready."

"Careful, Agent Chevalier, or I'll bump you back to trainee status, too."

That makes Sabine stop talking. I feel a smile bubble up, but Major Harken turns his furrowed brow toward me.

"Don't look so smug, Blaise," he says. "You're not ready for another mission by a long shot, but you're here and you're alive and you're what I have to work with. That's why I'm sending you out—is that understood?"

His words carve a hole in my chest, but somehow I find a way to nod. "Why do you need us in Cherbourg?"

"Laurent gave me new intelligence that requires our presence. This is the type of mission that will require two of us, and since I'm running low on agents I'm sending you along."

He's criticizing me yet again, but I'll take his sharp words over desk duty. "What do you need us to do?"

In reply, Major Harken reaches into his pocket and draws out two handkerchiefs. One side of them is printed with a pretty rose pattern, but the other side shows a map. This is a common trick we use in Covert Ops, disguising maps that lead to safe houses and key locations. If it's folded and worn a certain way—say, tied around your neck—the Nazis should never notice it.

The map on this particular handkerchief shows a northern region of France called Normandy, specifically a sliver of the coast. The city of Cherbourg is charted out clearly, from its massive seaport to its neighboring villages. And at the very bottom of the kerchief, I see two lines of coded text. An address, perhaps.

Major Harken taps a finger on the code. "The first line of text is the address to a safe house in Cherbourg. You'll rendezvous with a branch of the Resistance there, and they'll take you to speak with a man called Alexander Dorner."

Dorner. That's certainly not a French name. "You want us to meet with a German?"

"He's Austrian by birth. At least he claims to be," Major Harken corrects me.

That doesn't remove the bitter taste in my mouth. Hitler himself is Austrian-born, after all.

"This man also claims to be a Nazi officer with classified information for the Allies," Major Harken goes on. "He escaped from Germany to Belgium and then made his way into France, where he made contact with the Resistance."

Tilly shakes her head. "That's quite the story."

"Nevertheless it's a story we need to check out, because Dorner supposedly has information about Operation Zerfall. He's willing to trade this information for safe passage to England. A new life in Allied territory."

"How do we know that we can trust this man?" Sabine asks coolly.

"We *can't* trust him at this point, and that's why I need you and Blaise to interrogate him. If Operation Zerfall is as important as we think it might be, we have to follow every lead." He knocks his knuckle against the map, right over Cherbourg. "Find him. Question him. If his intelligence is worth considering, take him to the village of Auderville two days from now at zero four hundred hours, at these coordinates." He moves his knuckle toward the second line of coded text. "The Brits will send a submarine to retrieve him, just north of the village. One of their agents in the Special Operations Executive will meet you on shore and take Dorner to the sub via rowboat. After that, you can return to Paris."

I jot down Major Harken's commands in my mind. "What if we think Dorner is lying?"

Harken's brow arches. "Do you really need me to answer that?"

Ah. "Understood, sir."

"If it does indeed come to that, however, Sabine will do the job. That's an order. She has never had any trouble taking out a target, and we can't botch this task."

I dip an inch lower into my seat. He doesn't have to say my name to get the message across that he's talking about me.

Sabine places her palms on the table. "Then send me in alone, sir."

"No, and that's an order, too," replies Major Harken. "Because if this Dorner *is* telling the truth, then it'll be our highest priority to get him across the Channel."

"Why not dispose of him after he tells us what we need to know?" says Sabine. She gives a little smirk. "He's a Nazi. He doesn't deserve this new life that he seeks in England."

For once, I heartily agree with her, but Major Harken blows out a long sigh.

"Be that as it may, Dorner will be more useful to us alive than dead. He'll have details concerning the Nazis' plans and inner workings, which he can share with the SOE. They'll be able to use those details to our advantage." He flicks a rare look of annoyance Sabine's way. "Besides, we're not like the Nazis. We're not cold-blooded murderers."

Sabine isn't fazed in the least that he has compared her suggestion to murder. "Still, I can get to Dorner on my own. I don't need assistance."

"Getting to the drop-off point won't be a cakewalk, not even for you. There'll be patrols and barbed wire all over the coast, especially near a major seaport like Cherbourg. That's why this will be a two-agent job." He pauses, and his voice goes gruff. "If one of you goes down, the other will finish the handoff." Before Sabine can offer another word, he slides the handkerchief over to me. "Don't lose this."

"I won't." I fold the handkerchief carefully and hold it in my hands like it's the crown jewels of England. "Thank you for—"

"That's it for our briefing," Harken cuts me off. "Gather your things and brush up on your aliases. And, Miss Blaise? You better muster some makeup to take with you, too."

"Pardon, sir?" I say, blinking. I hardly wear makeup here in Paris. It wouldn't be very fitting of Sister Marchand and it wouldn't look quite right on Bretta, my schoolgirl alias that I've been forced to retire for a few months. Which means . . .

Major Harken snorts. "Lipstick, rouge, and whatever else you need to look the part. You'll be traveling under your Fleurette Dupre alias."

"I've never used Fleurette outside of training exercises. I can't really hold a tone or—"

"You're no Dinah Shore, but you can sing well enough." He must notice how I've gone pale because he adds, "It's either Fleurette or I'll leave you here at headquarters. Your choice."

I bite back my protest. "I'll be ready as soon as possible."

"Bring the guitar, too."

My stomach flutters because he's not talking about the guitar, exactly. He's talking about the guitar *case*, the one specially made for us by the Research and Development branch. From the outside it looks like an ordinary black case, and it looks even more ordinary on the inside with its plain velvet lining. But under that lining you'll find a hidden compartment that's the perfect size for hiding pistols or tear gas canisters or a plump bag of Aunt Jemima, another OSS invention that looks and cooks like regular flour but once you add a detonator and an accelerant you'll have a powerful bomb on your hands.

Harken nods at the three of us. "You're all dismissed. We'll convene again after you've packed."

Tilly claps me on the back to congratulate me before she darts to our room, but Sabine slinks out without looking at me. She's not happy at all that Harken has paired us together, but happy or not, we're stuck with each other. These are his orders.

And I, for one, don't plan on disappointing him.

I go to the weaponry first, which is tucked inside a space that used to be a cellar, and I can almost pick up the sharp smell of onions—but there certainly aren't any onions in front of me. Instead, on shelf upon shelf, there are over a hundred items that would make any Gestapo officer salivate: lightweight submachine guns, bombs in the shape of coal, candlesticks that explode when you burn them down halfway. I take a pistol attached with a silencer and grab a razor-thin dagger that I can stick into the sheath on my inner thigh. The pens come next. I take two that double as single-shot pistols before I reach for a couple that hide thin cylinders of tear gas. I make sure to handle those very carefully. One slipup and I'll be coughing up smoke.

The wardrobe closet is my next destination. The entire space is stocked with clothes, purses, shoes, and all sorts of other accoutrements necessary to disguise ourselves on the streets of Paris. Everything looks perfectly normal at first glance, but most of the clothes conceal a deadly secret. Our blouses and skirts are sewn with hidden pockets to stow stacks of bribe money or a handy knife to jab into an unsuspecting Nazi.

I pack quickly and dress even quicker: a cream silk blouse, a soft green skirt that's full enough to hide the dagger I've strapped to my thigh, and a pair of simple black shoes that contain a little surprise—two-inch daggers in each heel. I imagine thrusting one into the neck of Lieutenant Schuster. He'd never see it coming. At the last minute, I tuck a headquarters key and an alternate stack of ID paperwork into the secret blouse pocket. Hopefully, I won't have to use those papers.

With my valise packed, I'm left with one last task: becoming Fleurette. When I return to my room, I see Tilly by her bed, pacing like Major Harken. She's all ready to go, and she motions for me to sit on her cot.

"I'll help you with the wig," she offers. "I need to keep my hands busy or else I'll go mad."

"Delphine is stronger than all of us combined. You and Major Harken might be able to get her out by tomorrow night."

"We'll see." She pins back my hair, and there's no way she can hide her trembling fingers from me.

"You're going to find her. I just know it. Besides, Major Harken might be a pain in our backsides, but you won't find a better shot in France."

"Are you saying that Harken is a better shot than I am?" She tries to grin for my sake, but I've already heard the flutter in her voice. It's her tell whenever she gets nervous. She must sense this because soon she's schooling her features like we've been taught to do. "We better hurry or Major Harken will start shouting."

I want to assure Tilly again, but the truth is that I'm scared for her. Two lone agents against an entire city of Nazis? Those chances aren't good . . . and neither are mine, when I think about it. So I focus on my alias instead, sweeping rouge over my cheekbones and painting my lips red. Though I make sure to use a light hand, because makeup is in short supply across France, and it'd look suspicious to wear too much of it. In any case, we get most of our cosmetics from Laurent's daughter Christiane, who's a saleswoman with Isabelle Lancray and sneaks us samples whenever she can spare them. If we need more, we purchase them off the black market, which has grown by the month since the Nazi takeover.

When Tilly and I are finished, a glance in the mirror reveals a girl I don't recognize. Long golden waves cascade over my shoulders, framing a powdered face that looks far older than I really am, since Fleurette is a twenty-year-old singer who earns her living in Paris's smoke-filled nightclubs. She's the sort of girl who puts on heels every morning and wears lace nightgowns to bed, and who has had more paramours than she can count, while I've never had one. Theo made sure to scare off anyone who gave me a second look. A couple years back, Phillip Frakes tried to steal a kiss from me in the cafeteria after school—and I was thinking about letting him—until Theo spotted us and said real loud, *What exactly do you think you're doing, Frakey?* Phillip ran off, and I punched Theo in the arm for being so insufferably embarrassing, but he mussed my hair like always. *Some-one's got to watch out for you, kid*, he said. I wished I could've returned the favor when he went off to North Africa.

"Blaise! Good God, how long does it take to apply some rouge?" I hear Major Harken swearing in the corridor.

I tie the handkerchief map around my neck and grab my bags, and Tilly and I hurry out to meet him.

"There you are," Major Harken says when we reach him. He's standing next to the ladder, arms tightly crossed. "You have every-thing with you?"

"Yes, sir."

"Even your L pill?"

It's a grim question, but one that needs to be asked. I pat the small silk pocket on my blouse. "Right here."

"Good. I'm sending you and Agent Chevalier out to the train sta-tion first."

"We're ready, sir."

He looks doubtful at that, but thankfully he doesn't voice it. Quickly he briefs Sabine and me on the code phrases we'll use on the Resistance and the British Special Operations Executive to signal that we're friendlies. Then he jerks his thumb toward the hatch. "Get moving. I'll see you two back here in a few days."

Before we go, Tilly shakes Sabine's hand before she tackles me in a tight hug. I hug her back, wishing we had more time for a proper good-bye and wishing that she were the one coming with me to Cherbourg.

"Bon voyage," Tilly whispers to me. "Try not to smother Sabine in her sleep if you can. You may need to keep her around."

Despite everything that has happened these last twelve hours, I grin. "Go find Delphine and bring her home."

Major Harken shakes my hand, and he attempts to shake Sabine's, too, but she has already ascended the ladder. Apparently she's still cross with him for making me tag along with her. I climb up after her, and once I reach the top I try to wave to Tilly, but I find Major Harken staring at me. I wonder if he'll tell me good luck or offer a scrap of encouragement. Maybe he'll give an enthusiastic, *Get those Jerries for me, girls.*

Instead Major Harken looks at me with tired eyes and says, "Be careful. Watch your back. And don't get killed if you can help it."

With that ringing endorsement hanging between us, he disappears into the darkness.

SIX

After the hatch closes, Sabine marches to the side entrance with her powdered chin pointed upward. If Harken's warning has rattled her, she doesn't show it. She's far too busy scowling in my direction, obviously irritated that this is *our* mission instead of hers alone.

"Are you coming?" She taps her velvet toe against the floorboards. "Or do you need another minute to say your good-byes?"

I wouldn't mind giving her a great big shove right about now. "I'm sorry. I didn't realize that wishing Tilly well was a capital offense."

She sniffs. "It's likely best if the two of you didn't get too close."

"I don't remember asking for your input."

"Take it or leave it, but war is cruel." She whirls around to unlock the door and adds, "Why do you think Harken keeps us all at arm's length?"

I open my mouth to tell her that I know full well war is cruel, but it doesn't matter because she's already out the door. *Calm and collected*, I tell myself. Dealing with Sabine's sourness is a small price to pay versus desk duty, although this Dorner fellow better be worth the headache brewing at my temples.

The June sun follows us as we head to the métro, leaving a damp handprint on the backs of our necks. I scour the streets for any glimpse of the Nazis, but I see only a long line of Parisians queuing at a bakery. Their faces sag and their hands clench like claws around their ration cards, which is smart because you never know when a thief might try to snatch your ticket from you.

I doubt my parents would recognize the Paris that I'm standing in. My father was raised in the city, and my mother moved here when she aged out of the convent orphanage in Saint-Malo. She found work at a pâtisserie in Passy, where she'd sweep floors and wipe the glass displays that protected the famous Marie Antoinette macarons bursting with raspberry and rose cream when you bit into them. A few times, she even got to taste them. Nowadays you'd be lucky to come by a full cup of sugar, and even if you did, you'd have to trade your grandmother's china set for it.

When our car arrives at the Saint-Lazare station I expect Sabine to lose me in the crowd, but she sticks next to me like a bramble on a sock. She takes my elbow and guides me across the busy road that's filled with bicycles, many of them with suitcases balanced on the handlebars—Paris's wartime taxi service. The station bustles with a swarm of people today, including Nazis. The soldiers stop a group of passengers who've arrived in Paris and demand to search their bags for black market contraband—coal, tobacco, fresh meat. An old woman cries when they discover the eggs she has hidden in her purse. I can't blame her for that. I haven't tasted an egg in weeks.

Sabine leads us to the ticket counter, where we queue for over an hour with the other passengers, some hoping to head east to Verdun while others hoping to travel south to Vichy, home of the French government. But everyone knows that Nazis are the ones pulling the strings across the country, and Premier Pétain is nothing but a dressed-up marionette.

Using our fake francs, we purchase two tickets for the late morning train. The earlier one has been canceled due to track work, and so Fifine and I settle on an open bench, pretending to laugh at each other's jokes and sharing a pouch of dried plums that Laurent left for us.

Not long after we're seated, Sabine dips her chin toward me. Her expression is as calm as the Seine on a hot day, but she whispers daggers into my ear. "Over there. Five o'clock. See him?"

A shiver slithers down my back. I pretend to check the clasp on my valise as I search for the "him" that Sabine mentioned. There he is: a Nazi officer. He's staring at us. Rather, he's staring at *me*.

"We should move," I say quietly.

"Do you recognize him?"

I don't offer an answer right away. Could Father Benoit have turned me in after all? But he knew me as prim and proper Sister Marchand, not as Fleurette. "I don't think so, but we should leave. To be safe."

With my valise in one hand and my guitar case in the other, we head to the train platform, hoping to lose the officer in the crowd, but he weaves toward us. Worse, he has increased his speed. I search for possible exits, with my pulse stammering all the way.

"You head to the restroom," I whisper to Sabine, "and I'll continue down to the platform. If he arrests me—"

Too late.

"Mademoiselle! Attendez une minute!" the soldier calls out in passable French. He reaches me within seconds and gestures at my guitar case.

"Is there a problem, mein Herr?" I banish the quiver in my voice and bat my lashes. "Would you like to see my ticket?"

The soldier surprises me by offering me a grin so white that I wonder if he gargles with bleach. "Do you play, mademoiselle? The guitar?"

It takes me a few seconds to realize that he doesn't want to search my bags—that he wants to talk about my *guitar* of all things. "Not very well. Do you, mein Herr?"

"Guitar is a hobby of mine. I have three back in Munich." He combs back his golden hair, and I have no doubt that he's a real dish back in Germany since he has a face as handsome as Errol Flynn's, but I wish he'd leave us alone. Fortunately our train has arrived early. It's pulling into the station as we speak.

"I'm afraid we have to catch our train," I say.

"This one here?" He juts a thumb at it, and his grin widens. "It's mine as well."

I mask my disappointment. "How lucky for us."

"I'm spending the day in Cherbourg. I was waiting for another fellow in my regiment to join me, but I think he may have gotten lost. It's no matter, though." He leans in closer and adds, "I can always make *new* friends."

I almost groan.

"I'm Captain Oster," he continues, "but do call me Lothar. And you two are?"

"I'm Fifine, and this is my friend Fleurette." Sabine hugs my waist like we're bosom buddies, and she discretely jabs a finger into my ribs. I know what she's trying to tell me: The train is here and we need to get away.

"I'm afraid we better get in line, mein Herr, but have a wonderful time in Cherbourg," I say. I stoop down to grab my things, but he swoops in to take both my valise and case.

"I absolutely insist. As a gentleman." Before I can protest, he walks off with my bags and cuts through the disembarking passengers like a shark barreling through a school of minnows. I hurry after him, almost begging for him to stop, but he doesn't turn around until he reaches the first-class train car.

"I'll return your bags," he says slyly, "if you say please."

I'd rather kick him in the groin, but instead I force a smile. "Please?" I say, sweet as the Marie Antoinettes my mother told me about.

He holds out the guitar case, but before I can close my hand around the handle he snatches it back and laughs.

"You naughty thing!" Sabine says, catching up to us. Her tone is playful, but I can see the irritation lurking in her eyes. "You're going to make us miss the train."

"Don't you worry. I'll make sure that you won't." He motions to the ticket collector to help with our bags. When the ticket collector points out that Sabine and I don't have first-class tickets, Captain Oster scoffs and tells us to climb aboard anyway. "Forget about those dirty dregs down in second class. Women like you deserve to travel in style." He winks and heads up into the first-class car with my case in tow.

"Get on the train," Sabine whispers behind me.

I throw her a look. "With *him*?"

"He has our case. Besides, he has taken a liking to you. We can use that to wheedle information from him." Before I can protest, she nudges me onto the steps. "Now go. We don't want to miss this train."

Reluctantly I enter the car, and I see why the Nazis have claimed the first-class seats all for themselves. The floors are freshly cleaned, and there's plenty of space to stretch your legs—quite the luxury compared to the lower-class cars, where you're usually squeezed next to a man who sneezes on you.

Captain Oster has already removed his jacket and beckons to us from the back of the car. He ushers Sabine into the seat by the window and—how fortunate for me—he guides me into the seat right next to his. After I get settled, he plucks a silver flask from his pocket and hands it to me.

"To new friends!" he says, gesturing for me to take a sip.

I'm not in the mood for whatever he's offering, but I pretend to take a taste. "To new friends," I murmur.

For the next hour Captain Oster swigs from his flask and blathers on about every nightclub he has visited in Paris until he falls fast asleep on my shoulder, utterly soused. While he snores and Sabine nods off herself, I watch the train chug toward Cherbourg, relieved that I can finally shed the fake smile that I've worn since we left Paris. Soon I'm greeted by bright green fields and a ceiling of cotton-candy clouds, so pretty that it makes me forget about our mission for a moment, but I'm tugged back to reality when Sabine starts mumbling in her sleep.

She frowns. "Jean-Luc?" she whispers. Then again, louder this time. "Jean-Luc, be careful."

She's muttering nonsense for now, but soon she might mention something about headquarters or our mission ahead. I nudge her foot with my shoe until she stirs. "You were talking in your sleep," I tell her.

"Oh." She blinks hard at me, a little dazed. "I see."

I press a finger to my lips to quiet her, because I don't want to wake up Captain Oster, but it doesn't do any good. As our train pulls into the next station, he snorts awake.

"Where are we?" he asks with a yawn.

"Nearly to Cherbourg, sleepy one," I tease.

"I slept for that long? Must've been the brandy." He looks ready to plop his head back onto my shoulder again, but he straightens when he sees someone behind us. "Ah, Friedrich! Where have you been hiding all this time? Come meet my new friends."

Footsteps approach us, crisp and quick down the carpeted path. Lovely. Another Nazi to contend with. I look up, ready to gush about how wonderful it is to meet one of Captain Oster's colleagues, but my blood freezes when I see the man standing above me.

I know him. We met just yesterday, in fact.

Sweat gathers at the base of my collar. I tell myself that my eyes must be playing tricks on me, but there's no denying it. It's Lieutenant Schuster, all right.

Merde, merde, merde.

I pin a smile to my face in spite of the gymnastics my pulse is performing. The chances of this happening must be a million to one. I wish I could tap out a warning to Sabine in Morse code, but there's no way to reach her elbow. At least Schuster doesn't seem to recognize me—yet.

I cross my legs and let a sheath of my wig fall over my face, obscuring his view of me. "Why, how do you do, mein Herr?"

Schuster hardly glances at me before focusing on Captain Oster. "I thought we'd agreed to meet in the dining car. I've been waiting there this entire time."

"Oh, don't be like that. You found me now, didn't you?" Captain Oster leans back into his seat—and half onto me—while he tosses Schuster the flask. "Loosen up, my friend. We finally have a day off and you're acting like Major Bayerlein is breathing down our necks. Enjoy the company." He tilts his head toward Sabine. "Enjoy the pretty view."

Schuster's annoyed expression sweetens slightly as he takes in Sabine. To her he asks, "It's nice to meet you . . . ?"

"Fifine," she says, holding out her hand for Schuster to kiss, which he does gladly. "You're more than welcome to join us, but my friend and I must take a quick powder first. Won't you excuse us?"

Before the boys can answer her, Sabine whisks me toward the lavatory, with her hips swishing as she goes; and more than one soldier's head bobs up to stare at her. So very typical. We squish inside the cramped space, and Sabine gets to work applying a new layer of lipstick.

"What's the matter with you?" she says. "You went almost white when that Schuster fellow joined us."

I flush because I don't want to tell her about Schuster. I don't need her wagging a finger at me, but she needs to know the truth. "I ran into Schuster last night. On my way to meet Travert."

She utters a curse so ugly that even Harken would blush. "He *saw* you?"

"Not me. Sister Marchand. He stopped me while I was heading to the church."

She braces her hands against the small sink and sighs. "Do you know the danger you've put us in?"

"Me? This isn't my fault! How was I supposed to know that he'd end up on our train?"

"Hush now! We don't want the Germans overhearing us."

I want to shout that she's the one hurling accusations at me, but I sew my lips shut. Sparring with Sabine won't keep us safe. It's risky enough that we're talking in here. "We have to change cars," I say.

"That would look even more suspicious."

"If he recognizes me, though, we're done for."

"Then you better convince him that you're truly Fleurette and not anyone else"—she huffs and unbuttons the top button of her blouse— "and I'll do what I can to distract him."

"But if he—"

"Here's some advice," she says like she always does. Then she hands me a few tissues to place in my brassiere. "You've been given assets. Use them."

When we return to our seats, Sabine employs every one of her own assets and presses the entire left side of her body against Schuster's. "Did you miss us?" she says.

Schuster goes a little slack-jawed, but it isn't long before his gaze crawls toward me once again. My cheeks warm, and I pretend to giggle at some joke that Captain Oster is telling.

"You were gone for nearly an eternity." Captain Oster pulls me toward him, so close that I can smell the brandy on his breath. Beyond the window, I notice our train pulling into the station at Lison. Thankfully it won't be long until we reach Cherbourg. If I can keep Schuster at bay until then, we'll be fine. If not . . .

Captain Oster prattles on about making plans for dinner, but Schuster ignores him and leans forward, a hard look in his eyes. "Have we met before?" he asks me.

My heart jumps. "Have we? No, I don't believe so."

"You look familiar. I'm very good with faces."

"That he is!" says Captain Oster. "Friedrich has one of those— what are they called?—photographic memories."

Just my luck, I think, but I have to keep playing my part. "Perhaps you've attended a club where I've sung, Lieutenant. Are you familiar with Le Grand Duc? Or Ciro's?"

"Oh, Ciro's!" Sabine jumps in. She must have heard the accusation in Schuster's tone, and now she's trying to draw his attention away from me. "We should go there together, Lieutenant. We'll have so much fun. What do you think?"

Schuster ignores her bait and stares back at me. "I swear that we've met."

"Fleurette often gets mistaken for others," Sabine says, hooking her arm around Schuster's. "Why, just yesterday a girl stopped us on the street because she thought Fleurette looked exactly like her sister. Remember that?" She laughs, but for some reason Schuster shoves her away from him.

"What did you say?" he says to Sabine.

She falters. "Whatever do you mean?"

"I heard you." His head snaps toward mine. *"Sister."*

My pulse stops. Schuster's spine tightens like a tuned guitar string, and Sabine's eyes widen at her mistake.

Schuster shoots out of his seat and drags me out of my own by my wrists. "I knew I'd seen you before!"

I turn my frantic eyes toward Captain Oster. Maybe Schuster will listen to him. "Please, Lothar! Your friend is mistaken. Tell him!"

Captain Oster sloppily tries to rise to his feet. "Wait one moment, there, Friedrich. That's no way to treat our new friend."

"Open your blasted eyes! These girls aren't your friends, you fool," Schuster yells. The entire train car is now staring at us. Our cover is completely blown. The train begins moving again, causing Schuster to wobble, and I break free from his grip. But he's quick to shout, "Detain her!"

The soldiers erupt from their seats. Two of them stalk toward me with their hands on their holstered pistols while another shouts at Sabine to hold up her hands.

"Close off the exits!" Schuster cries.

I search for Sabine, and she nods at me. There's only one choice left.

I duck from one soldier's outstretched hands and drive the heel of my palm into his nose. Blood pours out of his nostrils and I hear him curse, but a broken nose won't be enough to stop him. I ram an elbow into his gut, and when he stumbles back I clip him on the head with one fierce kick, knocking him unconscious. Next to me, Sabine punches Schuster in the throat—I see a little satisfied smirk on her face—and she brings a knee into his groin. He crumbles onto the floor, but before she can finish him off with the single-shot pistol pen from her blouse lapel another soldier charges toward her, and he receives a bullet in the forehead instead. The Nazis open fire.

"The case!" Sabine hisses at me.

I leap for the guitar case and throw it open, but Captain Oster yanks me by the arm before I can reach for the secret compartment. I'm ready to punch him when he says, "Who *are* you?"

Before I can respond, a gurgle comes out of his mouth, followed by a splatter of blood. The drops spray onto my blouse, and then his whole body careens forward, tumbling next to my feet. There's a bullet hole in the back of his head, round and gaping. I look up to find Sabine tossing one pen aside and pulling out another.

"Move!" she says.

There's no time to gape at what's left of Captain Oster. While we dodge gunfire, I fire off both of my single-shot pens before grabbing the two loaded pistols from the case. I toss one to Sabine. We take aim and hit a soldier in the chest, but their shots keep coming, whistling closer and closer to our ears.

"We have to get off!" I shout over the gunfire. The train is picking up speed. If we don't escape soon, we'll break our legs trying to make the jump and the Nazis will happily arrest us—and I'm sure they won't reset our broken bones.

"Get the tear gas ready!" Sabine says. "I'll cover you."

There's no time to discuss other options. I dart for the back of the car, but a soldier's fingers claw at my ankle, trying to trip me. I yank out the sheathed dagger at my thigh and slash open his knuckles. He cries out and lets me go, and I sprint down the walkway, leaving behind my guitar case and the valise full of Fleurette's silks. Bolting through the door, I scurry into the narrow vestibule between the train cars. I use one hand to fumble for my tear gas pen while the other hand fires my remaining rounds to cover for Sabine. A heartbeat later, she hurls herself through the door, landing hard next to me with her purse bundled under her arm.

"Now!" she says.

I yank off the pen cap, which sets off the canister of gas inside of it, and I toss it back into the first-class car. A white gas spews forth, and I hear the soldiers screaming and coughing before I slam the door behind us. The tear gas should buy us some time, but how much of it I don't know. A few minutes at most.

"This way!" Sabine says.

For once, I listen to her without protesting. I hike up my skirt to free my legs, and we speed into the next car, leaping over the surprised passengers and their luggage that idles in the aisle. When we reach the end of the train, I hear a faint shout far behind us.

"They're coming!" I yell to Sabine. Two soldiers are stumbling toward us, still coughing from the gas but pursuing us nonetheless. I throw my dagger at the first, and the blade hits home, plunging below his collarbone. He falls to his knees with a scream, but the other soldier merely leaps over him and keeps coming for us.

"To the back!" Sabine tells me.

We hurtle through the door that leads outside. The wind snatches at our hair and tosses strands of our wigs into our faces. I tear the whole thing off and let it fly out of my hands. The ground beneath us is a dizzying blur, and I remember the L pill in my pocket, but we can still make it off this train. Sabine pushes me forward until my stomach hits the metal railing, the last barrier between me and the tracks.

"Don't lock your knees," she tells me.

"Wait—"

"There's no time!" She turns back to fire a round, and I quash the alarm lodged in my throat.

Calm and collected.

Calm and collected.

Oh, never mind.

I clamber over the rail. The wind blasts against my body, stealing tears from my eyes, and even though I haven't done it in months, I make the sign of the cross.

"Hail Mary, full of grace," I whisper.

With that prayer on my lips, I jump.

SEVEN

It's a matter of seconds between jumping and landing, but I have to make each one of them count. During training in Washington, DC, we spent an entire week leaping out of moving cars to prepare for a moment like this. I racked up plenty of cuts to show for it, too, but this is no training exercise with a soft pallet to catch my fall. The ground rushes up, full of weeds and rock and hard earth, and I scramble to remember what I was taught.

Bend my knees.

Protect my head.

Twist my body around, preparing to roll when I land. If I don't, I could snap an arm or ankle. Or even my neck.

I hold my breath and wait for the impact. When it comes, the air gets knocked out of my lungs. I tumble over the grass, bruises forming with each collision. My head spins, and it keeps on spinning long after I come to a stop at the bottom of the muddy hill.

Seconds pass before I can breathe again. I'm lying on my stomach with my face smashed against a slick of mud. I clench my fingers and toes. Nothing appears broken, but when I try to sit up my vision goes sideways and I throw up the meager breakfast I had at headquarters.

My forehead sinks back into the mud, and I tell myself to get up. The train might be gone, but it won't take long before the Nazis double back to find us. And that's when I hear a scream.

Sabine.

I push myself up, and a shooting pain throbs at my left wrist. I can tell that it's sprained, but tending to it will have to wait because I spot Sabine not far ahead, lying curled on the ground. We're both alive, at least, but we're not alone. Schuster has followed us.

That lunatic must've jumped from the train, too, judging by the way he's limping. He doesn't seem too bothered by his leg, though, because I can see the murder written in his eyes even from where I'm standing. With his hands outstretched, he grabs Sabine by the neck and starts choking her.

I ignore the agony in my wrist and stagger toward them, watching helplessly as Sabine tries to fight him off. She begins to turn purple, and I clench my fists because they're the only weapon I've left—we had to leave all our pistols and knives behind on the train. But then I remember that I'm not as defenseless as I'd thought.

"Schuster!" I scream. I'm nearly there. "It's me that you want!"

His face jerks up and a scowl spreads over it. Underneath him, Sabine doesn't move, and I don't know if she's unconscious—or worse. While Schuster drops her and drags himself toward me, I kick off both shoes and twist off one heel. When he lunges at me, I'm ready. I jump backward and swipe at him with the hidden blade, but he's just as quick, and my knife hisses through air.

He comes at me again, and this time I don't have the room to spin away. We fall to the ground. Stars hover in my eyes, but I blink them away because he's trying to rip the knife from my fingers. Wriggling my knee free, I heave it into Schuster's belly. While he's stunned from the blow, I stab the blade between his ribs, turning his grunt into a scream. I twist the knife deeper, causing as much damage as I can, because that's what I was taught.

Schuster rolls off me, blood pouring from his wound. There's so much that it pools around him, but I haven't dealt the killing blow yet. He could survive like this, at least for an hour, enough time for help to arrive. By then, he could tell the Nazis what direction Sabine and I have fled in and give them an exact description of what we look like.

I hold the knife tight. He has to be finished off.

"What are you waiting for?"

I whirl around, the knife hot in my hands, to find Sabine heaving herself toward me. She holds one arm tight against her side, but at least she's upright and breathing.

"You're—"

"Alive. Yes," she says. She jerks her chin at Schuster, who's moaning and clutching his side, trying to keep the blood from leaking out of him. "Be done with it."

I kneel next to Schuster with my heart pumping fast. I can draw the blade across his neck or thrust it into his heart. A quick slash or twist and he'll be gone. He's already halfway there. I raise the weapon, but my palms begin to sweat, just like what happened with Travert.

"Give me the knife," Sabine says.

I jerk my hand away. This is my job, not hers. I wipe the sweat off my hands and position myself above Schuster. I couldn't ask for an easier target. He has lost too much blood to give me any fight. I locate the softest spot on his neck.

Quickly now, Lucie.

"We're running out of time," she huffs.

I thrust the blade in before she can take it from me. Schuster splutters out blood and nausea climbs through my stomach, but I harden myself against the animal sounds that he makes. If I don't, I might lose the rest of my breakfast.

Finally Schuster stops breathing, and Sabine nudges me aside to thrust her fingers at his jugular.

"He's dead." She says this without feeling and cleans her hand on the grass, leaving a smear of blood on the thick green blades. "Take the knife. We can put it to good use."

I nod but make no move to yank out the blade. I blink at my hands. My traitorous hands. Schuster was going to kill us both, and yet I hesitated. Again.

Sabine frowns, then sighs. "It'll get easier. The killing."

"Thanks for the pep talk," I shoot back. I don't want her pity.

"I wasn't mocking you. Do you think that my first mission was easy? It wasn't until my fourth that I didn't want to vomit right afterward."

Slowly, I study her. Sabine, getting a case of the nerves before a hit? I wonder if she's saying that for my benefit, but she has never been one to spare my feelings. "You could've told me that before my first mission." Who knows? It could've helped.

"I did try," she quips. Before I can call her a liar, she starts snapping orders at me. "Help me with my shoulder before the Germans send reinforcements."

"Is it broken?"

"Dislocated. I assume you were trained for this sort of injury?"

"Of course." My OSS instructors taught me first aid and beyond: cleaning wounds and sewing stitches and setting bones, because spies in the field don't often have hospitals at their disposal. It has been months since I've used my skills, but I don't tell that to Sabine. Instead I fetch her a stick to bite down on and tell her to shut her eyes.

"I'll keep them open, thank you," she replies.

"Suit yourself. Ready? On the count of three. One . . . two . . ." With one rapid motion, I realign the joint.

Sabine utters a filthy curse that would make an old French sailor blush. "You told me on the count of three!"

"Did it work or not?"

"It did," she says, glaring knives at me. "But next time, if there *is* a next time, I'd rather be ready for the pain than be taken by surprise."

"Next time, you can pop in your shoulder by yourself," I mumble, but it's not loud enough for her to hear. It doesn't matter anyway. Sabine no longer pays me any attention. She has reached into her purse—our only piece of luggage that has survived our escape—and takes out the compass and handkerchief Harken gave her. She uses both to scour our new surroundings, an unceasing patchwork of sheep pastures and apple orchards that Normandy is famed for. It almost reminds me of home.

When we were young, Maman would bring Theo and me to a farm outside the city where we'd pick strawberries as big as our thumbs. Back then Papa would join us, too, and he'd treat us all to Italian ices at Mr. Benedetti's café on the way home. This was before their restaurant closed and the drinking began. The memories of those outings course over me, but those strawberry fields didn't carry the scent of fresh blood on them like the one I'm standing in now.

Sabine swears under her breath, and I glance up.

"We're nearly fifty kilometers from Cherbourg," she tells me.

I feel like cursing myself. Looking the way we do, with dirt and blood smeared all over our clothes, we can't exactly hop onto the next train and expect to go unnoticed. We'll have to walk to the safe house through this Nazi-infested region of France.

"Do you have extra papers at least?" she asks.

Thankfully I do, as does Sabine. But not even these papers will help us reach the safe house any faster. It's not like we can double back to the train station and buy more tickets.

"We need to walk northwest." Sabine chops her hand through the air.

"Are you sure?"

"Certainly. I know this area."

"You've been here before?"

"Not *here* exactly, but yes. My father's family hails from the town of Brix. We'd spend weeks along the coast during the summer, my brother and I."

Well, that's something I never knew before. Sabine has never mentioned a brother to Tilly or me. She rarely speaks about her family or her life before Covert Ops, as if she sprouted out of the earth at the start of the war, fully formed and ready to kill Allied traitors. She's like Major Harken in that way, and I wonder if she has taken a cue from him by keeping everyone she meets an arm's length away from her.

But her revelation about her brother is neither here nor there given where we're standing. "Shouldn't you have mentioned that you've been to Normandy?" I ask.

"I didn't think it would concern you or the mission," she says with a shrug. Then she speeds ahead of me, showing no sign that she dislocated her shoulder recently or that she wears a ring of bruises around her neck.

After I stick the knife into my shoe and put them both back on, Sabine and I forge deeper into the countryside. Once we've put a few miles behind us, we turn out our pockets and dump out the contents of Sabine's purse to survey our remaining supplies. It isn't much at all: one pistol pen, one revolver with two remaining bullets, the dagger from my shoe, and a thin stack of forged francs. It's paltry pickings compared to what we left on the train. I can't help but wince thinking about all those grenades, pistols, and our bag of Aunt Jemima that now belong to the Nazis.

A gunshot pops in the distance, and Sabine shoves everything back into her purse. "Go, go!" she whispers.

I stumble to my feet but tears sting my eyes when I put too much weight on my wrist. When Sabine looks for me behind her, she scowls.

"What are you doing? We have to hurry," she says.

"I'm trying!"

"Try harder." She returns to my side and attempts to push me along, but I jerk away from her.

"If I'm holding you back, then go on without me," I snarl.

"Don't be ridiculous."

"Just go! Isn't that what you wanted in the first place?"

She looks like I've smacked her. "Why must you assume the worst about me?"

I gape at her words. *Me* assume the worst about *her*? "Ever since I set foot in Paris you've treated me like a pebble in your shoe!"

"How can you think that after all those times I've tried to help you?" She throws her hands up in the air, and I figure that she'll leave me for good now, but she does the complete opposite. She clenches on to my arm and drags me forward. "Enough of this. Major Harken gave us his orders. Move."

I try to wrest myself free from her, but Sabine only tightens her hold. I'm sure this is Harken's doing. He must have told Sabine to stick to me like glue, and that's why she's towing me through a copse of trees that look older than Charlemagne himself. Yet all the while, her question lingers in my ears. How exactly has she "helped" me over these last few months? She's always sniffing at me and correcting how I pour my tea and saying that I should hold my dagger *this* way. If that's what she calls helpful, then she can keep her henpecking to herself.

As we draw closer to Cherbourg the tiny villages grow into plump towns. More than once we have to lie flat on our stomachs as we hear a truck rolling in the distance. We've been walking for hours, but we're still miles away from the safe house.

"Stop! We have to stop," I say, panting.

"There's no time to catch our breath."

"It's not that. Look around us." I wave at the sweeping fields that we're standing in, as vast as a ripe green sea. I count three farmhouses within eyeshot, and who knows if the people living there are friendlies or German collaborators?

Sabine won't hear of it. "Let's push a little farther."

"And risk someone spotting us?" Harken may have left her in charge of this mission, but I won't let her risk our necks over this. "A little farther" could lead us right into a Nazi trap and then a prison cell. "The Nazis need only a pair of binoculars to find us out in the open."

She plants two fists on her hips, looking ready to carry me to the safe house herself, but even she must see how futile it is to keep pressing forward. "Very well," she says grudgingly. "We better wait until nightfall, but we can't stay here." She points a little ways north. "Follow me."

We settle in the shadows of an abandoned church that lies half crumbled in a fallow pasture. Its windows are long gone and a furry layer of moss has covered its stones, but it's cool and quiet and we couldn't ask for much more than that—aside from a pitcher of water and a plateful of Maman's fricasseed chicken and a great helping of her *tarte normande* for dessert. That was Theo's favorite meal, and Maman would cook it for his birthday every year. On his birthday this year, however, not long after Theo passed, Maman had spent hours shut in her bedroom while Papa had left for who knows where.

I took over both their shifts at the bakery and begged Mr. Richard not to let them go, which he halfheartedly agreed to because it wouldn't look very patriotic to fire the parents of a dead soldier.

At least Ruthie stopped by to keep me company. She didn't say much—that's Ruthie's quiet way—but she swept the floors and smiled at the customers even though she was hurting as much as I was. I couldn't help but think about the life she and Theo could've had. A house by the beach? A couple of children with Theo's smile and Ruthie's smarts? They would've called me Aunt Lucie. Thinking about all of that nearly did me in that day, especially with the weight of Theo's last letter in my pocket, but Ruthie must have sensed this and placed a warm hand on my shoulder. I wondered then what it might've felt like to have a sister.

Sabine and I take shifts sleeping. When it's my turn I try to get comfortable, but a cloud of gnats buzzes around my head and darts in and out of my ears. I manage to get in a few winks, but my eyelids are heavy when Sabine shakes me awake.

"Quiet," Sabine whispers. "It's me."

I take a long look at her, then all around us. The world has shifted since I fell asleep. The sun has vanished and has been replaced with a scattering of stars. The air has chilled, too, breathing goose bumps over my skin and making me long for a knitted blanket to wrap around myself. And that's not all that has changed.

"Where did you find those clothes?" I ask. Sabine is wearing a faded red dress with brown buttons down the front. She's also sporting new cotton stockings rather than her shredded old ones from the train.

"I took them from a clothesline. There's a little farmhouse not far from here," she explains. Then she presents me with a plain blue dress and a matching knit sweater. "We'll need these more than the farmer's wife I took them from. I left a few francs for her troubles."

"Someone could've seen you." I'm not only thinking about the farmer or his wife catching Sabine in the act. There could've been one or two Nazis billeted at that farmhouse as well. When the Germans invaded France, they didn't bother building barracks to house their soldiers. Instead they did what Nazis do best—they stole. They claimed apartments, houses, and even entire hotels for themselves.

"You think I'd be so careless?" says Sabine. She holds out the clothes for me to take. "Do you want these or not?"

I mumble a *merci* and snatch the dress from her. I'm so eager to shake off my dirty clothes that I forget to feel guilty that we've stolen a poor Frenchwoman's clothing, but field agents like us have to make do with what we have at our fingertips. After we've buried our bloodstained things, I change into the dress, which hangs off me like a paper bag. But it's clean and the sweater is soft and I hug myself at its welcome warmth. This is more than I could've asked for, but Sabine unveils another surprise that she has tucked behind the church's broken wall. A bicycle.

"I took this, too," she tells me. "It's a little rusted but it works."

I whistle at the sight of it. "You're sure no one saw you?"

"What do you think?" She smirks and shoves the handlebars at me. "Here, take it."

"Me? You're the one who found it."

"Must you argue with me over every little thing? Once the sun rises, it will be best for us to split up. The Germans will be searching for two girls traveling on foot."

I shake my head at her. "I can't take the bicycle."

"You can and you will. You're injured."

"I sprained my wrist, not my feet. Besides, I thought Major Harken wanted us to stick together."

"Major Harken isn't here." She thrusts the handlebars into my palms, along with additional supplies, like her compass and our last pistol pen. "Go. That's an order. I won't be far behind you."

I grab the handles because Harken did say she's in charge, but I'm still unsure why she doesn't take the bicycle for herself. At headquarters she's always rapping my knuckles if I try on one of her wigs or use one of her cups to drink from, but I know she's made up her mind and there's nothing I can do to change it. If she doesn't want the bicycle, I'll gladly take it. "Thanks. For the ride."

She's already shooing me off. "Stop dawdling. I'll meet you at the house, unless I make it there first."

Knowing Sabine, she isn't kidding around—and she might just beat me to Cherbourg. With one last farewell, I start down the hill and onto the dirt road. I can't help but glance back, though. I raise my hand to wave at her, and I'm surprised to hear her shout back at me.

"Don't say that I haven't helped you."

She turns her back and starts cutting through a field, and I realize finally why she insisted I take the bicycle, and a surge of guilt swells in my heart.

Maybe I've assumed the worst about her all along.

September 6, 1942

Dear Luce,

I'll give you three tries on where I'm writing you from. Ready? ███████*?* ███*?* ████████*? Nope. You'd be wrong on all counts. If you can believe it, we're in jolly old* ████████*, homeland of Sir Chive himself. We're training with the* ████ *before we have to ship out again. I sure don't mind a few days back on dry land, looking for some tea and crumpets in my off time. I don't even know what a crumpet is, but I hope it tastes better than mess hall chow.*

How's Ruthie? Did you see her yet? I think the two of you should start talking about our big California plans. She's worried about leaving her ma behind, but I think you can convince her. What's not to like about sunshine and palm trees and me? We could be strolling down the street and bump into Jimmy Stewart or Bette Davis. It'll be nothing like Baltimore. Not one lick.

I'm thinking Ruthie could find a job as a dressmaker, and you could work as a typist. I know you could pick that up quick. I'm not sure what I'll do yet. No bakery jobs for me, though. I don't plan on making another baguette ever again—and I don't want you to, either. We're going to get away from all that.

It might be a little while before you hear from me again. We're not sure where we'll be heading, though Gordo still has his money on ████████

██████. Wherever we end up, I don't want you or Maman worrying over me. Promise? We've got the best boys in the world fighting for the ol' U.S. of A., and we'll be flying the Stars and Stripes in no time. You should start planning my parade! I want floats and baton twirlers and a whole truckful of Maman's galettes. That's not too much to ask for your big brother, is it?

Theo

EIGHT

I pedal until the sun peeps over the Norman hills and until my wrist swells like a tire on a hot day. Then I grind my teeth through the pain and pedal some more, riding past the orchards filled with unripened apples and the thatched-roof village that probably hasn't changed much since the Middle Ages. Paris feels a half-world away, especially with the ocean nearby. I can't see its glimmering waves, but there's a crispness to the air, salty and fresh, that I've never smelled back in the city, unless you count a stroll through the morning fish market.

About halfway to Cherbourg, I lean the bicycle against a tired tree stump and recheck the map on my handkerchief. The cloth has been stained with dirt and sweat, but I can make out the crisscross of roads and the lines of coordinates that Harken scrawled onto it. I trail my finger over the safe house coordinates. I should arrive in a matter of hours, and my stomach tightens at the thought of the provisions waiting for me there: bread, maybe some cheese, and a pitcher of sweet, sweet water.

Dorner will be waiting there, too—for Sabine and me both.

I glance at the path behind me, expecting to find Sabine catching up to me with another bicycle that she has somehow stolen, but when I look behind me I see only the apple orchards.

"Bon voyage," I whisper. I'd forgotten to tell her that before we parted ways, and I hope I'm not too late for it now. It's strange. Yesterday I was more than ready to get rid of her, and now I'm feeling a bit sorry to leave her behind. But I tell myself that she'll be all right. She's Sabine, after all. If anything, the Nazis who cross her path should be afraid of *her*, rather than the other way around.

Just as I head down the road again, I hear the unmistakable hum of a truck. A glance over my shoulder sends a sinking feeling into my gut. It's the Nazis, all right. I plaster on a smile, like I'm nothing but a country girl enjoying the summer sun, but I wonder if that'll be enough. They could ask to see my papers, to demand where I'm going. The truck comes up behind me, and the soldier in the passenger seat sticks his head out the window, a cigarette poking out of his mouth. My heart pumps fast, but as the truck overtakes my bicycle, he winks at me.

"What're you doing tonight, baby doll?" he shouts. Then he makes a hand gesture so rude that I blush all over. If Theo were here, he'd pummel that German until his hands bloodied, but my brother isn't here to protect me anymore, and he hasn't been for a long time. I've had to learn to fend for myself, from dodging Papa's fists to appeasing Mr. Richard and now to keeping one step ahead of the Nazis. That's why I smile at the soldier instead of pointing my pistol pen at him like I really want to do.

When I reach the city limits, a briny breeze ripples through my stolen dress and I catch my first glimpse of Cherbourg. It looks like a postcard I could send home to Maman, with the sky and sea a blazing blue and the pretty town houses pressed together like sweet buns straight out of the oven. Out in the harbor, dozens of ships float quietly on the calm waters, reminding me of the bottled letters that Theo and I threw into the harbor when we were kids. Did any of them ever make it this far?

Once I guide my bicycle into town, however, my quaint postcard of a city gets torn to pieces. It's clear that the war has brought destruction to Cherbourg. I pedal past a brick shell of a shoe factory—a casualty of the bombings, I'm sure—and over streets littered with fresh rubble that leaves my shoes caked in dust. The Nazis and Allies have been playing tug-of-war with the city, hoping to gain control of its port. At the rate they're going, though, I wonder if there'll be anything left of Cherbourg once they're finished.

I avoid the Germans the best I can, but I can only avoid so much. My fists clench around the handlebars each time I spot one of their trucks or a pair of their uniformed patrols, and I lead the bicycle around corners and into sour-smelling alleys to get away from them. These side streets take me farther and farther from the safe house, but I'd rather get there in one piece than not at all.

By the time I track back to the coordinates it's well past noon, and I wonder if Sabine has already caught up with me. I spot the safe house, but I don't knock straightaway. I ride past it to size up the place. It's a sliver of a building, four stories tall, and skinny as a matchstick. I look over the windows and roofline to detect whether it has been compromised—maybe a broken window or a radio antenna poking out where it shouldn't be—but the place looks clean, at least from the outside.

My pulse scatters at what I'll find on the other side of those walls, but I march up to the front door and rap three times. Footsteps shuffle from inside, and the door creaks open an inch, revealing a snow-haired woman peering up at me through the crack. She's a tiny thing, with a long nose and round unblinking eyes like a heron's.

Suspicion paints her voice cold. "I'm not interested in what you're selling."

"Madame, I'm not here to sell you anything." I step closer and dim my voice to a whisper so that I can tell her the code phrase that Harken instructed me to give. "The piano will be tuned this September."

Her expression does an about-face. A smile springs onto her lips, and she tells me the correct code phrase in return. "I look forward to playing more Chopin." Then she tugs me inside the house under the wings of her shawl. "Whatever took you so long? Come in, come in."

Once I'm tucked inside the woman's cozy house, I'm greeted by a stone fireplace that holds a spitting-hot fire. There's a pot hanging above the flames, and the scent of whatever is cooking inside of it— hearty and meaty—makes my mouth water. The woman drags me to her kitchen table and introduces herself as Ava Rochette while she plies me with a cup of water and a bowl of onion stew. Clucking over me, she insists on wrapping up my injured wrist, all the while explaining how she joined the Resistance in Cherbourg a year ago, not long after her two grandsons were taken to Germany in the draft.

"I decided that if I couldn't bring them back from Germany myself, I'd fight the Germans here the best that I could," she says with a long sigh. But she saves a smile for me. "What am I to call you, dear?"

I nearly give her Fleurette, but I remember that alias has been compromised. Instead I say, "Marie-Louise," the name on my extra papers. I scan the room for any sign of Sabine. Even on foot, she should've arrived by now. She's quick and she knows this area, and I half expect her to bound down the narrow set of stairs. "Did my colleague arrive earlier? She has dark hair and goes by the name of—"

"*Non*, you're the first. I was told yesterday to expect two girls from the Parisian Resistance, but when both of you failed to come I thought that the Nazis must've gotten to you."

"We escaped from them." *Barely*, I almost add. I don't correct her, either, about my being in the Resistance. Outside of Laurent, only a handful of French know about Covert Operations' existence—and we'd like to keep it that way. I drain the rest of my water and thank Madame Rochette for it while I dig into the stew. "I'll need to speak with Monsieur Dorner as soon as possible. Is he being kept nearby?"

She chuckles. "You could say that. The Resistance put him in my attic."

I nearly drop my spoon. "He has been here this whole time?"

"Yes, right on top of our heads." She points up to the second floor. "I agreed to take him in after another safe house came under suspicion."

"The Resistance left him with you, alone?"

"Oh, I can protect myself, don't you fret," she says, sipping at her grilled-barley tea and nodding at the enormous butcher knife that takes residence beside her copper sink. "Dorner has been expecting someone to come interrogate him."

"Your Resistance contacts haven't questioned him yet?"

"They did, but just enough to decide to contact your liaisons in Paris. Do you wish to see Dorner now?"

My appetite vanishes, and I set down my spoon. See him *now*? If Major Harken were here, he'd tell me to wait for Sabine. *Don't you forget that I left Chevalier in charge*, he'd say, before reminding me of the two missions I've botched already.

"Marie-Louise?" says Madame Rochette, waiting for my answer.

I almost tell her that my hands are tied until Sabine's arrival because that's what Major Harken would want me to do.

But is it really?

I realize then that it isn't Major Harken muddying my thoughts and holding me back. It's my own doubts. They've been dogging me since my first mission and they've grown louder since my run-in with Travert, but I know I need to give them a great big heave out the window. I didn't claw my way through training and now to Cherbourg to turn tail and wait in the corner. Theo was no coward, and I won't be, either.

I get up from the table. "Lead the way, please," I tell her.

I follow Madame Rochette upstairs and into a bedroom so narrow that it barely fits an iron bedframe and an ancient-looking set of drawers. Heavy curtains cover the closed window, turning the air stale. Madame Rochette uses her shoulder to scoot the drawers aside, which reveals a false panel in the wall. She pries it open with her fingernails.

"Hello?" she calls out. "It's me. Madame Rochette."

The windowless attic lies in shadow. From the back of the space, a man steps forward, and as he enters the room I stiffen at the sight of him.

This has to be a mistake. This can't be him. Major Harken made Dorner sound like a grizzled Nazi officer my father's age. I peer back into the attic, waiting for someone else to join us, but the attic is as empty as a bombed-out tank.

Madame Rochette makes the introductions. "Monsieur Dorner, the Resistance has sent a representative to see you."

The man tilts his head at me. "They sent a woman?" he says in French.

"Yes, a woman," I say sharply. I'll count that as the second notch against him, the first being that he's a Nazi. "*You're* Dorner, then?"

"Yes, Alexander Dorner."

We'll see about that, I think. I thank Madame Rochette and march into the attic. The space is cramped—just a closet, really—and the ceiling slopes at a sharp angle, so my head nearly grazes the rafters. The room lacks for a window, but a few beams of sunlight filter in through the old slats of the roof.

I frown all over again. Dorner can't be much older than Theo was before he died, and I have to admit that he reminds me a little of my brother, too, with the sandy hair that won't lie flat and the lanky frame that could use a good bit of filling out. But that's where their similarities end. Theo never wore glasses, while this Dorner fellow sports a tortoiseshell pair. My brother also had that trademark glint in his eye, but there's no trace of that in this man's eyes. No, Dorner's are big and blue and innocent, like a little choirboy's. However, if he truly is who he says he is, then those eyes will be far from innocent.

Dorner straightens and smooths the wrinkles of his button-down shirt. "May I ask what happened to Philippe and Louis, the ones who escorted me here?"

"They have other tasks to attend to," I lie.

"They promised me that—"

"I don't care what they promised. You're under my authority now. If you have an issue with me, I can alert the Gestapo of your presence."

"Please," he says swiftly, "don't. I think we'd all like to avoid them if necessary." He offers me a polite smile, which I don't return. "I don't want to start out on the wrong foot."

"It's too late for that."

"Then let me apologize." His offer sounds genuine enough, but it does little to stamp out my suspicions. He's too young, for one thing. He's too polite, for another. And for a man on the run, he's far too calm. He should be jittery like Monsieur Travert, who nearly soiled himself after I dropped my Sister Marchand routine. But maybe Dorner is made out of tougher material than Travert was. He'd have to be to survive the journey out of Germany and into France. Or maybe all of his nerves subsided when he saw that the Resistance had sent in a woman. If that's the case, I'll be sure to kick those nerves right back into him. We practiced interrogations for weeks at training, and now I'll put them to good use.

Dorner uses a handkerchief to dab the sweat from his forehead. "I hope you'll accept my apology, mademoiselle . . . ?"

I leave his question hanging between us while I walk about the room, noting which floorboards creak and which ones don't, allowing the silence to stretch and grow to unnerve him.

"You can call me Marie-Louise," I tell him, and leave it at that. I search for where we can sit. *Establish the hierarchy*, I think. Since Dorner is a whole head taller than I am, I gesture for him to take a seat on a turned-over fruit crate that he's using as a nightstand while I take the rickety dining chair left abandoned in the corner. When we're both seated, I'm the one with the height advantage.

"I should thank you for meeting with me," he says. There's that smile of his again, but we'll see how long this prim-and-proper routine will last. What I'd give for a pack of chemically laced cigarettes, but they were all left on the train.

"You can keep your thank-yous," I say bluntly. "I'm not meeting with you as some favor. I'm here because you claim to have important information."

"I do indeed."

I scowl. "I'll be the one to determine that. So allow me to tell you how this meeting will proceed. I'll ask the questions; you answer them. If at any point I detect a lie out of you, we'll take a short walk to the Gestapo office in Cherbourg. Are we clear?"

He attempts another smile. "May we discuss my passage to England?"

"Don't get ahead of yourself, Dorner."

"Please, you can call me Alex."

"I'll call you Greta Garbo if I want, and we'll talk about England when I feel like talking about England." I've had about enough of him changing the topic, and I'm sure Harken would tell me that Dorner is obviously stalling. That's when I begin with a simple question to kick off this interrogation. "What's your full name?"

"Alexander Maximilian Dorner."

"Your age?"

"I'll be twenty-one next month."

He's even younger than I'd guessed. Granted, as the war has dragged along, the Nazis have been sending out younger and younger soldiers to the front lines, but I don't know how a twenty-year-old like Dorner could have jumped up the ranks so quickly that he'd know about Operation Zerfall.

"Where are you from?" I ask next.

"Innsbruck, Austria, but I was raised in Munich. I was attending university there when the war broke out."

"What were you studying?"

"I was working toward a doctorate in pathology."

That certainly raises my brow. "A doctorate? At your age?"

"I started two years ago," he says. There's the slightest edge of pride in his voice, and I figure that he must have begun his university schooling at age fourteen or fifteen. So he's educated. *Very* educated. But that doesn't mean that I can him trust him any more than I did a minute ago. If anything, I need to raise my defenses even higher.

"When did you join the military? At the outbreak of the war?" I ask.

He sits forward slightly, puzzled. "When did I join the military?"

I channel Harken and say, "Didn't you hear me the first time?"

"I'm afraid you must be mistaken. I never joined the military. I *worked* for the military, yes, but I wasn't a soldier."

I almost call him a liar. If he isn't a soldier, then how could he have heard about a military operation like Zerfall? An alarm bell clatters in my thoughts, but I quiet it for now. I need to get to the bottom of this.

"That's not what I was told," I say coolly.

"Then there must've been a miscommunication."

I lurch forward in my chair. "Are you accusing me of lying?"

"No, I—"

I slap him. A burst of pink appears on Dorner's cheek, and his mouth hangs open. That should show him not to underestimate me. Unlike Nazi women, I'm not here to keep his home and his bed warm.

"If you're not a soldier, how did you come to work for the Nazis?" When he doesn't answer me straightaway, I lift my hand again and I say, "Answer me."

He flinches and says, "Yes, mademoiselle. My university adviser was a member of the Nazi party. When I told him I needed assistance with funding, he secured a placement for me at a *Wunderwaffe* laboratory."

I've seen that word before—*Wunderwaffe*—in Harken's office, stamped on one of his classified files. He never said much about it— just that it was a covert Nazi initiative to create "wonder weapons," like missiles and superheavy tanks—although I hadn't heard anything about a laboratory.

I ask, "What did you do at this laboratory?"

"Research. I was an analyst there. I studied diseases." His fingers roam toward his shirt buttons, plucking at them. A nervous tic, perhaps? I have to dig deeper.

"I need details, Dorner."

He draws in a breath. "For the most part I worked with numbers. Statistics and raw data." Another breath. "I never worked directly with a live subject until two months ago."

"What do you mean? Dogs? Monkeys?"

"No." He clutches on to a single shirt button and squeezes it between his fingers. "Humans."

The blood seeps from my face. The Germans have been experimenting on *people*? I know I shouldn't be surprised. I've witnessed the Nazis' cruelty with my own eyes, but that doesn't stop the queasiness from rolling through my stomach. I can't let Dorner see how this revelation has affected me, though, so I sit up straight and tuck away my disgust. I need to maintain the upper hand at all times, even if I don't know a lick about pathology and diseases. Those weren't exactly topics the nuns taught at school.

What I can do, however, is lie.

"The Resistance has heard about these experiments," I tell him, leaning back into my chair.

"You have?" There's surprise in his tone.

"Do you truly think we'd be that naïve about the Nazis' secret operations?"

"But the laboratory where I worked . . . it was different from the others. We weren't merely studying diseases."

"Then what else were you doing?"

"We were undertaking a special mission." His fingers move absently from his button toward his collar. He pulls at it, like it's too hot in the attic. "The scientists called it Operation Zerfall."

I resist the urge to grab his shirt and shake the information right out of him. "I see," I say slowly, trying to keep my cards close to me. "Go on."

"If I tell you, I want to discuss my going to England."

I decide to humor him. "You've been agreeable so far. We can talk." Because "talk" is just that. I won't be agreeing to anything. "But first, what's Operation Zerfall?"

"It's best to show you." He rises from his crate and reaches underneath a pile of blankets to grab a thick folder, and he presents it to me like he's holding the key to Berlin itself.

"What's this?"

"Evidence."

I toss him a bored expression, but my pulse thrums as I open the folder. Inside, I find stack upon stack of paperwork that's filled with numbers and graphs, all of it speckled with mud, which probably came from Dorner's getaway out of Germany. I turn the pages until I find one with text—and I see that it's written in German. *Merde.* My own German might be good enough to eavesdrop on the soldiers standing on a Parisian street corner, but it's nowhere near good enough to read this. I'll have to wait to find a translator before I can decipher it.

Dorner must see my frustration. "Turn toward the back. There are photographs."

True enough, when I reach the end of the pile, I find dozens of photos waiting for me there. My fingers go cold touching them. I expected to find aerial pictures of Nazi bomber targets or photos of a terrible weapon that the Germans have concocted—isn't that what Zerfall must be? Instead, I find hospital patients surrounded by a team of nurses. The patients' arms and legs have been strapped against their cots; and their hair has been shaved off. Some of them are even missing eyes or entire limbs. But that isn't why I'm grimacing.

It's the look on their faces.

It's how their mouths are splayed open in silent screams.

I want to look away, but I make myself continue. With each new photo, my gut tightens more. How many people did the Nazis conduct their "testing" on? What was the purpose of all these gruesome experiments?

"The patients were mostly war criminals," Dorner murmurs, as if that should lessen the blow.

I frown. *War criminals* could mean anything to the Germans: downed Allied airmen, Resistance members, soldiers like Theo. Civilians, even, who've displeased the Nazis in some way.

"I wasn't in charge of finding the subjects," Dorner says quietly.

"Is that the excuse you use to comfort yourself?" His response doesn't inspire any sympathy from me. I continue looking through the photos. I don't think they can get any worse until I come upon the very last one.

"Mother Mary," I whisper.

While the previous photos featured solely men, the one before me now is of a young girl. Her hair hasn't been shorn like the others. It's tied in a tight braid that hangs limply down her back. Her dark eyes stare up at me, tears falling out of them.

I squint at the photo. No, those aren't tears. They're too dark.

It's blood.

I slam the folder shut.

"*Es war alles so schrecklich,*" Dorner says, slipping into German. *It's all so terrible.* The innocent student that he introduced himself as has been with replaced with the trembling boy in front of me now. Had he been putting on a brave face before? That question recedes from my thoughts, however, as the image of the little girl haunts me.

"What happened to her?" I ask. Rage surges inside me. "To all of them?"

"Zerfall."

I shake my head. "Zerfall is a military operation."

"In a way, yes." His throat is dry as he searches for words. "The laboratory and the research we conducted, it was all for one purpose . . ."

The folder weighs heavy in my hands as I piece together everything he has told me. His studies in pathology. The photos of live subjects. The mouths frozen with screams. It's so clear to me now. Operation Zerfall isn't a ground invasion or an airstrike or anything else that Major Harken had imagined. It's much worse than that.

Zerfall is a plague.

NINE

The folder tumbles from my lap and spills around my shoes, the photographs landing in a horrific ring around the chair. Dorner leaps up to collect it all, but I don't move to help him. It's hard enough to breathe, much less lift a finger.

So this is what Hitler has in store for the Allies: millions infected, millions bleeding, millions dead. Knowing the Nazis' taste for killing, they might just succeed. How can the Allies fight a disease with our bullets and tanks?

The rage multiplies in my heart, a burning furnace that makes me want to smash everything in this room, Dorner included. He may have turned his back on these experiments, but he did play a hand in bringing about Zerfall. If it weren't for Major Harken's orders, I'd be putting my skills to good use and strangling the life out of Dorner this very minute.

But what if Dorner is lying?

That question rises at the back of my mind, and I clutch my fingers around it. There's the possibility that Dorner could be spinning a magnificent yarn for a free ticket to England. He could be a Nazi agent sent to France to gain my trust and admittance onto British soil. It wouldn't be the first time the Germans have tried to infiltrate the Allies, but why would they give Dorner such an outlandish cover? The Germans are smarter than that. Far smarter.

I wish I could get Harken's input—and where's Sabine when I need her? She should've arrived by now. I stare at Dorner's folder, and I know that there isn't time to waste. Whether Dorner is telling the truth or whether he's a German spy, I need to get to the bottom of all this. My work here is far from over.

"You've told me quite the story, Dorner," I start.

His head shoots up. Confusion fills his big eyes. "Story? You think that I've been lying to you?"

"It's possible."

He takes the folder. "You have the proof in front of you. You have it right here."

"These documents could've been doctored."

"Why would anyone go to the trouble of that?"

"For safe passage to England."

The last piece of his proper exterior begins to crack. "I risked my life leaving Germany. I committed *treason* coming to you, and you believe I did all this to travel to England?"

"There are spies everywhere."

"I'm not a spy!" Anger twists his features, but he has enough resolve left to rein it in. "Why is that so difficult for you to believe?"

"You had a prestigious job in Germany. You had a long career ahead of you, yet you gave all of it up along with everything else that you knew."

He goes quiet. Then, deliberately, he opens the folder and turns to the photo of the little girl. "Here is my reason. This is why I left."

"Because of one patient?"

"For all of them." He closes his eyes. "Though I'll never forget her. She was ten years old. A Jehovah's Witness. She never spoke or cried like the others, but every day she would look at the clock on the wall. For days I wondered what she was waiting for. Perhaps her family to come through the doors? But her parents and brother had already succumbed to the virus." He clears the wobble from his voice. "Later I realized that she was waiting for death."

Silence takes me by the throat. I think about what that little girl went through, from losing her family and then losing her own short life that had barely started. And for what? For the "crime" of her faith? I can't help but think about Ruthie and what would've happened to her and her mother if they'd lived in France instead of America.

My hands knot into fists so tight that I lose all feeling in them. I did the same thing after Theo's funeral, too. Maman had bought flowers and a tombstone, but we didn't have a body to bury beneath it. That's what the army told us. My brother was laid to rest in some grave in the Algerian desert, but I bet that little girl wasn't even given that.

I turn my attention back to Dorner. All of his politeness has been stripped apart and replaced with the haunted man in front of me. Admittedly I'm glad to see him looking so miserable.

"I've seen the Zerfall patients with my own eyes," he says, "and I've worked next to the scientists who developed the disease. If you have your doubts, then let me clear them."

It's the perfect answer, spoken with the right amount of gusto, but I know Major Harken wouldn't fall for a pretty answer so easily.

"Tell me about the virus," I say. "How did the Nazis create it?"

He wipes clean the lenses of his glasses. "They didn't *create* the virus, per se. We don't have the ability for that. What they did instead was send research teams to places throughout the world where deadly diseases sometimes occur. The Orient, for instance. The jungles of South America."

I'm not quite sure where he's leading me, and so I motion for him to go on.

"One team in particular discovered a disease that struck at the mouth of an African river. So in 1938 they built a facility there to observe it, and eventually they gathered enough research to bring three live patients to Europe for further study."

A tingle washes down my spine. "The Nazis have been at work on this mission for years?"

"Since before the war started, at the Führer's behest. He was the one who named the initiative Operation Zerfall."

I grow cold all over. Leave it to Hitler to concoct something like this. It's not enough that he has conquered half of Europe. He wants to bring everyone else to their knees as well.

"What are the symptoms of Zerfall?" I ask.

"A fever to begin with. It's usually accompanied by a cough and sore throat."

I jot down as much as I can in my memory. "What else?"

"There's not much else. Not in the first phase."

The pen in my mind comes to a hard stop. "What happens in the second phase?"

"That's typically when the bleeding starts from the orifices, from the eyes and nose especially."

I try to ignore the shudder rolling through me. It's no wonder why the patients in the photographs looked so wracked with pain. I don't even want to think about my next question, but I have to ask it. "And after that? The third phase?"

Dorner's fingers tug at his shirt buttons again, and I know his answer can't be good. "There isn't a third phase. After the second phase sets in, a handful of patients may survive, but most will succumb to the disease."

I sink back into my chair, and there's no use hiding my horror. I don't know much about diseases, but Zerfall sounds worse than the Spanish flu and the Black Death put together. Then a new question knocks at my thoughts. "If the virus is that contagious, why aren't the Nazis afraid of contaminating their own forces?"

"Oh, they're well aware of that." He shifts his attention away from me and onto his muddy shoelace. "That's why it has taken years to launch Zerfall. The disease is ready to spread, but our team couldn't do that without risking the lives of German troops. So they had to develop a cure first."

"There's a *cure* for Zerfall?"

"That's the key to the entire operation. Every German soldier must be inoculated against the virus before the Führer unleashes it on the Allies." He turns through the folder's papers until he stops upon a photograph that I must have missed before. "This is the mastermind of Zerfall. This is the man the Allies should look for."

He holds up a blurry photo of a gray-bearded man who looks like Santa Claus's younger brother, with a face as round as a Christmas pie.

"Dr. Elias Reinhard. He's the head of the laboratory that I worked for," Dorner continues.

Reinhard! I remember Travert mentioning that name to me. I pull the photo out of Dorner's hand and scrutinize it until I've memorized the lines of Reinhard's face. If he truly is the monster that Dorner has painted him to be, then the Allies will need to learn as much as they can about this doctor—and kill him.

"When will Dr. Reinhard be ready to launch the disease?" I ask.

"A few months, I believe."

"Two months? Four?"

"I don't know. I wasn't privileged with that information."

I point at the folder. "You know all of those details, but you don't know when this whole fiasco will start?"

"I was an assistant, and a low one at that. And I stole those documents, remember?"

Merde. "If you don't know when Reinhard will deploy the operation, then do you know *how* he'll do it?"

"I was never told the exact details, but I do have an idea."

"Well?"

"He'll deploy the victims themselves."

I'm not sure if I've heard him correctly. "Deploy them in what sense?"

"Reinhard will transfer the first-phase patients into Allied territory when they're at their most contagious. He'll parachute them into London or pack them into transport boats headed toward the British seaports."

"The disease is spread by air, then?"

"No, from contact with bodily fluid."

"Then we'll tell the Brits to burn the boats and shoot down the others."

"I'm no military strategist, but they won't be able to get them all. I should mention, too, that the patients don't even need to survive the journey. The corpses are infectious as well. Someone would have to bury them, and that someone could easily pass on the illness to others."

I breathe in but still feel breathless. This Dr. Reinhard has thought of everything, hasn't he? "Where's Reinhard's laboratory located? Don't tell me you don't know. You worked there."

"I know the coordinates. I memorized them, in fact," he says.

It's the exact news that I wanted to hear, but there's a cautious edge to his voice that I'm not sure about, like a cornered dog with its hackles raised.

"What are these coordinates?"

He stares at me with those big blue eyes of his, but they don't look so innocent right now. "I'll tell them to you once you've agreed to my terms."

"Terms?"

"I want to go to England. I want immunity and citizenship, too.

In return, I'll gladly work with British intelligence and tell them everything they need to know about Zerfall. I believe that's fair."

I glare at his audacity. "That isn't how this works. *You* came to *us*. Not the other way around. Give me those coordinates."

"If I do that now, who's to say that you wouldn't stick a knife in my throat? I have to protect myself. You must see that."

This isn't going according to plan. Harken told me to interrogate Dorner, which I've done, and then deliver him to the British if he's telling the truth, which might be likely but has not been determined. Only now Dorner is withholding information from me—information that I need—and I don't like it one bit. Then I realize my mistake. I let our interrogation tip much too far in his favor. I let him sweep me up in his story about Zerfall—but I'll show him who's in charge.

I reach into my pocket for the pistol pen that Sabine gave to me, twisting it open to reveal the barrel inside and pointing it straight at Dorner's Nazi heart.

"Give me the coordinates," I tell him.

He raises his hands but shakes his head all the same. "Shoot me now and the coordinates die with me."

"I don't need to shoot to kill." I point the gun at his kneecap. "I can shoot to maim. You can survive well enough with one leg, but you'll be in so much pain that you'll wish I'd turned you over to the Gestapo."

Just when I think I've got him, he lays another one on me. "If you shoot me—in the leg or the arm or wherever else—I won't tell you the name of the double agent within your Resistance."

"What are you talking about now?"

"I learned something at the laboratory, not long before I left," Cautiously he brings his hands back down into his lap. "There was a patient there, a Frenchman. He claimed to be part of the Resistance movement, and said that he had smuggled himself into Germany to bomb a rail station."

"How does this have anything to do with the coordinates?" I nearly slap him again—or maybe I should go with a punch to the gut—but Dorner is quick to continue.

"When this man learned that he was next in line to be injected with the Zerfall virus, he broke. He started spilling secrets left and right—and he was apparently a higher-ranking member of the Resistance."

"So?"

"He told us that there's a double agent within the Allies' espionage network. This agent is in France. In Paris, to be exact."

In *Paris*? He certainly has hooked my attention with that, but I don't put the gun away. I keep it right where I want it pointed. "You really expect me to believe the words of this man? A 'patient' at your laboratory who the Nazis likely beat and tortured?"

"He told me something else," Dorner says. "He said that this double agent isn't French."

"Then what is he?" I scoff. "Finnish?"

"Either British or American. The man wasn't sure which, but that must narrow down your choices."

My heart thunders. "The Americans have barely entered the war."

"They could've parachuted their spies into France."

"You seem to be making many assumptions above your pay grade."

"Are you willing to take the risk that I'm lying to you?"

He has me there and, by the way his back has gone straighter, he knows it, too. I think of the most awful French words I've heard. The chances that he's lying to me are high, a desperate move he's making to push me to take him to the coast. But what if he's telling me the truth? What if there really is a double agent within the Resistance? There aren't many foreign members within the group—a couple brave Brits and a handful of other nationalities. Canadian. Dutch. And yes, American.

Could it be someone within the OSS? Within Covert Ops, even?

I shove that thought aside and curse Dorner for even planting it in my head. Delphine is rotting in a Nazi prison, and Sabine might be joining her soon. My agent sisters are risking their necks every hour of every day, and I trust them far more than this Austrian standing in front of me. And yet I can't ignore what he has told me.

"Do you want to bargain with me, Dorner? Then let's bargain. Tell me this supposed double agent's name, and I'll make the arrangements to get you to England. If not, I'll choke it out of you."

He tilts his head to one side, measuring my offer. "Here's what I have in mind. Bring me to the Brits—alive and well—and I'll give you both pieces of intelligence."

"That's not how this is going to work," I say through tight teeth. If he wants this to go to blows, then so be it. We'll see how long it takes before he squeals like Travert.

I lurch onto my feet, ready to throw him to the floor, but before I touch him there's a pounding below us. Someone is at Madame Rochette's front door. Sabine, maybe? I shake my head. She'd never make that much racket.

"They're here!" Dorner says, his body tightening.

I close the distance between us and place a firm hand over his mouth. I don't need to ask who "they" are.

It's the Nazis.

TEN

Not a second later, there's a crash below our feet. Boots march through the front door of the house, quick and heavy drumbeats that can only belong to the soldiers. The shouting soon follows, in angry clipped German. I can barely hear Madame Rochette's response.

"What's the problem, mein Herr?" she says. "No, no, I live alone. My husband passed away years ago, and my only daughter resides in Toulouse. Her sons, my grandsons, were both taken in the draft."

There's another shout. Something I can't make out.

"Of course you may look at my papers," replies Madame Rochette. "I keep them in my kitchen drawer."

And not too far from her butcher knife, I think. I bet Madame Rochette could stick that knife of hers into the Nazi in a few seconds flat, but there should be more than one German downstairs and she won't be able to take them all, not without a whole block of kitchen knives.

"What should we do?" Dorner whispers.

I glower at him to keep him quiet.

"You must have weapons," he says. "Give one to me."

Is he insane? Arm him, a Nazi I'd just met? Somehow I doubt that his professors taught him hand-to-hand combat at university.

"Let me handle them." I silence him with a glare, and thankfully he doesn't say anything after that. If he had kept jabbering, I might have placed him in a chokehold. Actually, I wouldn't have minded doing that. I could've squeezed my fingers around his neck until he coughed up the name of the double agent.

Madame Rochette's voice takes on a sweet edge. "That's my bedroom upstairs. I've had a bit of a rat problem, so do take care." Despite her warning, the soldiers soon infiltrate the second floor. I wince as they overturn the bed and yank out drawers from the dresser, the same sounds I'd hear whenever Papa flew into one of his rages.

"Search for any signs of the Resistance!" one of the men says.

I can hear every one of their movements, every step that they take. There's just a thin wall that separates us from their fury. I stare at the panel to the attic, hoping to keep it closed through sheer will-power alone. I clutch the knife from my shoe in one hand while I hold my last remaining pistol pen in the other. One shot. That's all we have.

There's another crash. Somehow I know that they've shoved aside the dresser that's hiding us from them. I set my jaw. If those soldiers come barreling in, I'd rather go out fighting than surrender.

"They're coming!" Dorner whispers. "Give me a weapon!"

"No, follow my lead." A hasty idea springs into my mind. Who knows if it will work, but . . . I stow the knife in my pocket but keep my grip on the pen. "And stay quiet."

The panel flies open, and a single Nazi aims a rifle at our heads. *"Hände hoch!"*

Dorner and I lift our arms into the air. The panel is narrow enough that only one soldier can squeeze in at a time, but I notice two more Nazis behind this one. That's three soldiers total. The odds could be much worse, but all three of them carry rifles and pistols while we have next to nothing. I need to play this very carefully—and I better hope that my hands won't start trembling.

Before the soldier can get another word out, I break into sobs.

"Please, God, don't hurt us!" I cry out in broken German. "We'll surrender!"

The soldier isn't fazed as he steps into the attic. *"Hände hoch!"*

"Don't shoot!" I cry. I'm still holding the pen, but I can't fire it just yet. I have one shot, and I need to draw him closer somehow. *Think, Lucie.* Then I blurt out in my paltry German, "I'm with child!"

Dorner's eyes widen under his glasses. The soldier does the same, but he keeps his rifle close to him.

"Don't hurt my baby!" I break into even louder sobs and annoyance flickers across the Nazi's face, but I'd rather have him annoyed than jumpy and trigger-happy.

"Tais-toi!" the soldier shouts in French. He stalks toward me, raising his rifle to swing the butt of it at my wailing mouth, and I know I've gotten him. Flicking off the pen cap, I banish all of my thoughts, because I can't lose my nerve now like I did with Travert.

The bullet pops out of the pen barrel and flies into the soldier's chest, right into the heart. He collapses in front of me, with his rifle clattering onto the floor. The remaining two Nazis try to push their way inside the attic. I grab the knife from my pocket and hurl it at the incoming soldier. The blade strikes him in the soft spot at the base of his neck. It's not a death wound—it'll take him minutes to bleed out—but the soldier is young, probably younger than I am, and he panics. His shots go wide as he tries to dig out the knife, which only makes things worse. The blood flows free and fast, and while he's busy trying to plug up the hole in his neck Dorner lurches forward.

"No, wait!" I hiss. Is he insane, making a run for it now? But he doesn't make a break for the door. He's reaching for the fallen rifle.

The third soldier pushes himself inside, ready to spray us with bullets. I yank the first dead Nazi up to use as a shield for Dorner and me, but he's too busy unjamming the rifle trigger.

A swear tears out of my mouth. "Get down!"

This is the end. We're cornered.

But the gunfire never comes. The third soldier gasps and topples onto his fallen comrades. There's a butcher knife lodged in the back of his head, like a stabbed melon. There's a new figure standing in the attic, with a bloodied lip and a bruised cheekbone. And I've never been happier to see her.

"Sa—" I start.

"Odette," Sabine finishes for me.

Right. Compromised aliases, new names for both of us. I march over and give her a hug. We've never embraced before; in fact we've never stood this close to each other willingly. Maybe that's why Sabine startles at my gesture, but I don't care one bit. I was beginning to think I would never see her again.

"Where were you?" I ask. I flinch at the sight of her face, especially at the purple blotch that rings her left eye. I want to pepper her with questions. Was she arrested? Where did she get those bruises? But Sabine beats me to the chase.

"I'm all right," she says in a way that tells me it's not up for discussion. Then she unravels herself from my arms and looks Dorner up and down. "Is that him? Is it Dorner?"

Dorner blinks from me to her. "How do you know my name?" Then, to me, he asks, "Who is she?"

"A colleague of mine," I say quickly. I see that he's still holding on to the jammed rifle, and I snatch it away from him before he does something foolish with it. "And she just saved your life." *Our lives*, I might add.

Footfalls travel up the staircase, and Madame Rochette soon stumbles into the attic. She looks much paler than when I saw her last, and she goes even whiter at the sight of three dead Nazis in her home.

"Nom de Dieu!" She makes the sign of the cross and clutches on to Sabine's arm to steady herself. "It appears you arrived in the nick of time, Odette."

"I would've been here sooner if I hadn't been . . . delayed," Sabine says.

I want to ask her what she means by that, but we have to get out of this house first. "We need to leave," I say to the three of them. "The Nazis will send more soldiers once these patrols don't return."

Madame Rochette gives a trembling nod. "Come, quickly. There's another safe house outside of the city."

"What about the bodies?" I ask.

"I'll tell the Resistance to dispose of them."

"What about you?" Guilt gnaws at me for what we've exposed her to. "You shouldn't stay here—"

"After I've taken you to the safe house, I'll go to my sister's." She peers cautiously out the window and begins herding us down the stairs. "We must hurry."

Once we've piled up the bodies, Sabine and I change into a couple of Madame Rochette's old dresses and pick over the Nazis' weapons. We strap their pistols to our thighs and tuck their pocketknives into our brassieres. The rifles are far too big to carry with us, but I miss the weight of their bullets just the same.

Sunlight leeches from the sky as we dive into the shadows. Madame Rochette leads the way, walking a block ahead of us with Dorner next to her while Sabine and I follow suit. I figured it would be easier to hide in plain sight as separate pairs than the four of us crammed together. We've already passed five corpses on the street, their bodies propped up with spikes through their throats. As if that weren't warning enough, the Nazis had scrawled a message and tied it around one of the victims' feet: *For aiding and succoring the Resistance.* I can only imagine what they have in store for a spy like me.

There's another reason why I suggested we travel in pairs. I need a moment with Odette. The streets have nearly emptied, and we're alone on our block, but I hush my voice just the same.

"Did they arrest you?"

Sabine stiffens. "Yes."

"What did they want?"

"What else could they want? To see my papers. To question me."

"When?"

We walk into the shadows of a bombed-out apartment building, and she steps over a sharp piece of rubble, choosing her words just as carefully as she chooses her steps. "Not even an hour after we parted ways. There was a patrol, and there wasn't time to hide."

"What did you tell them?"

"Nothing important. I gave them Fifine's cover story."

For ten whole hours? But I remind myself that Sabine is Sabine, Harken's favorite. If anyone could lie for that long and get away with it, it would be her. "How did you escape?"

She winces, and I know I've dragged up a brutal memory. "How do you think? I used my 'womanly charms' on him. Is your curiosity satisfied?"

The color leaves my cheeks. "I didn't mean to pry."

"Then don't. I'd prefer to forget about all that, and I'd ask you to do the same." For a second, her hardened mask falls off to reveal a trembling girl underneath. "Please."

I blink at her. I don't think she has ever said please to me before. Or to anyone. That's why I swallow the barrage of questions in my throat. I can't help but think that if she had been the one to take the bicycle into town, then I probably would've been the one who got picked up by the Nazis—and I'd have the bumps and bruises and bad memories to show for it.

Sabine wraps her arms around herself. "Tell me about Dorner. What have you discovered?"

I inhale a deep breath because I'll need it for what I have to say next. Then, once I make sure that the street is completely empty around us, I give her the bare-bones version of what Dorner has told me: about the laboratory, about the virus, and about what will happen next. With every detail I give, Sabine simply stares ahead, but I can see the muscles in her jaw twitching.

"So this is what they have been working on. A weapon we'll have no defense against," she mumbles. "You believe what he has told you?"

"He has a folder full of paperwork and photographs, all taken from this secret *Wunderwaffe* laboratory." I nod ahead of us to where both he and Madame Rochette are walking. Despite the danger it will bring us, Dorner still has his papers on him, wrapped in a tarp to keep them dry and tucked inside the back of his shirt, secured with a belt. I don't like the idea of having all that intelligence out in the open, but both the SOE and Covert Ops need to see the evidence for themselves. Once they see that photo of the young girl crying blood . . . I sweep that image away, though, because I haven't told Sabine everything yet. "There's more. Right before you arrived, Dorner told me that the Allies have a double agent among us. In Paris."

Sabine finally looks at me. "Who? Someone in the Resistance?"

"Maybe even higher up. He told me he'd give us the name when we arrive at the Channel. He wants full immunity in England."

I wait for Sabine to bluster and to call Dorner a list of terrible names for bribing us like this. I may even have to hold her back from choking the double agent's name out of him. Instead Sabine doesn't do much of anything. She goes quiet as she looks over at Dorner. He's a half block ahead of us, with his arm linked around Madame Rochette's, like a grandmother and grandson out for a stroll. He does glance back at us every other minute to make sure that we're following, and I cautiously wave him on.

"Do you trust him?" she asks.

I chew on that. Yes, Dorner has answered my questions and has shown me his folder of proof, but that doesn't mean we should throw our arms around him and welcome him to the Allies. But here's the other side of that coin—can we take the risk of *not* trusting him? Of ignoring the Zerfall virus?

That's at the heart of all this. We can't.

"We have to trust him," I whisper back. "If this disease gets out, we could lose everything, not just the war." I think about Zerfall making its way to the States. My mother could get sick, along with Ruthie. The thought of them crying blood and joining Theo in a cold grave makes my teeth clench. It was bad enough losing my brother— and having him die thinking that I was angry with him. I can't lose anyone else that I care about. "I know you outrank me, but you have to take my word on this."

Sabine's chin juts slightly upward, and I'm ready for her to launch into me finally, telling me that I'm forgetting my trainee status. But she doesn't. "Very well. We better move quickly to the coast."

"You're not going to insist on looking through his folder?"

She sighs through her nostrils. "That would be ideal, but how exactly can I interrogate Dorner out on the street? I'll have to take your word concerning his story."

She must notice the surprised look on my face because she goes on to say, "If Dorner turns out to be lying, I'll strangle you both. Is that clear?"

Now, there's the Sabine I know, which puts me a bit more at ease. And she's right. There really isn't time for her to give Dorner a full grilling.

Sabine speeds ahead to catch up with Madame Rochette, and I hurry after her. To the right of us, a clock tower sings and I count down the hours until the rendezvous with the SOE.

My heart goes grim, but I urge myself to pick up our pace. If we don't get Dorner to that drop-off, the entire war might as well tilt in Adolf Hitler's favor.

ELEVEN

Madame Rochette takes us to an old stone farmhouse that sits west of the city. Behind us, all of Cherbourg has gone dark. The entire city is under a mandatory blackout meant to shield the port from Allied bombers sneaking over from England. I search through the feathery clouds for any sign of our planes, but the sky is clear tonight. Thankfully. If we're caught in the bombers' cross fire, there is no amount of Hail Marys that will save us from their payloads.

We arrive at the safe house unannounced, but once the elderly farmer sees Madame Rochette he whisks us inside and serves us each a ladle of fish stew. Apparently this isn't the first time he has taken in fugitives, and he fortunately doesn't ask us many questions. Once our stomachs are filled, Madame Rochette kindly asks him to give us a pouch stuffed with supplies. Food. Water. A map. Even a weapon—a boning knife. Then we wait. Agonizing as it might be, we don't have another choice. In the summer months, the sun doesn't set until late here; and we'll need to surround ourselves with darkness to hide from the Germans' quick eyes.

Once that dark sets in, we thank the farmer and sneak back into the night, where we part ways with Madame Rochette. She's off to her sister's apartment, but before she leaves I give her two pecks.

"We can't ever thank you enough for what you've done," I start.

She gives my hand a firm pat. *"Vive la France,"* she says, and hurries onto the road without looking back. I can't blame her for distancing herself from us. She has risked her own life to save our necks, and now she won't be able to return home. At least not until the war is over.

Using the starlight to guide our feet, I hurry us westward, over the gently rolling hills that crisscross with neat rows of shrubbery to mark one farmer's land from the next. As we thread through one line of bushes, Dorner comes up beside me.

"I'm not sure it's wise to be traveling after curfew," he whispers, pushing his glasses up his nose.

"Do you want to get to England or not?"

He stumbles on an overgrown root. "We're going now?" I steady him and nod. There wasn't time to explain to him earlier that the SOE had already made arrangements to retrieve him tonight. "Precisely how will I get across the Channel?"

"By submarine. The British are on their way as we speak."

"Then you believe what I've told you about Zerfall." He sounds pleased by this, but I'm not here to stroke his ego.

"Remember your end of the bargain, Dorner. Tell them everything you know about Zerfall, and they won't kill you."

"Get me to the Brits and the coordinates and that name is yours." He matches pace with me, step for step. "You can call me Alex, you know."

"I know," I say, and I don't look back.

We swing south to skirt past the Querqueville airfield, where the Nazis swarm like hornets defending their nest, and we continue on to the grassy fields that run parallel to the Atlantic. The smell of the ocean hangs right under my nose, briny and sharp, and the sea winds have chilled the air around us. Once we've passed the airfield, I open the map and trace a lone finger along the path that we'll take from here to the drop-off point, drawing an invisible line from where we're standing over to the slim peninsula that juts off from the main palm of Normandy like a crooked finger. We'll need to reach the very tip of that finger in a matter of hours.

"Looks like there's another fifteen miles to go," I say to Sabine.

Sabine gives the map a hard look. "More like sixteen."

A few days ago I would've rolled my eyes at her, but we don't even have time for that. Fifteen or sixteen miles, it won't be easy terrain. There'll be rocky hills and thick brush that snatches at our ankles and—from a glance at the darkening sky—there's a summer storm brewing that should slow us further. "We better move fast if we want to make it on time." I say that for Sabine's benefit as much as Dorner's. I'm surprised that she hasn't insisted on leading the charge to the coast, but she seems content to let me do it. Whatever happened during her arrest has truly rattled her, and I'm tempted to ask if she'd like to rest, but she settles that for me.

"I can keep up," she says stiffly, and focuses her attention on Dorner. "He's the one we should worry about."

"There's no need for that. It's my neck on the line," Dorner says.

"And ours," Sabine points out before she shoulders the canvas pouch that carries our belongings, which also includes Dorner's folder and our remaining weapons. We have the knife that the farmer gave us, along with a pistol pen that Sabine has managed to save from headquarters. That's all that stands between the Nazis and the three of us.

We forge ahead a few more miles, then Sabine lifts up her fist, her signal for us to get down. I yank Dorner to the ground and squint over the hills to see a light bobbing along the beach. It's probably a patrol who's naïve enough to be using a flashlight, and even though he's moving in the opposite direction from us I know better than to start breathing easy. There could be a group of his friends waiting for us ahead.

Dorner turns to me. "Shouldn't we keep moving? It looks like there's a storm coming in." Heavy clouds lurk over the sea, blocking out the stars as the storm moves toward dry land.

An idea strikes me. "No, let's stay here until the rain comes," I say, and both he and Sabine frown. "The rain will give us cover, and we'll need as much as we can get since it's too dark to see the patrols."

"Our first priority should be getting to the drop-off point," Sabine points out. "It's nearly zero one hundred hours, and our rendezvous is in less than three hours. There's not much time."

"I know, but we won't have to wait long before those clouds come in. We'll stay put for twenty minutes tops."

"Fifteen," she counters.

"Fine, fifteen. Catch your breath and rest a little. I'll keep watch."

While Dorner sips some water and Sabine finds a dry patch of grass to sit on, I perch myself near the top of the hill. Ten minutes tick by. I scan the fields to search for another flashlight, but the countryside is quiet and dark—and once I've relaxed a little—beautiful, too. These soft hills, this hum of the ocean . . . I'm starting to understand why Papa only spoke of France when he was drunk and why Maman spoke so little of it at all. Did it hurt them too much to talk about it?

I wonder how they're doing. Mostly I worry about my mother. She must be lighting candles at St. Raphael's every day for Theo and me. I can see her so clearly, the frayed shawl over her shoulders, the desperate prayer she murmurs over and over again. Guilt settles into my stomach at leaving her without saying good-bye. I'd left her a note saying that I was going to California because I didn't have the nerve to tell her that I'd be going off to war like Theo had done. I knew that would crack her heart right in half.

Say a Hail Mary for me, I wish I could tell her, even though all of our prayers did nothing for my brother in the end. And yet, out here in these Nazi-infested hills, I figure one of my mother's prayers is better than nothing.

"Where are you?"

I jolt up.

"Where are you, Jean-Luc?"

It's Sabine. Both she and Dorner have drifted off, but she's the one talking in her sleep and asking the whereabouts of someone named Jean-Luc again. Whoever he is and whatever he means to Sabine, he could be the reason why we're discovered. I crawl on all fours toward her and give her a good shake.

"Shh, you were talking in your sleep again," I whisper. From the sound of her whimpering, her dream wasn't a pleasant one.

She props herself onto her elbow. "Was I?"

"You were saying someone's name. Jean-Luc."

She goes very still. "I see."

"It can't happen again. If the Germans heard you talking about your boyfriend—"

Her eyes flash dark. "Jean-Luc isn't my boyfriend."

"Whoever he is—"

"He's my brother."

"Oh." I didn't even know that she had a brother a couple days ago, but this is the second time that she's mentioned him now. Does she have nightmares about Jean-Luc like the ones I have about Theo? "You sounded worried about him in your dream."

Her shoulders tense like a cornered cat, ready to hiss at me, but when Sabine speaks, her voice is as small as a newborn kitten's. "I haven't heard from him in weeks," she admits. Then she turns her face away. "He joined the *maquis* last Christmas."

I'm impressed. I don't know Jean-Luc, but I already respect him. A few months back, the Nazis began drafting able-bodied French— mostly men but a few women—to send to Germany for manual labor. Thousands have ignored their orders, though, and have turned to guerilla fighting instead. They call themselves the *maquis*. "I'm sure you'll hear from him soon. There must be another backup at the postal service."

"Yes, perhaps."

I can tell that my words have done little to comfort Sabine, and I remember exactly how she feels. After Theo went off to war, I'd run to our letter box every afternoon to see if I'd gotten something from him. When I didn't hear from him in a few weeks, I imagined the worst. Maybe a grenade had taken him. Maybe machine gunfire. Then the nausea would hit me, and I wouldn't be able to eat the rest of the day.

"If Jean-Luc is half as tough as you are," I tell her, "then I'm sure that he's all right."

She doesn't thank me or turn around, but I think I see a flutter of a smile before she digs out a canteen and takes a long sip. She offers me some, but I shake my head. Sabine doesn't put the canteen away, though, choosing to run her finger along the side of the container.

"I have a question for you," she says suddenly. "Why do you keep that glass bottle in your room?"

My own shoulders tighten. She's talking about the bottle in my nightstand. I didn't think Sabine would've remembered that, but nothing really gets by her, now, does it?

"Do you not have glass bottles in America?" she asks.

"Of course we do."

Sabine gives me a quizzical look and my shoulders inch up farther, but I wonder what's the use of holding on to this secret. Theo's gone, and who knows if the three of us will survive the night?

"It's something my brother and I did," I say finally. "When we were kids, we would write letters to our relatives in Saint-Malo and put them inside of glass bottles. Then we'd toss them into the harbor. Whoever could throw the farthest would win."

"Win what?"

"Nothing. Just pride that you threw the farthest that day." Not surprisingly, since Theo was four years older than me, he usually won.

"Why wouldn't you mail the letters?"

I shrug. Because we didn't have the money for postage. Because we'd never even met our relatives. "It was a silly thing that kids do. Didn't you and Jean-Luc ever do something like that?"

"Sometimes, yes." She looks back out into the ocean, and I wonder if she's remembering something from her past. Whatever she's thinking about, she doesn't share it with me. "So you have family in Saint-Malo?"

"Not anymore." My mother hasn't stepped foot in that city since she left for the US with my father. I'm sure they arrived in Baltimore all shiny with hope. And for a while, they truly lived the American Dream. They opened up their own café, Les Delices, where they pushed out dozens of ham omelets and *croque-monsieur* every day. There were plans to open up a second location, maybe even a third down the road, but that was before the Depression. The bank notices came quickly after that, forcing them to find work at Pascal's, for Mr. Richard's next-to-nothing wages. Not long after that Papa started hitting the bottle. "How about your family? Are they still in Normandy?"

"My father is." A sour note creeps into her voice. "He lives on my family's land and cares for my grandfather."

A brother, father, and now a grandfather. Sabine has an entire family somewhere in France. Although I do notice that she doesn't mention her mother.

"Jean-Luc and I are supposed to inherit the farm one day," she adds.

An image plants in my head of Sabine holding a pitchfork and wearing boots and an apron. "You? A farmer?"

"Don't laugh. That land has been in my family for over a century."

"I can't quite see you planting turnips."

"We grow *apples*." She shoots me a glare before her eyes go soft. "My mother taught me how to prune the trees when I was little. Before she returned to Algeria."

My mouth feels dry. "I'm sorry."

"Don't be. I don't blame her for leaving Papa."

Sabine's family history seems to grow grimmer and grimmer, and in some ways it reminds me of my own. We have fathers we hate and brothers we love. And I wouldn't blame my *maman*, either, if she ever decided to leave Papa. I wish I had known all of this when I first came to Paris. I wish she had told me.

Sabine brushes her fingers over the thick grass underneath us. "When the war's over, Jean-Luc and I might try to find her."

"You should go," I say. *Before it's too late*, I want to add. I can't help but think about Theo's letters and how he talked about us visiting Saint-Malo and seeing where our mother had grown up. I hope that Sabine and Jean-Luc's plans will end better than ours did. I hope she won't have to live with the regret that I do now. I should've written Theo back sooner. I should've told him that, of course, I'd forgiven him. I didn't know that we'd have so little time left.

The first patter of raindrops falls around us. Both Sabine and I look up. It won't be long until those clouds rip open and douse us from head to toe. I go awaken Dorner, but I freeze in place when the sound of voices enters my ears. The sound of laughing.

I flatten myself against the chilly ground, and Sabine does the same. Who could be out here at this hour? Soldiers, probably, but I cling to the hope that it's a pair of farmers who got a little too drunk and a little too lost.

"Can't believe we have to be out in this weather," one of the men says in French.

French! I nearly smile. I'd much rather hear French out here than German.

"Move your feet. The sooner we're done with the watch, the sooner we can tell the captain that we're finished and maybe he'll let us go home."

I curse silently. They may be speaking French, but that doesn't mean they're friendlies. They're likely the French police, the Nazis' hired help. My hands roam quietly for the pistol pen, just in case, but maybe I won't have to use it. We might go undetected with the darkness cloaking us, and if Dorner doesn't snore.

"Bijou!" one of the men calls out. "Where is that girl?"

Girl? Is there a woman with the patrols? Holding my breath, my gaze falls upon a moving shadow. My skin shivers when I hear a dog's whine.

Bijou's whine turns into a bark.

"Bijou!" The patrols trundle back toward us and the beast starts to growl, a low rumbling sound that tells me she isn't a dainty lapdog that you'd find under Marie Antoinette's arm. Hardly a second passes before Bijou is upon us. I swing the pistol toward her, but before I can pull the trigger, she pounces on me, saliva dripping from her mouth. I manage to hold her off, but the gun topples out of my hand in the process.

Shouts fill my ears. The patrols cry out, and Dorner lets out a yelp as he awakens to the madness. Sabine pushes him out of the way and hurls herself at the Frenchmen, twisting one man's arms behind his back and snatching the rifle from his grasp. She swings it into the back of his head, knocking him out cold. While the other patrol fumbles for his pistol, Bijou snaps at me again, inches from my neck. The thought hits me that all of my training, all of my work in Paris, might come undone at the jaws of a French guard dog.

A gunshot claps through the air. Bijou howls, then whimpers and staggers away. I blink furiously, expecting to see Sabine with the smoking gun. Instead, I find Dorner standing over me with his glasses askew and my pistol pen in hand.

"Are you hurt?" he says, panting.

I don't get the chance to answer him. The second policeman takes off running. Sabine aims her stolen rifle at him, shooting twice, but the night is on his side. The bullet goes astray, and he begins crying for help, screaming for reinforcements.

Merde. Over on the next hill, I see them. Flashlights. Shouting. More police.

I grab Dorner's arm and reach for Sabine's. "There's more coming! We have to run."

Sabine pushes us away from her. "Take him to the drop-off!" she says to me. "I'll route the patrols away from you."

"We go together!"

"No, Dorner has to make it to the coast. There's nothing more important than that. One of us stays with him, the other leads the Nazis away."

"Then I'll route the patrols. I took the bicycle last time." If she's trying to "help" me again, it's not going to work.

"What are you even talking about? I'm faster than you. I can out-run them. Go, before we lose more time. That's an order!"

The shouts hit a crescendo. We can't waste another second, but I can't let her go. She has a stolen rifle to her name and nothing else.

"But—"

"He's the mission! Don't forget that."

She's right. We're Covert Operations. The mission always comes first—and this might be the most important one we will ever under-take. "Watch your back."

Her face is grim when she tells me, "The same to you. Now go."

I won't make her say that again. Taking Dorner by the wrist, I lead him west toward Auderville, toward the beach, toward the finish line. I won't look behind me, either, because if I do, I might just turn back.

"Will she be all right?" Dorner breathes out.

"Of course she will," I say softly. "She's the best we have." And that's the truth. Then, with the ocean crashing into our ears, we run.

TWELVE

We fly over the wet hills. Our legs stumble on the slick grass and stone, and our ears echo with the fresh shouts of the patrols. Every step we take leads us farther away from Sabine, and my heart hurts at that thought. She might be fast, but not even she can outrun their bullets.

A part of me wants to double back to Sabine's side, but the other part of me knows that we have to stay ahead of the soldiers. There might be a handful of them now, but the Nazis will soon send in reinforcements. More soldiers. More dogs. More bullets that we won't be able to dodge.

The rain keeps falling. Our clothes soak through and cling against our skin, but I don't even think about stopping until we're so out of breath that we might collapse. I search for a place to hide, but there aren't any trees or crumbling buildings to shield us from sight. We're out in the open with fields all around us, so I drop to my knees and flatten onto my stomach. Dorner doesn't need any coaxing to do the same.

"We'll rest for a few minutes," I say between breaths, "and no more." A peek at my watch tells me that we need to make up for lost time. We have an hour and a half until we have to reach the beach. There won't be any second chances if we miss that submarine.

While Dorner wipes the rain from his glasses, I scan the horizon for any trace of a flashlight or headlight that could give away the Nazis' location, but I find nothing except for the black clouds overhead and the shadows of the surrounding hills. Though I know that the patrols could be skulking around the next corner, like coiled-up snakes waiting for us to step on them.

"Any sign of Odette? Will she attempt to rendezvous with us?" whispers Dorner.

I shake my head. Sabine wouldn't take that risk. She'll lead the Nazis away from us with her last breath if necessary. A twinge plucks at my chest, and I hope with everything inside of me that she'll be able to escape. If she doesn't . . . I won't let her sacrifice be in vain.

"We could go back," Dorner says.

"No, we can't. The mission always comes first," I echo Sabine. I search through our pouch for a canteen, but find mine empty. I sigh and toss it aside.

"Here, have some of mine," Dorner says, offering his own canteen that he has attached to his belt loop.

"Save it for yourself," I say reluctantly. I've been trained to go without water, but Dorner hasn't.

"There's plenty." He nudges the canteen into my hand and won't drop the matter until I draw in a slow sip. "How much farther until we reach the submarine?"

"Not far," I lie. We'll be cutting it close. "Don't worry. I'll get you there."

"That isn't my main concern."

I almost choke on the water because if that isn't his main concern, then there must be something he isn't telling me. "What is your concern then?"

"The British. Once you hand me over to them, they could arrest me. Throw me in prison."

"Tell them what you've told me. Show them the photographs."

"Will that be enough?" He swats his hand against the damp grass and peers at me from the corner of his eye. "Perhaps you could put in a good word for me. You must have a contact with them if you were able to arrange for my transport across the Channel."

"It doesn't matter what I say. What matters is what's in your folder."

He chews on that for a moment. "I suppose you're right." His mouth kicks up into a half smile. "Although a good word can't hurt. I'd sincerely appreciate it, Marie-Louise."

"We'll see." I suppose I could radio the SOE once I get back to headquarters—*if* I can get back there, that is—but I meant it when I told him that what I have to say won't matter much in the end. His evidence will have to speak for itself.

Dorner seems to drop the matter for now. "Do you have any more of those pen contraptions in case we run into the patrols again?"

"You used my last one."

"A pity. I've never seen anything like it. Does the Resistance make them?" He tilts his head like he's puzzling out the results of an experiment. "They seem rather handy."

"They are handy," I say, but I don't tell him where I got the weapons. His question might be innocent, but I can't spill Covert Ops' secrets. "By the way, good shot tonight."

"It was nothing." He wipes his glasses again, and I see that one of the lenses has cracked down the middle. "I was lucky."

"I wouldn't call it lucky. I'd call it good aim." *Excellent* aim, really. I point at his glasses. "You only had use of one eye with that lens cracked."

"It's not a strong prescription," he demurs, and tucks the glasses in his shirt pocket as if to prove his point. "And you give me too much credit. I haven't shot a gun since I was a boy, back when my brother took me hunting." His voice cracks. "He was drafted by the Nazis a year ago. I hope that he's all right."

I nod, though I can't quite echo his sentiments. What if his brother's regiment had fought Theo's? It's a miniscule possibility, but it's still there, reminding me of the fact that Dorner and I stood on opposite sides of this war just a month ago. That makes me wonder, too, what Theo would think if he saw me sitting here and sharing a canteen with a former Nazi scientist. He'd probably call me crazy, even if I explained everything about Zerfall to him. *Watch your back, Luce,* he'd tell me, and that thought makes my heart ache. I only wish I had been the one watching Theo's back the day he was shot. I wish *I* had been there to push him out of the way—because he would've done the same for me.

I get back onto my feet and offer my hand to Dorner. Maybe I can't take a bullet for my brother, but I can deliver Dorner to the SOE and get the coordinates to the laboratory. It's too late to save Theo, but it won't be too late to save the thousands of soldiers and civilians who could die of Zerfall.

We hit our grueling pace once again with only the crashing of the waves to keep us company. For a man who has seemingly spent most of his time in a laboratory, Dorner manages to keep up with me. When we stop again, I'm the one who needs more water and not the other way around.

Dorner rests his hands on his knees while he steadies his breath. "I don't mean to slow us down."

"You haven't," I say.

"You don't need to lie for my sake. If it weren't for me, I'm sure you would have swam across the Channel by now." He sees me smirk and goes on. "It's true. I've yet to see you make a mistake."

I almost snort, wishing Major Harken could hear that. "Tell that to my supervisor."

"You two don't get along, I take it?"

"Not always." I wait for him to ask me more, but he doesn't. He's smart enough to know that it isn't his place, but the silence between us stretches and swells—and the memory of my Class 3 infraction stretches and swells with it. I never even told Tilly about what happened that night. I was too ashamed.

That's why it takes me by surprise when I hear myself tell him, "I was supposed to take out a target a few months ago. It . . . didn't go as planned."

"Take out?"

"Kill."

His eyes widen. "Ah."

My throat grows tight as I think about that mission. It had been my first solo assignment, and it took place about a month after I landed in France. I left headquarters that rainy evening with a bounce in my step. I was so sure that I'd be pinned with a new title by the end of the night. *Agent Blaise.* I knew it would soon be mine.

My target's name was Allard, a known collaborator who had gained the trust of a few Resistance members only to send them to prison. His reward? Money and a pat on the head by the Germans. Allard should have been a simple kill—he was old and slow and already sickly with a disease that made it hard for him to breathe. Harken had laid out the plan for me, too. I'd follow Allard into a busy métro car and knick his ankle with the tip of my umbrella, breaking open the skin so that the poison on the umbrella tip would seep into his bloodstream. Easy as the alphabet song.

It had started off without a hitch. I had worn my hair in two French braids and put on my pressed school uniform. My pièce de résistance, though, was a light pink umbrella edged with ruffles that I had sewn on myself. Tilly told me that she didn't recognize me at all. I took that as a compliment.

Rain showers had drenched the city that day, packing the métro full with grumbling passengers. I followed Allard into a second-class train car and elbowed three men aside to get a seat close to him. Right before we reached his stop, I made my move. I maneuvered myself behind him while clutching on to my umbrella. My thumb hovered over the button that would release the needle tip.

But as I aimed the tip at Allard's ankle, I broke out in a cold sweat. *First-time nerves*, I thought. My trainers told me that this might happen, so I breathed in deep and reminded myself of what Allard had done. A traitor like him didn't deserve to live.

I tried aiming the umbrella again, but everything worsened from there. My fingers shook. My neck reddened. I didn't know what had come over me. Thinking about Allard's crimes made little difference, so I thought about Theo. I would never see my brother again, yet someone like Allard kept on breathing. That gave me just enough wherewithal to press the button and swing it at Allard's foot.

It was too late. The doors opened, and Allard plunged onto the crowded train platform. I scrambled to catch up to him but ran into a young woman instead. She couldn't have been much older than I was. Both of us fell to the ground, and I was about to run off when she cried out and clutched her calf. Somehow my umbrella had grazed her skin, and now a thin line of blood was staining her stocking. It was just a nick, but dread filled me to the brim. Within a day or two, she wouldn't be able to get out of bed, and it wouldn't be long until she stopped breathing completely. The poison was that potent.

I stood frozen on the platform, watching that coward Allard shuffling away while this girl dusted herself off. I had my orders, but I couldn't leave her to die.

A heavy hand fell on my shoulder right then. I spun around to find Harken standing over me. Apparently my first solo mission wasn't a solo one after all. He had been tailing me all along, and see-ing the scowl on his face, he must've regretted sending me out already.

"Sir—"

He shoved a tiny bottle into my palm. The antidote. "Take care of the civilian."

"I'm sorry!"

"No apologies. Not here."

"But—"

"You've done enough. Find the girl. Fix this."

He gave me a push. I made it five steps before I turned around to apologize again, but Harken was long gone. By the time I returned home, everything had been settled. I had caught up with the girl and swiped the top of her foot with my umbrella tip—this time with the antidote rather than the poison. Harken had taken care of Allard. It wouldn't be long before Allard would be found strangled in a run-down café restroom, but Harken wouldn't let me off easily just because our target was dead. He sent me to desk duty so fast that my head spun, and that was where I stayed until he finally agreed to give me another chance with Monsieur Travert. Not that that had gone much more smoothly.

"Did you catch your target?" Dorner says, cutting through the quiet night.

"We did," I reply dryly.

"Ah," he says again. "The Resistance . . . trains you for this type of thing?"

I tense. He's likely asking me that out of scientific curiosity, but I don't like the implication behind the question. Yes, the OSS and the Resistance trains their agents to kill, but we weren't the ones who started this war. "Don't the Nazis train their soldiers to kill people?" I retort.

"I hadn't thought of it that way," he murmurs. "My apologies."

I wave him off. There's no more time for *I'm sorrys* and chitchat. I urge us back into a run.

With the coastline just beyond our fingertips, we draw so close to the ocean that the spray of salt water dusts our faces. A curtain of fog greets us, too, and I hope it will grow thicker. It should mask our arrival at the beach.

I spot a village ahead. If the map is correct, it will be Auderville—and that means we're nearly there. North of town, we reach the cliffs that buttress the ocean and we skim along the tops of them until I find a rocky path down to the beach. I hurry down the jagged boulders, but my hand slides off a slick rock and I nearly lose my grip. Dorner is quick to catch my wrist, though, and I mumble a *merci*. That's twice now that he has watched my back tonight. I wonder what Harken would say to that. Frankly, what would I have said to that before I met Dorner?

By the time my feet meet the sand, we're late. I tell Dorner to stay put while I forge ahead alone. I'll be faster that way. As long as I can flag down the SOE boatman, that'll buy us a little time. But the fog is thick and gray, cutting my visibility to next to nothing, and I see only dark waves in front of me.

The Brits aren't here.

I fumble with my watch. It's 0405. We're five minutes late. Could they have left already? My knees give out and sink onto the frigid sand. We've come too far to find an empty beach. Sabine may have given her life so that we'd make it here.

All that, for nothing?

"Marie-Louise!"

My senses come alive, and I curse myself for leaving Dorner behind. I race back to find him, thinking that a patrol has followed us, but when I reach him he's pointing frantically at the water.

"There! Do you see it?" he says.

I squint toward where he's pointing—and I see it indeed. It's a rowboat coming ashore, guided by a lone boatman. I nearly crumple to the sand one more time, but I can't let my relief get the best of me.

"Stay here," I tell Dorner again. As the boat swiftly approaches shore, the man rowing catches sight of me. He goes rigid and begins reaching for something at his waist—a gun?—and I spill out the passcode that Harken gave me.

"There might be rough waters tonight!"

His hand falls to his side, and I hear a sharp sigh. "But the sea appears calm enough to me."

He's SOE, all right. I march into the waves, shivering as the cold water climbs up my dress, and I help him tow the boat onto the beach. "You sure are a sight for sore eyes," I say, my words nearly drowned in the crash of the waves.

"So are you," he replies in accented French. "I had a devil of a time coming to shore with that storm, but my superiors would've boxed my ears if I came back empty-handed." He blinks into the fog. "Where is . . . ?"

"He's here. I wasn't going to let you boys miss out on this parcel." As if on cue, Dorner steps into our view. I'm about to make the introductions when the boatman stops me.

"That's for my commanding officers to know, miss. My orders are to get him on the boat and back to the sub as quick as I can."

I call for Dorner to get onto the boat, but he doesn't come running. Rather, he tucks his head down to ask me, "This gentleman will take me to England? You're certain of his credentials?"

There isn't time for any more caution. "He knew the correct passcode. He's SOE. You have my word on that."

He straightens, then nods. Just three days ago I would've thought this impossible—a Nazi scientist placing his trust in an Allied spy— but I suppose I've come to grudgingly trust him, too. He may have played a hand in setting Operation Zerfall into motion, but with his help we'll stop the virus from spreading. Who knows? Maybe Dorner's intel will tip the war into the Allies' favor—but that doesn't mean that I've forgotten our bargain.

"Now give me the coordinates," I say.

He sweeps the wet hair from his forehead and gives me the numbers, then repeats them twice. "The laboratory isn't far from the city of Verdun."

"By the eastern border?"

"Yes, very close to Belgium. But you should know that you won't find the laboratory at the coordinates I gave you," he says.

I go numb all over. "What?" In mere seconds, my numbness shifts into a red-hot anger, and I'm ready to slap him and shove him onto the sand.

"Let me finish! The entire facility was built *underground*."

"You wait until now to tell me that?" I wish I had slapped him before because now I'm so dazed that I couldn't muster the energy if I wanted to. How are the Allies supposed to destroy a laboratory underground? We won't be able to use our bombers. We'll have to take out the lab with ground forces, but it could take years for our soldiers to infiltrate France. We're still trying to claw our way into Italy.

"Listen to me. You can access the laboratory through an outbuilding at the coordinates. An elevator will take you to the facility. But it's heavily guarded." He digs out his precious folder of documents, still dry from the tarp we wrapped around it, and yanks out a few pages. "Take these. They're schematics of the building."

"What am I supposed to do with them? Give them to the Brits?"

"Take them before they get wet! I made copies." He waits until I fold the pages and stow them under my dress before he continues. "Show the papers to the Resistance in case . . . in case something happens to me before I get to London."

"You'll get to London just fine," I assure him.

"Just in case there's a U-boat attack."

"Very well," I say grimly. At this point, the boatman is waving his arms and getting ready to push off. I have to make this quick. "Give me the name of the double agent."

Dorner bends down so that our foreheads nearly bump. "T.J.H. Those are the agent's initials. I'm sorry but I never did find out the full name."

"Mademoiselle, monsieur!" the boatman interrupts us.

But I can't let Dorner go just yet. My fingers dig into his arm. "You're sure? You're absolutely sure?"

"Yes. I saw the documentation."

My head spins so fast that I feel nauseous. I stumble, but Dorner reaches back to steady me. "Are you all right?"

How do I even answer that? Dorner appears ready to say more, but the boatman has come up behind us and pulls him toward the boat. Soon they're aboard and the boatman begins rowing, yet Dorner never takes his eyes off me.

"Thank you!" he calls out. "I'll never be able to repay you, but remember . . ." The mist swallows him up along with whatever he wanted to tell me. At this distance I wouldn't have been able to hear him anyway.

T.J.H.

Dorner may not know the name of the double agent, but I certainly do.

Thomas Julian Harken.

November 18, 1942

Dear Luce,

It turns out that Gordo was right all along. We've landed in ████████ —
in █████ *if you're wondering, and I'm sure that you are. That's why I
haven't been able to write to you sooner.*

*The French gave us real trouble after we landed. I thought they were sup-
posed to be our allies, but Sergeant Stanton told us that the Nazis are
making the French soldiers fight us over here. Something about how*
██████ *is a French colony. I'm sure I'm botching that explanation, but
I'm not as book smart as Ruthie is.*

*You can tell Maman to breathe easy, though. I may have a few bruises,
but I still have all of my fingers and toes. We've been given some time off
while we wait for our transports to arrive, so the boys and I've gone swimming in the* ████████████ *and have been stuffing our mouths full of
mandarin oranges. There's sand everywhere, too. It gets in our eyes and
our shoes and all over our food. It makes me think about the time when I
convinced you and Ruthie to skip school and we caught the bus to Ocean
City, but the wind got so bad that we couldn't eat a bite of Ruthie's picnic.*
██████ *is sort of like that. No camels sighted yet.*

*I'm back at camp now, and we've taken in some of the French wounded.
Most of them don't speak a word of English, so I've been translating to*

help out the docs. One of the soldiers said that he's from Saint-Malo and that got me thinking. Maybe we might've known him if Maman had never met Papa and never left France, but I guess you and me wouldn't be here at all if life had turned out that way.

I'm sounding like a sap now, aren't I? It must be the ██████ sun. I'll write again soon. Until then, give Maman and Ruthie my best and take care of yourself. I'm sorry that I can't be there to protect you from Papa. More sorry than you know, little sis.

Love you.

Theo

THIRTEEN

I return on foot to Cherbourg, dazed. The sky overhead is as blue as the jewels at Versailles, but I might as well be walking through fog.

T.J.H.

Those initials punch through me every time I blink, and they haunt me as I wind my way back to the safe house, where we parted ways with Madame Rochette. The farmer there is kind enough to let me rest for a couple hours, but I don't want to put him in any more danger, so I borrow a few francs and take a fresh change of clothes that once belonged to his dead wife. After that, I leave for the train station straightaway. There's no time for rest—not after what Dorner has told me.

I board a second-class train car and ignore the greasy-haired man sitting next to me who keeps knocking his knee against mine. For the entire trip I try to make sense out of what Dorner revealed to me. Major Harken, a double agent? A *traitor*? I can't see him turning— not for the money and not for the favors, like Travert. That's the part that doesn't make sense. What could the Nazis have offered him to make him give up his country?

Maybe Dorner got the initials mixed up, or maybe there's

another T.J.H. within the Parisian Resistance. This could just be a coincidence.

Can it be that simple, though?

I should contact the OSS, but it's not exactly easy to talk to them. I'd have to radio them, and it could be days before I'd get an answer. Besides, Harken controls our radio.

If Sabine were here, she could send a message to our London office.

Except I don't know where she is. I don't know if she's alive.

I thrust that thought into the dustiest corner of my mind. I need to focus on returning to headquarters first. And then . . . and then I'll decide what my plan will be. I don't know what I'll find when I return—whether or not Sabine has made it safely, whether Tilly and Delphine have made it back in one piece, and whether Harken will await me there—or what I'll say to him.

With a whine of its wheels, the train pulls into the Paris station and I begin my trek back to headquarters. The sun drags low behind me and has nearly dipped below the trees by the time I reach the 6th arrondissement. I walk alongside the calm waters of the Seine, trying to organize my scattered thoughts. Suddenly someone bumps into me from behind. I'm sent sprawling forward and I'm about to mutter a curse, but I don't hit the sidewalk. The very same someone who ran into me grabs me by the arm to steady me.

"My apologies, mademoiselle," a girl says, "but you should watch where you're going."

"Watch where *I'm* going?" I whirl around to face this dolt, but once I turn I forget what I was going to say.

"Surprise," Sabine says. She links arms with me and leads me down rue Saint-Jacques toward headquarters.

It's like she's a street cat, popping up whenever I least expect her. She must have nine lives, too, because this is twice now that she has escaped from the Germans' clutches. A dozen questions spring to the tip of my tongue. I know I need to wait until we arrive at headquarters to release them, but one wriggles out. "When did you make it home?"

"This morning."

I break into a smile for the first time in days. "You beat me back." Of course she did. "Did you . . . ?" My smile fades because I have to choose my next words with care. There's an elderly couple sitting on a bench across the street from us, and you never know if there's a Nazi patrol waiting around the corner. "Did you run into any trouble?"

"I ran into plenty, but nothing I couldn't handle."

"When we left you—" I stop because I've said too much already. "I'm so glad to see you again. And . . . and I have something to tell you."

"Oh? I've something to tell you, too."

With our secrets dangling between us, we return to the bookstore and descend into the dark lair of headquarters. The smell of dust and mold creeps into my nose. I used to hate this scent, but now I take in a long breath of it. *Home.* But that cozy feeling doesn't linger, because Harken's initials crop up in my mind again.

Sabine lights the candles on the hallway table. "Tell me what happened to Dorner. Did you make it to the coordinates?"

"We did. He should be in London by now, telling the SOE every-thing that he told us."

"Good. That's very good." She shuts her eyes in relief, but the moment is fleeting. "What about the double agent?"

My mouth goes dry. "He gave me the agent's initials."

"That's all? He said he'd give us a name!"

"The initials are T.J.H."

Sabine goes quiet as she puzzles out the letters, and it doesn't take her long to unravel them. "Major Harken?" she whispers.

I wait for her to swear up and down, or maybe she'll defend Harken until her face purples, but she doesn't do either. She's oddly calm about what I've told her. Something must be off.

"You don't seem very surprised by this news," I say.

"I'm not." She doesn't elaborate, merely crooks a finger in my direction. "You better follow me."

I remember that she had something to tell me, too, and so I follow her down the dim hall and toward Harken's private quarters. He always keeps his door tightly locked, but Sabine picks the lock with ease and strides inside. I stop in place.

"Did you break into Harken's office?" I ask.

"I had no other choice. He wasn't here, and I needed to check the radio in case the OSS had a message for us."

"Did they?"

"No, but I heard something else on the frequency." She takes out a piece of paper from her blouse pocket and presses it into my palm. "Here. It was in Morse."

I stare at the paper. My own Morse code is rusty, but I manage to translate it after a few tries:

TJH: Tuileries Garden. Usual time. Your payment is ready.

The room tilts, and my head goes with it. "You heard this on the radio? You're sure?"

"Undeniably. I heard it three times." She nods at the suitcase that holds Harken's radio. To use it, she would've needed to drag the suitcase up to the ground floor to get a signal. I imagine her stooped by the window, pointing the antenna discretely out while she turned the dials to pick up any messages—and coming across this one. "You do know what this means, don't you?"

"Of course I do," I mumble. Although I still can't quite believe it. "Is the message still being broadcast?"

"Perhaps. I can't be sure."

"I need to hear it."

"Don't you trust me?"

"I trust you with my life." And that's the truth, after what we've been through these last three days. "But we're talking about Major Harken committing treason, Sabine. We need to be absolutely sure before we throw around any accusations."

"You're holding the proof in your hands." She motions at the Morse-coded message she has given me. "Dorner's intelligence confirms it. How do you explain that?"

I don't have an answer for her. The thing is, I can't clear Major Harken's name . . . and yet I know this man. Never in a thousand years would I think that he's a spy. And to be honest, I thought Sabine would share my doubts.

But Sabine seems to have made up her mind already. "You simply don't want to see the truth, do you?" She crosses her arms, and a sharp blaze of hurt punches my stomach. She's talking to me like I'm a fool, and frankly I'm tired of her hot-and-cold routine. I thought we had worked past it.

"Listen to me—" I start, but my voice falls silent when we hear five crisp knocks on the hatch. Someone's here. Maybe Tilly.

I tuck Sabine's scrawled message into my pocket and head out, but Sabine makes a grab at me.

"Lucie!" she hisses. "What if it isn't a friendly?"

But I heard the five knocks loud and clear, and all I can think about is Tilly—that she's alive and that she has come home—except when the hatch unlocks I don't find her descending the ladder rungs.

It's Harken.

"Blaise?" he says gruffly, hobbling onto the floorboards. He must've injured his left ankle, judging by the way he favors the right one. There's a notch of surprise in his dry throat. "You're alive."

"Yes." That's all that I can say. An accusation teeters at the edges of my mouth, but it doesn't come out. My head still reels from what Sabine has showed me. "Where's Tilly?"

He moves past me and limps down the hallway toward his quarters. "We took different trains from Reims to better cover our tracks. Did you find Dorner?"

"We did," says Sabine, stepping out from the shadows of his room.

Harken breathes a sigh of relief, but his face soon scrunches into a scowl. "What were you doing in my quarters?"

"I had to check the radio, in case another agent contacted us."

"I see." He shows no hint of alarm. If he's playing dumb, he's doing an excellent job of it. "And did someone?"

"No, but I heard a most intriguing message," Sabine says.

"Sabine, wait—" I start. I didn't want to confront him now. Not until I heard that broadcast myself. But I also thought that we'd have more time before Harken arrived at headquarters. I search over his face, and I realize that he does have some questions to answer—whether he's innocent or not. "Sir, we have a lot to discuss."

Despite his exhaustion, Harken nods. "Into my office. Let's talk."

We all file in. Harken settles into the chair behind his desk while Sabine and I stand in front of him, where I study him intently, noting the hunch of his shoulders and the dark bags beneath his eyes. I still can't see him as the double agent, but neither can I ignore what Dorner and Sabine have told me. If Harken has indeed turned, then he needs to pay for his betrayal. I'll escort him back to the US for his court martial myself.

Before I can open my mouth, though, Harken beats me to the chase. "Look, I'll be quick," he says, rubbing the bridge of his nose with his first two fingers. "Delphine is dead. By the time we had a rescue plan set in place, the Resistance in Reims discovered that she had succumbed to her injuries. Agent Fairbanks and I tried to head back to Paris after that news, but there was a bombing on the railways that delayed our return." He spits out the information rapid-fire, one fact after the other. We don't even have time to process that another one of our agents is gone. "Tell me about Dorner and Operation Zerfall."

"How can we be sure that Delphine is dead?" Sabine is quick to reply. "Did you see her remains?"

"We didn't have that sort of access. I've taken the Resistance at their word—and that's final. Now brief me on your mission. What did you do with Dorner?"

"I interrogated him, and we found his story to be valid." I feel Sabine elbow me in the ribs, silently telling me to get on with it, but if she wants me to throw out the accusation, then we'll do it my way. "He told us—"

"So what's Zerfall?" Harken interrupts.

"That's classified information," Sabine says.

"Classified?" Harken's brows cross. "On whose account?"

"On mine," she replies.

"If you're making some sort of joke, I'm not laughing," Harken says darkly.

"I'm not laughing, either," she says.

"You know what? I don't appreciate your tone, Agent Chevalier. Maybe you've forgotten that you're speaking to your superior officer."

"Superior?" Sabine barks out a laugh. I don't like how she's escalating this situation, and I'm about to tell her to cool it, but Sabine snatches the reins of the conversation and gets straight to the point. "No, I believe I'm talking to a traitor."

The room goes silent. Harken's eyes gather with storm clouds as they fly toward Sabine. Mine do the same. Has she gone entirely mad?

Harken pounds both fists on his desk. "Excuse me?"

"You heard me, you traitor," Sabine retorts. "Show him the paper, Lucie."

Harken turns his attention to me. "Blaise, you're in on this, too?"

"We all need to calm down!" I say, my voice carrying over theirs. Before they can get another word in, I spill out everything. "Dorner said that we have a double agent in our ranks—an agent with the initials T.J.H."

It takes a second for my revelation to sink in to Major Harken, but once it does, he turns bright red from neck to forehead. "How dare you even—"

"Show him the message!" Sabine interrupts, turning to me. When I don't move quickly enough for her liking, she digs into my pocket and shoves the paper at him. "I heard that with my own ears over the radio. A message from the Germans to you."

Harken crumples the note without reading it. "I won't even dignify your accusation with an answer. It's *that* ludicrous. Now, get out of this room before I toss you out of Covert Ops completely."

"I'm not leaving until you confess what you've done," Sabine counters, not budging.

"Stop it, the both of you!" I yank Sabine's elbow because we're getting nowhere with this method of attack. I don't know what she was thinking, charging him like that. Did she truly expect him to confess to us? But Sabine has the strength of a viper and shrugs me off.

"How much are they paying you?" she shouts at him. "How much did it cost to buy you?"

Harken turns a violent shade of scarlet. Then everything happens so fast. A fuse bursts inside of him and he slaps her hard. At that very moment, the anger in his eyes shifts to shock, but Sabine is just as quick to react. She yanks out a tiny pistol from her skirt pocket, one that she must've gotten from the weaponry upon her return to headquarters. Except she isn't using it on a German officer or a Nazi collaborator. She's pointing the barrel straight at Harken's heart.

"What are you doing?" I cry to her.

She ignores me. "Put your hands up where I can see them. *Sir.*"

Harken looks ready to throttle her, but he does as she says, bringing his hands over his head slowly. Then he shouts knives into the air. "You're out of the OSS completely, Chevalier! Pack your bags before I throw you out myself. That's an order."

"You just threw me out of Covert Ops," Sabine says, a smirk on her lips. "I no longer take orders from you, you filthy traitor."

"Blaise!" Harken says, his hands still in the air. "Seize Chevalier's weapon. That's our property she's holding."

"Don't listen to him!" Sabine jumps in. "Do you see what he's doing? He's trying to drive us apart."

"Calm down, the both of you!" I take a step toward them, but I keep a steady eye on the gun. I don't want Sabine to swing it toward me. "Sabine, put down the gun. Major Harken, keep your hands up."

"Do you hear what she said, Chevalier?" says Harken.

"But you do have to answer her questions, sir," I say to him. "*Our* questions. Let's get this straightened out. Why are you receiving messages from the Nazis?"

"Unbelievable! The two of you have gone completely mad!" He points a finger at Sabine. "Get that gun out of my face, Chevalier. Or you're going to regret it." His hand lowers slightly, and he eyes his desk drawer.

Fear wraps around my throat because I realize what he's doing. "Sir, no!"

I might as well be shouting to a wall. With lightning quickness, he thrusts his hand into the drawer and his fingers coil around something—a gun?—but he never gets a proper handle on it.

Sabine's pistol explodes three times. The sound clashes in my ears, a trio of pops. Harken stumbles back and drops to the floor.

"Major!" I cry.

Sabine's pistol clicks empty. Horror fills her features, but it's fleeting. Soon, there's nothing but steel on her face.

Harken moans, and I stagger toward his desk.

"He's a traitor," Sabine whispers, but she doesn't stop me from rushing next to him. His hands clutch a circle of red that's blossoming over his shirt. Traitor or not, my stomach lurches. I search for something to staunch the wound but there's too much blood.

"Blaise—"

"Save your breath!" I press my hand over his wounds, but I can't stop the bleeding. He needs a doctor, a whole team of them.

He needs a miracle.

"Blaise," he whispers. I grip his hand, but his fingers fall limp against mine.

"Hold on, sir. We'll get help!"

With great effort, he tilts his head until his eyes land upon mine, but they're already fluttering shut.

"I'll find Laurent," I tell him, but we both know that it'll be useless.

"Blaise," he whispers. Blood trickles out from his lips. "Don't . . . trust her."

His hand drops to the floor, thudding dully and going still.

"Sir?" I whisper. Trembling, I reach to check his pulse, but even before I touch his skin I know that he's already gone.

Major Harken is dead.

FOURTEEN

I squeeze Major Harken's fingers, but there's no response. I shake him, then slap him.

Nothing happens.

"Sir?" I hear my voice turn shrill. *"Major?"* My hands are slippery with his blood, the redness staining the cuffs of my sweater.

"Is he dead?" Her voice punctures the air, and I blink toward it. Sabine stares at Harken's body, the pistol still resting in her hand. Something breaks inside me at the sight of it. I lunge at her and snatch it from her grasp before I toss it across the room.

"Yes, he's dead. Harken's dead!" I say.

My shrillness seems to cut through her haze. "Keep your voice down! Do you want every Nazi in Paris to hear you?"

I jump to my feet, wishing I hadn't tossed that pistol away, because I wouldn't mind using it right now. "You *killed* Major Harken and you're telling me to keep quiet?"

"He was reaching for his gun!"

"How do you know that's what he was reaching for? You shot him before we could see anything!"

"I was defending myself!" To prove it, she steps over Major

Harken's body like it's a piece of litter in the street and yanks open the drawer, where she fishes out his personal pistol. "Do you see now?"

"It's not like you gave him much choice, pulling your gun on him like that!" I knock her hand away, and Major Harken's last words echo in my ears. *Don't trust her.*

My mind whirls. But could I have trusted *him*?

I brace my hand against Harken's desk. Everything I've known for three months has been yanked apart and turned upside down. If I had some time to think or breathe—

"Dear God, what happened?"

A new voice rips through my ears, and my head snaps toward the door. My first thought is that the Nazis have found us, that they heard the gunshots and now we're done for. But I don't find a soldier in the doorway.

"Tilly?" I choke out. Major Harken said that she was following behind him, but I never even heard her come in. She must've made her way into headquarters while the rest of us were too busy screaming at one another.

Tilly doesn't answer me. Her entire being is transfixed upon Harken's body. "Major?" she whispers. Her face is a pale moon, and she stumbles toward his body, but I block her path by wrapping my arms around her. "What happened? Why is he—"

"He's gone," I whisper. "He's dead."

She pushes me away and falls to the floor next to him, her hands shaking as they cover her mouth. Then she grabs him by the collar. "Major Harken!"

"Tilly—"

Her eyes are wild when she looks up at me. "How did this happen?"

I point a trembling finger toward Sabine. "She shot him."

Tilly's head whips the other way. "You . . . *shot* Major Harken?"

"He was a double agent!" Sabine explodes, tossing both arms in the air. "Lucie and I learned that there was a traitor among us, with the initials T.J.H."

Tilly's lips split apart. "Who told you that?"

"Dorner."

"The Nazi you were sent to find? You believed him over Major Harken?"

"That isn't all," Sabine is quick to say. "I heard a transmission over the radio—a message from the Nazis to Harken, promising payment for betraying Covert Ops. Tell her, Lucie."

"Don't you drag me into this!" I say. "Harken could still be alive if you hadn't waved that gun at him."

Sabine shakes her head in disgust. "Why do you insist on protecting a traitor?"

"There wasn't definitive proof of that!" I reply. "There should've been an investigation."

Sabine snorts. "Harken could've escaped by the time that happened. Very well, if you want more proof, then listen to the radio yourself." She carries the suitcase holding the radio out of Major Harken's office and drags us both up to the main floor of the bookstore, ignoring Tilly's tears that splash onto the floor. I don't tell

Sabine to stop. It may be risky to use the radio at a time like this—who knows if the Nazis will be listening for our signal—but I need to hear this message. I need to know if Harken has died in vain or not.

If he has, Sabine will have to pay for that.

Sabine warms up the radio while the three of us gather just beyond the open hatch. She fumbles with the dials, searching for the correct frequency, until her eyes alight. "It's here!" She thrusts the earpiece at me. "Listen."

I shove the device into my ear, and the tapping of Morse begins immediately. I struggle to keep up with the symphony of dashes and dots.

"Is it the message to Harken?" Tilly says, her voice breaking. "What does it say?"

I'm too busy translating the message to give her an answer. *Tuileries* . . .

Sabine's head bobs up. "Did you hear that?"

I shush her. *Garden* . . .

"There! A truck," Sabine whispers. She pokes her head beyond the false door and peers out the closest window. "We need to get back downstairs!"

"I need another minute!" I say. *Tuileries Garden* . . .

"Those headlights are turning back around. We need to move!" Sabine practically pushes Tilly down the ladder before she reaches for the radio to stow it back in its case.

I bat her hand away. "I need more time!"

"We don't have any to spare!" With that said, Sabine yanks the earpiece from my ear and closes the suitcase. "Don't stand there, Lucienne. Move!"

She has to physically pull me into the hatch, however, because the last word that I deciphered still clangs in my ears, tuning out everything else surrounding me.

Usual . . .

Sabine was telling the truth about the Nazi message. I may have heard a snippet, but it was word-for-word as she had translated.

My head goes dizzy. Sabine is telling me something, but my ears are full of cotton. Even as Harken lay dying in my arms, I couldn't believe the accusations. Not him, of all people.

"You were right," I whisper to her.

She pauses. There's no smug look on her face. No triumph. "I didn't want to be," she says, helping me onto the ladder and passing me the radio. Her head remains above the hatch, watching, listening, waiting. She swears. "It's them! Go, go!"

I stumble down the rungs, missing the last two completely and tumbling onto my backside. While Tilly helps me up, Sabine shuts the hatch and locks it tight.

"The Nazis are outside!" Sabine says. "They must've picked up our signal."

"What do we do? Major Harken always told us . . ." Tilly stops midsentence, and I give her a quick squeeze on the arm.

"We need to take out all of the files and grab as many weapons as we can," I say, breaking out of my daze. I can be angry later. First, we have to make it out of headquarters alive.

"Yes, we need to follow protocol," Sabine says. Somehow she has squelched any panic from her features, a trick Harken mastered, too. How else could he have made it as a double agent? "Matilda, handle the files. Lucienne, go to the weaponry. Fill three suitcases with whatever you can fit inside them."

"What about you?" I say to Sabine.

"I'll get the kerosene."

"No, leave that to me." A blot of color has returned to Tilly's cheeks, and her fists are rooted at her sides. "If we're going to blow headquarters sky-high, that'll be my job."

She gets no argument from Sabine or me. While Sabine heads for the file cabinet in the meeting room, I grab our extra valises from the wardrobe and bolt for the weaponry—in go the grenades and a few knives, in go the pistols with silencers, and in goes a miniature machine gun, along with a plump bag of Aunt Jemima. It doesn't take long for the valises to groan from the new weight, but I'm not finished yet. I have pockets, don't I? I stuff them full of pistol pens and gas pens and another knife for good measure. Even then, I've hardly made a dent in the weaponry. I place a solemn hand on top of one of the shelves. This room deserves a better end than going up in flames.

Boots stomp into the bookstore overhead.

They're here.

Gathering the valises into my arms, I hurry toward the storage room. Shouts echo above me, and the footsteps clatter throughout the store. Our hatch is well hidden, but it's a matter of time before the Germans find our headquarters. Sabine shoves aside a crate of potatoes and guides her hand along the stone until she locates a hidden latch that accesses our escape tunnel. With a sharp yank, a door pops open in the wall, just wide enough for us to crawl through.

"Where's Matilda?" she asks.

As if on cue, Tilly appears behind us, panting and grasping a near-empty canister of kerosene. She pours the rest of it by the doorway and tosses the can aside.

"Did we forget anything?" she says, and I pat the bags.

"What about the L pills?" asks Tilly.

Sabine shakes her head. "There's no time."

With a valise under her arm, Sabine slides onto her stomach to fit into the dirt-packed tunnel. It's my turn next. While Tilly strikes a match, I wriggle my bag and myself into the tight space. I'm about to scramble up the tunnel, but then I freeze at what I've forgotten.

"Are you stuck?" Tilly says behind me.

I frantically try to worm my way back down. "Theo's letters! I forgot his letters!"

"I already dropped the match. We need to go!"

Those pieces of paper are all I have left of my brother. Even if that last letter of his brings me to tears every time I read it, I can't let it get blown to smithereens. But Tilly's telling me to move and I know we might get caught in the explosion if I don't get up this tunnel fast. And yet, I'm frozen.

"Lucie, please!"

I clench my eyes shut and force myself to crawl. *The letters are only letters*, I tell myself. *Just paper.* Though that doesn't stop my heart from splitting in half.

I slither over the damp until I emerge through a rain grate in a sour-smelling alleyway, about one street over from the store. I help Tilly out, and I stop thinking about Theo's letters for a moment because I can see a dim red glow coming from deep within the tunnel. Soon that fire will reach headquarters—and we need to be far away before that happens. I may have taken a bag of Aunt Jemima with us, but there's ten times more left back in the weaponry. Once the fire reaches it, every arrondissement in Paris will witness the flames.

"Run!" I whisper.

We take off with our bags bumping against our legs. When we catch a glimmer of headlights ahead of us, we break the other way toward the Luxembourg Gardens, trailing our fingertips against the brick wall to guide our feet. We're four blocks away from the bookstore when the explosion hits my ears. Tilly falls to the sidewalk. Sabine drops her valise. I stumble into a lamppost and throw my arm over my head to shield it from the spreading heat. Behind us, a fire plume blossoms above the roofline, glowing like a jewel against the black velvet sky. Then another plume rises up, shooting ash and dust that showers onto our heads. I wonder if the remnants of my brother's letters are mixed in with it.

The flames lick higher and illuminate the stately façade of the Palais du Luxembourg, just across the street from us. I pull Tilly to her feet while I search over the palace windows. The Nazis have claimed the building for themselves, of course, and they'll be sure to send in a swarm of patrols once they see the fire we've made.

"We have to keep moving," I say.

Sabine nods. "The escape route to Laurent's."

The escape route that Harken taught us, I think. Should we even trust it? Is Laurent a double agent as well? But Dorner never mentioned Laurent's initials, and at this point we have no one else who would take us in.

"Tilly, go west. Sabine, go east," I tell them. I don't like the idea of parting ways again, but we'll draw far too much attention if we travel as a trio. "Watch your backs."

As bits of paper fall down around us, we take off in our separate directions. I pick up my pace until I hit a run, fleeing from headquarters and from the only home I've known in France. I allow myself one last glance, and my gaze takes in the sight. All of those books, burning. All of my letters, gone. All traces of Harken, charred to ash.

I tell myself that he got what he deserved. He was like Monsieur Travert, the scum of the earth.

But when my eyes well with tears, I let them fall.

FIFTEEN

It's the same cat-and-mouse game, and I'm the mouse once again. I skitter through the Marais district, zigzagging left, then right, with one arm clutched around my valise. I don't stop. If the Nazis catch me and take one look inside my bag, I'll be done for quicker than a goose on Christmas.

A dozen blocks from headquarters, the guttural bellow of a truck engine sails into my ears and I press myself flat against the wall of a jewelry shop. Once again I'm grateful for the power outage that has curled a black fist around the city. My legs twitch, ready to flee, but I hold my breath and wait. The Nazis will be expecting us to run; they'll be searching for movement on the dark streets.

And I won't give it to them.

The truck slows and rounds the corner, and I pull up a map of Paris in my head to chart the shortest path to Laurent's. He lives in the 11th arrondissement, not far from Saint-Paul-Saint-Louis, the same church where I met with Monsieur Travert. Was that only four days ago? It feels like an entire year has passed since then. We've lost Delphine and now Harken, and even headquarters is gone.

I cross the Seine under the watchful gaze of Notre Dame, and at last I veer onto a cobblestone street that's lined with humble row homes. The houses were built so closely that the residents have stretched clotheslines from window to window, like telephone wires connecting one house to its opposite across the road. Damp blouses and cotton trousers hang inches above my head, and I have to brush aside a pair of brown socks to reach Laurent's house at the end of the lane.

When my feet hit the front step, there's no need to knock. Laurent's thirty-year-old daughter, Christiane, is already there to whisk me inside. Right as she shuts the door, the words tumble out of me. "Our headquarters were compromised. Harken is—"

She pulls me away from the door. "I know, *cheri*. Matilda told me."

"Tilly's here?"

"She arrived ten minutes before you did. She asked for my father, but he's working late at the club again." She sighs and touches a shaky hand to her curly hair, strands of which have already gone gray. This war has aged her fast. "Tilly told me everything. I thought she was babbling nonsense at first, but now that you're here, too . . . It's all true, then?"

I don't know what to say. So I simply nod.

She kneads her fingers against her temples. "I don't know if I can believe it."

I don't blame her. I don't think I would've believed all this, either, if I hadn't seen the life leak out of Harken myself, or if I hadn't heard that radio message. "Where's Tilly now?"

"I put her in the attic. I didn't know where else to hide her."

"Can I see her?"

"Of course, but let's get you cleaned up first."

Christiane takes me to the washroom sink. I don't know why she's insisting that I clean myself up, but then I look down and realize why. Harken's blood has dried on my hands, is caked under my nails, and is streaked across my shirtsleeves. I must look like I've murdered someone with my bare hands.

Christiane dips my fingers into the copper sink and scrubs each of them with soap, leaving the water tinged pink. Seeing Harken's blood wash off reminds me of his last moments. Him, struggling for breath. Clutching the hole in his stomach. A bitterness reaches into the back of my throat, and I wish I could toss that memory across the Atlantic.

I can't mourn for him. I won't—not for a traitor like he was.

"We'll head upstairs now," Christiane says while she towels off my damp hands. "Once Sabine arrives, I'll go to the club to fetch my father."

After she deposits me in the attic, I search for Tilly in the darkness. The attic is small and reminds me of the one in Madame Rochette's house, but the sweet charred scent of Laurent's pipe floats through the air, and I hold on to this small comfort.

Tilly doesn't stand to greet me. I find her curled at the foot of an old chaise.

"Any word on Sabine?" she whispers.

"Christiane went downstairs to wait for her."

She wraps her arms around her knees, making no move to sweep the hair that has fallen over her face. "I didn't think it could get any worse after we lost Delphine. Now headquarters . . . Harken . . ."

I slump next to her, and I realize how exhausted I am. When was the last time I got a full night of sleep? Before I came to Paris, probably. Maybe even before that. When Theo was alive and I wouldn't wake up from seeing him in my nightmares.

"How long was Major Harken a double agent? The entire time he was in charge of Covert Ops?" she asks.

"I don't know," I say. "I don't know if we'll ever know."

"I *killed* people at his bidding, Lucie," Tilly goes on, her voice as fragile as the lace coverlet on the chaise's arm. "Were they even our enemies?"

I drape an arm around her. "Don't think like that. Harken got most of our targets' names from the Resistance, some even from Laurent. The people we took out were far from innocent."

"How can we be sure? Six people are dead because of me. Six lives that I can't get back." She looks down at her own hands, and the pads of her fingers are stained with Harken's blood, too. She grimaces at the sight of it. "I have to find the washbasin."

"Christiane told us to stay in this room."

"I can't have his blood on me." She reaches for the door and I try to pull her back, but it doesn't matter in the end because both of us freeze at the sound of footsteps below us. Two shadows ascend the ladder into the attic, and I'm relieved to see the both of them. Sabine and Laurent. He must have come home early from the club.

"Les filles," Laurent says, hoarse. He hugs Tilly and me, and she collapses into his arms, softly crying into the crook of his neck. Sabine and I, however, watch them at a distance.

Minutes pass before Laurent pulls away from Tilly's embrace. "Can we be sure of Harken's betrayal?"

"More than sure," Sabine says. Again, she's astonishingly calm. At least one of us is at her best during a crisis like this. "We all heard the radio message that the Nazis sent him."

"It's true," I add quietly. "I heard it, too."

Laurent's shoulders curve inward. "Of all the people who could have betrayed us, I thought the major would be the very last."

Tilly rubs her eyes with the heels of her palm. "Me too."

"He had all of us under his spell," says Sabine, "but no longer. The truth might be painful, but we're better off knowing his real intentions."

"I'll speak with the Resistance," says Laurent. "We must get you three to safety as soon as possible. I'll see you to the Spanish border myself if I have to."

"Leave France, you mean?" I say, blinking.

"But of course. You'd be risking your lives by staying in Paris, or in the country altogether, for that matter. Now that Covert Ops is no more—"

Sabine steps forward. "Covert Ops is very much intact."

"Without Major Harken, though—"

"We don't need Major Harken. We have the three of us," she continues. "That's plenty to carry out the mission ahead of us."

"Mission?" Tilly says.

"Dismantling Operation Zerfall." Sabine looks to me. I gape at her for a heartbeat. She can't mean what I think she means. After what we've just been through . . . But it isn't long before I find myself nodding. Even with Harken gone and headquarters blown apart, Covert Ops survives in this very room—and we have unfinished business.

Swiftly Sabine and I take turns explaining what we learned at Cherbourg: the Zerfall virus, the secret laboratory, Hitler's plans for the Allies. When we finish explaining the details, both Tilly and Laurent are left breathless.

"What will become of us?" Laurent whispers.

"This is why we must shut down the laboratory where Dorner worked," Sabine says.

Laurent balks. "Take down an entire Nazi facility? The three of you against their citadel?"

"It has to be the three of us," I hear myself say. "We don't know if Dorner made it safely across the Channel. The Germans could've sunk the SOE's submarine. Even if he did reach the English coast, it could be months before the Allies gain access to the laboratory. They have no land access to the laboratory's coordinates, and they have to destroy the building from within. It's too far underground for the bombers to have any effect."

Laurent nods grimly. "Then how do you plan to destroy it?"

Tilly's eyes come to life. "A well-placed bomb should do the trick. You brought the Aunt Jemima, didn't you, Lucie?"

"We have a bagful," I reply.

Laurent rubs his chin. "It might not be my place to say this, but the three of you will be throwing yourselves into the lion's den."

What he says is true. The chances of us taking down the laboratory must be close to nothing, but I can't run away to Spain. The photos that Dorner showed me flash through my mind, stopping on the picture of the little girl crying blood. And remembering that, I know that my decision is made.

"We joined Covert Ops knowing the risks," I tell him, "and we'll need your help in getting to Verdun. We have the right coordinates but taking the train will be too much of a risk."

Laurent sighs but relents. "I'll see what I can come up with."

We spend a sleepless night curled up like motherless kittens in the attic, each of us snapping awake at the softest sound: a dripping faucet, the creak of a fan, the gunshots in our dreams. Sometime in the middle of the night I jolt awake to find my shirt damp with sweat. I see Major Harken all over again, dying, his blood everywhere. I hug my pillow and wish that Theo were here to squeeze my hand, like he used to do when I was little and Papa went off on one of his binges. I look left and right to Tilly and Sabine, both fast asleep. I have the two of them, at least. Along with Ruthie, they're the closest things I have to sisters.

Come morning, Christiane shakes us awake and leads us silently down the stairs and through the back door of the house with our valises in tow. Once outside, we find ourselves standing in front of an old truck with rust scattered over its body.

"My father is already in the driver's seat," Christiane says. Her voice is hushed, as the rest of the neighborhood slumbers on. "I put some food and fresh clothes inside for you."

"How in the world did you find a vehicle of this size?" Sabine says, the exhaustion in her eyes disappearing as she takes in the truck.

"Called in a few favors."

"A few *big* favors," I whisper. "I don't know how we can thank you."

"There's no need. Simply keep yourselves safe." Christiane pecks us on our cheeks. "You best hurry. The fewer people who see you at this hour, the better. Be careful getting in. You'll have to ride in the back, I'm afraid. It may be bumpy—and possibly hostile—but you'll be kept out of view."

Possibly hostile?

Christiane seems to sense the question hovering on our lips, and she answers it by opening the back of the truck. Inside, there are six stacks of wooden boxes piled neatly in columns, each one as high as our necks. I don't know what could be hiding inside of them until I hear a low hum coming from the box closest to me.

"Honeybees," says Christiane. "They belong to one of the members of the Resistance. The cover story will be that my father is transporting the bees to an apiarist near Verdun."

"We have to travel to Verdun *with* the bees?" says Tilly.

"It was my father's idea. I thought he may have lost his wits, but the bees should keep you safe. If you're stopped, it's not likely that the Nazis will conduct a thorough search."

There's not much time for a good-bye. Christiane isn't the sentimental type, and she shoos us past the humming hives and toward the sliver of space at the back of the truck, where we sit shoulder to shoulder. We find a pouch of food, a full canteen, and laundered dresses that we change into, careful not to bump into the crates and the hundreds of bees droning inside of them.

"All settled?" Christiane whispers.

"All settled," I answer for all of us. "Thank you, Christiane."

"Give those Germans a swift kick for Papa and me," she says before she steps back.

The door closes with a thunk, and we're thrust into darkness.

SIXTEEN

———

The truck bumps and bounces along the road, and we bump and bounce along with it. There's no window to sneak glances out of, but we try to measure how far we've gone by the pavement under the tires—from the smoother streets of Paris to the rough roads beyond the city and then the dirt paths that crunch and scrape as we draw closer to Verdun.

We're stopped twice by the Germans. Both times the three of us grip onto our preferred weapons. Sabine, the machine gun. Tilly, a grenade. Me, a pistol in each palm. But we don't have to use them. Once the Nazis order Laurent to throw open the back of the truck, it doesn't take them long to bolt.

"Dear God, what's that sound?" one soldier says.

"Those are beehives, mein Herr. I'm transporting them to a cousin of mine who purchased them from me," Laurent replies smoothly. "She's hoping to expand her honey production."

"Did you say beehives?"

"Yes, ten of them in all. Do be careful. I believe one of the honeybees has landed on your lapel."

There's a yelp. "Close up your truck and get on your way!"

———

About an hour after that, the truck tires roll to a stop and I hold my breath for the thousandth time. Have the Nazis stopped us again? A cramp tightens in my calf, but I ignore the pain and clamp my fingers around my two guns.

The back of the truck opens, and the afternoon sun spills onto my face. We've been staring into the dark for so long that my eyes hurt for a good five seconds before they adjust to the light.

"Girls? We're here," says Laurent.

I wobble out of the vehicle, punching my thighs as I go to get the blood circulating in them again. Outside, I get my first glance at Lorraine, one of the eastern French provinces, with Verdun located in its northwestern corner. Sloping hills surround us, rolling east toward the German border. Verdun should be a few miles away from here, somewhere west of this worn-down farming road. We told Laurent to keep driving until the town was well out of his view. If anyone saw us, how could we explain three girls hitching a ride in the back of a truck full of bees?

A breeze rustles through the dozens of trees along the roadside, and a flock of sheep chews on fresh summer grass over on a nearby hill. It feels like Laurent has dropped us in the middle of a French storybook, but I'm sure the Nazis are somewhere nearby. They could even be right underneath my boots for all I know. Dorner did say that the laboratory was underground.

As Sabine stretches and Tilly fetches our bags, I catch a glimpse of myself in the reflection of the driver's window. I've put up my hair in a tight braid, and I'm not wearing a pinch of makeup. But this is the

Lucie that my brother would recognize. This is me. If I'm to die today, I'll do so looking like myself.

Laurent gathers us together. "The coordinates you gave me are due east from here. I'm afraid I don't see any other roads that will lead us closer. This is as far as I can take you."

"You've done plenty already," I tell him.

"You should head back before nightfall. We want you to be as far away from this road once we reach the laboratory," says Sabine.

Laurent lingers anyway, pecking us on our cheeks as Christiane did hours before. "I have a second cousin who lives north of here, in the village of Stenay. She's a member of her local Resistance. If you need shelter, go to her farm and tell her that Christiane and I sent you." He gives us the address and waits for us to repeat it back to him, even though I know the chances of me using it are slim.

After the truck vanishes over the hill, Sabine uses a compass and map—given to us by Christiane—to chart the coordinates that Dorner gave me. With a tilt of her hand in the correct direction, we form a line and follow after her, saying nothing as the forest grows thick around us and the gnats start buzzing about our heads. We've walked more than a mile when Tilly points toward a gravel path that she spots at the bottom of the rise we're standing on. Sabine and I nod at her in silence. If there's a path, then there must be something ahead of us.

We trek a bit farther until Sabine raises one fist above her head, her signal for us to stop. She crouches and crawls to the very top of the next hill, where she checks her map again and motions for us to join her.

"It's straight ahead of us," she whispers.

I peer over the edge. True enough, it's there. Just like Dorner said. The hill bottoms out into a flat slice of land, completely emptied of trees and completely encircled by a barbed-wire fence. A lone brick building lies at the very center of the land. It reminds me of the old post office back home, a blink-and-you-miss-it sort of place. But this is no post office, and I know better than to skip over it. Dorner told me that building will be our access point to the laboratory underground.

"It doesn't look like much, does it?" Tilly says under her breath. "Look at all of those guards, though."

She's right. There are soldiers on guard all along the fence, more than a dozen by the looks of it, but we figured as much as we discussed our options on the long drive out here.

"We'll stick to the plan," I tell them. "We get in. We set the Aunt Jemima. We run." Except it won't be that easy—I see that now, as I squint at the compound again. On the building's roof, I spot a widow's walk—a sniper's nest, probably. We won't have any trees or outlying buildings to shelter us from the gunfire, which leaves us with two options: shooting the sniper dead or sending in a bomb to destroy him. At this distance, however, both choices are long shots. "We need to figure out how to get over the fence and take out that sniper."

Sabine scrutinizes the roofline with me. "We're too far. Not even the best shooter within the Resistance could make such a shot. How about using a bomb?"

I quickly nix the idea. "We could destroy the whole building, and the laboratory would remain intact underground. We need to obliterate the whole thing from the inside to kill any traces of that virus." I wait for one of them to contradict me, but they say nothing. "Are we agreed, then? We have to get down to the laboratory and set up the bomb there. We need to make sure Elias Reinhard goes down with it."

Both of them nod at me, so we're united on that front. All that remains now is figuring out how to get rid of the sniper before he takes us out with three clean shots. The trouble is that we'll never get close enough to the building while he's alive. Unless . . .

"We need a distraction," I whisper. "How much Aunt Jemima powder can you spare, Tilly?"

"Not much. Why?"

"What if we bomb a corner of the fence? That should draw enough attention away from us so that we could make it to the building."

"That could work, but the Nazis could cut off access to the laboratory," Tilly says.

"Then we'll have to be quick about it," I reply.

"No one can be *that* quick," Sabine says while she takes another hard look at the compound perimeter. I'm about to ask her if she has any suggestions, but then she points far to our right. "I may have another idea. At three o'clock, just outside of the fence."

Tilly lets out a low whistle. "Why, won't you look at that?"

It's a patrol. I can't tell what he looks like at this distance, but he does appear to be alone.

"I see just the one. Shouldn't there be more?" I ask. Then I notice something I hadn't before.

"He's . . . relieving himself," Tilly says. "Guess he wanted some privacy."

"Precisely," Sabine says. "The other soldiers can't see him from where he's standing. Stay here." Then, without explanation, she takes a pistol out from her valise—one that's equipped with a silencer—followed by a long knife. She sprints away from us without another word, racing through the forest on silent feet, leaving us to gape at her. I start to rise myself, but Tilly stops me.

"Let her go," she whispers. "She must have a plan."

I wonder, however, if Sabine has gone insane. Tilly and I watch nervously while Sabine slinks toward the soldier in question, who's zipping up his pants and stooping down to tie his shoe. Sabine darts behind a particularly thick tree, and there's a flash of metal in her hand. The knife.

Just then, the soldier stands straight. Something must've caught his attention, and I have to bite my lip to keep from shouting a warning to Sabine. He reaches for his gun and cranes his neck toward the forest—toward Sabine. But she doesn't need any help from Tilly or me. Whirling around from the tree, she takes aim and throws the knife, sending it whipping through the air and straight into the soldier's skull. He doesn't make a sound, simply crumples like a toppled domino.

I breathe in sharply. That was a perfect shot. Not just good or accurate but *perfect*. A spark of hope ignites inside me that we might survive this day after all.

Minutes pass, and when Sabine returns to us she's sweating and out of breath. In her arms she carries the dead soldier's uniform, along with a small pouch she must've taken from him. She tosses the clothes at Tilly.

"Those should fit you," says Sabine.

"Fit me?" Tilly says, slightly aghast.

"To get us into that laboratory. You'll take Lucienne as your prisoner." Sabine sniffs when she notes the baffled look on Tilly's face, and on my own. "We have to get close to that building, don't we? This should get you access. When you get close enough I'll set off a grenade at the far corner of the fence. That should distract the guards long enough for you to get underground and plant the bomb." She pats our valises. "Leave me with a few of the rifles and pistols. I'll take out as many as I can up here and join you as soon as I can."

I say nothing while her plan settles into my mind. It's a preposterous one, yes, and the odds of us pulling this off are nearly impossible. But it might be our best hope of getting inside the laboratory.

Tilly's voice is quiet when she says, "They'll find us out as soon as they hear me speak German. I'm far from fluent."

Not to mention the fact that she isn't a male soldier, but that's the least of our problems now. "Hopefully it won't get to that point. I'll make sure to set off the grenade long before you have to say anything." Sabine tosses Tilly a ring of keys. "I found this on the Nazi as well. That should be able to get you through the front gate."

Tilly gingerly takes the keys. "It could work, I suppose."

"It'll *have* to work," I murmur. If we had more time, we could come up with a better strategy to get in and get out of Reinhard's nest, but every minute that ticks by is another one wasted.

Tilly heaves a sigh. "Then I better see if this fits." She strips out of the clothes Christiane gave her and dons the German uniform piece by piece. It fits her surprisingly well, minus the too-long pants and the jacket that strains against her chest. She turns in a circle for us. "Well?"

"Passable," I say. As long as no one takes a good long look at her.

"We'll need to do something about your hair, though," Sabine offers.

Tilly nods, takes the dagger hidden by a strap next to her ankle, and begins cutting off her hair. It falls to the ground around her in a bright ring, and she hides the aftermath under the soldier's helmet.

"We better hurry." Sabine points ahead. "Are you two ready?"

Ready?

Am I ready to become the Nazis' target practice? Am I ready to set off a bomb that could blow me to pieces?

Am I ready to die?

No, I don't feel ready at all, but I don't think Theo did, either, when his unit landed in Algeria. I doubt he was ready to die a few months later, but there will be tens of thousands of Theos dying in the coming months if Operation Zerfall launches and spreads across England and the States.

But not if I can help it.

I *will* be ready. I have to.

We divide up the weapons. Tilly and I hide an assortment of them underneath our clothes—knives, pistols, tear gas pens—and we stow more in the soldier's bag, including the pouch of Aunt Jemima and two gas masks. Meanwhile, Sabine carefully extracts a small fist of powder to blow up the fence, bundling it up in a handkerchief. She also gathers her share of grenades and rifles and tosses me a couple extra magazines, which I tuck into my boots. We decide not to wait until nightfall to execute our attack. There's no point in delaying the inevitable. We can't give the Nazis another minute to finalize Operation Zerfall.

There's no time for a good-bye. Sabine goes one way while Tilly and I head in the other direction. If all goes well, Sabine will catch up to us down in the laboratory. If not . . . we go on without her. We'll carry on Covert Ops' mission to the very end.

We draw to the edge of the forest, inching toward the empty field and toward the Nazis' eyeshot. To properly play this part, I walk a step in front of Tilly with my hands in the air while she holds one of our rifles against my back.

I glance at her. "Are you ready?" I say, echoing Sabine.

"Do you truly want me to answer that?"

"Fair enough." We've reached the gravel path that leads to the fence. The patrols ahead have spotted us, and one of them springs up toward the gate to meet us. I scan the fence line, waiting for the explosion, but there's none. Where is Sabine? She told us that she'd set off the explosion before we reached that fence.

The soldier's hand glides to his holstered pistol. *"Halt! Wer ist das Mädchen bei dir, Himmel?"*

I know enough German to decipher that he's asking us to stop. My feet hesitate, but Tilly presses the gun into my spine, nudging me forward. The soldier is pointing at us now, shouting in tense and fast German. This time I can't translate what he's saying, but by the bark in his voice I know that we're skating on inch-thin ice.

"Halt sofort an, Himmel!"

Tilly clears her throat, but both of us know that we're goners once she opens her mouth. Then it hits me. Maybe she can't talk, but I still can.

"Please, sir! I don't know what I've done wrong!" I cry out in French and fall onto my knees. Keeping my hands up, I force a sob out of my throat. It's the same routine I used in Madame Rochette's attic, and I hope it'll work for us now. "Don't hurt me!"

Tilly plays along with my distraction, yanking at my arms, shoving the rifle butt against my back. The soldier at the fence shouts at us louder, but there's a dismissive look in his eye that wasn't there before. Nothing to see here, just a hysterical woman who has wandered to a place she shouldn't have. But how long is he going to accept this routine before his suspicions return? Fortunately I don't find out the answer to that—because Sabine finally delivers on her word.

An explosion hammers into my eardrums. A burst of angry fire blooms along the far corner of the fence, knocking one of the patrols onto the ground and melting the barbed wire into metal puddles. The soldier in front of us falls backward, his helmet rolling off his head, and he forgets about Tilly and me entirely as he hurries to the thick black smoke. Three of his colleagues peel off after him, shouting orders and grabbing their rifles. Not only that, when I search over the sniper's nest I see the sniper's rifle pointed away from us and toward the fence. This leaves us with a few precious seconds to get inside the compound.

"The keys!" I say to Tilly. Sabine, to her everlasting credit, launches another grenade, not far from the first. The soldiers scatter—some toward the first explosion site, some toward the second. It's chaos for them and the perfect cloak for us.

We scramble to the lone building without any trouble. When I reach the main metal door, though, I pause. I know better than to throw it open. I'm sure there will be a wall of soldiers on the other side, with their guns pointed straight at us.

"The tear gas!" I say to Tilly, but she's one step ahead of me. She shoves a mask at me and dons the other one, and I barely have time to tighten the straps on mine before she thrusts a live gas pen inside. We throw ourselves against the door to block the soldiers from getting out. Soon their fists slam against the metal and their screams claw into my ears, but we don't budge until those screams turn into coughs and those coughs shift into nothing. I nod at Tilly, and we yank the door open. Two soldiers stagger out and fall onto their knees, retching. They don't even see us—their eyes are swollen shut.

Tilly sweeps a spray of bullets inside the building while I take care of the ones who've escaped. I breathe out and aim, and I think about Theo. About the Nazis who killed him. I squeeze the trigger three times into the Nazis' backs before my hands can think about trembling. One soldier tries to run, but he falls after I fire into his back. When he goes limp, I expect the nausea to hit my stomach, but it doesn't come.

After Tilly gives me the all clear, we duck through the door. Curls of gas still swirl inside the room. There's not much inside aside from two desks and the five bodies on the ground. No, six bodies. The last soldier alive coughs and reaches for his dropped pistol, but I rush forward and kick it out of his grasp. Tilly comes behind me and finishes him off with a bullet right through the head, like she was taught. She then pockets the gun for herself while I grab another one from off the floor. We'll be facing a lot more Nazis today, and we need all the firepower that we can get our hands on.

"This way," I say, remembering the schematics Dorner gave me. I spent most of last night memorizing them and plotting out a plan of attack. I lead us around the corner, and we find ourselves in front of an elevator. Tilly grimaces, and I know what she's thinking. An elevator is the last place we want to be—a tight metal box that we could easily get trapped in—but we have no other choice.

I press the down button and the doors slide open like they've been waiting for us. We step inside. While the elevator creaks and groans, the lone lightbulb above our heads swings back and forth, blinking in and out. It feels like an entire decade passes before we reach the bottom, but at least it gives Tilly and me time to go over our weapons. We have five pistols between us, along with a handful of pistol pens and tear gas pens, not to mention a half dozen knives strapped to various body parts. And the bomb, of course. Still, I wouldn't mind adding Sabine's little machine gun to the mix. Or I'd settle for just plain Sabine.

Once the elevator stops and its doors screech open, Tilly and I glue ourselves against the walls to brace for the gunfire that'll come at us. But there are no shots. No shouting soldiers. There's no sound at all except for the hum of the lightbulb.

Tilly looks at me, confusion written all over her, but I don't have an answer for her because I'm just as puzzled. With my pistols nearly jumping out of my hands, I dart a glance beyond the doors, but I find an empty corridor. The hallway is bathed in white and sterile as a hospital floor, but in a hospital you'd find gurneys and wheelchairs and waiting rooms. Here, there's none of that, just a big hollow space.

Where are the soldiers? The scientists?

"This doesn't make sense," I whisper.

Tilly nods. "Let's plant the Jemima and get out fast."

Uneasiness spreads through my stomach, but we have a job to do and we can't do it from the elevator. Our boots squeak over the waxed floors that have been polished to a sheen, and we pass door after door, each one shut tight. I don't want to even imagine what lurks behind them: vials filled with Zerfall, samples of blood, autopsied corpses.

I cross over a wide hallway—this one as cold as the one we're walking in—but as I pass over it I hear gunshots. Dozens of them. I duck down at once and search frantically for the source. Not behind us. They're coming from down the hall I just crossed. And that's when I notice that Tilly never made it over with me. She's still on the other side, a gun in each hand.

"I'll cover you!" I say to her, motioning for her to join me.

"There's too many! I'll hold them off!" She tosses the pouch at my feet and fires off five rapid rounds.

I pick up the pouch and go cold all over. This was supposed to be a three-woman job, but Sabine's somewhere outside and now Tilly has to hold off the soldiers. I sling the pouch over my shoulder and think about my brother again. It's all left to me now—and I won't let him down.

The laboratory has woken. I leave the soldiers behind me to find more ahead. Two jump out from one corner, and I barely have time to shoot one before the other is on top of me. We tumble to the floor, and I drive my elbow into his stomach and a fist into his chin. One more bullet, and he slumps next to me, his blood ruining the fresh wax beneath his body.

I right myself and run, zigzagging down one corridor before spinning into the next. As the Nazis close in on me, I dash through a pair of double doors and slam them behind me, throwing the lock, even though a little lock won't keep the Germans away for long. The room is utterly dark, and I search desperately for a light switch but come up empty. I swear, but tell myself it doesn't matter. I can get by with touch if I have to.

I empty the pouch and grope for what I need: the accelerant, the detonator, and the bag of Aunt Jemima. Almost there. Just one more ingredient. *Fire.* My fingers pry upon a book of matches, and I tear one off. I need to move fast. Once the bomb is set, I won't have much time between finding Tilly and making it back above ground. But even if I don't make it out, if this whole building collapses on top of me . . . I'm going to make Theo proud.

Get it done, I think. *Get it done now, Luce.*

I bring the match head to the strike strip when suddenly the lights turn on, so bright that they blind me. When I force my eyes open, I find myself in the middle of a giant box of a room, as barren as the halls I ran through. Except there's an enormous chalkboard in front of me, which spans an entire wall of the room. There's a message written on it, too.

Jedem das Seine, Geheimoperationen

All of my blood runs cold. My German might be far from fluent, but I parse out the meaning behind those words. *To each what he deserves, Covert Operations.* The match falls out of my fingertips, because the Nazis shouldn't know that Covert Ops infiltrated France.

Unless . . .

Footsteps stomp down the hallway, and soldiers fly into the room, a blur of gray uniforms. I scramble to pick up the match and finish what I came here to do, but the Nazis are too fast. One of them seizes me from behind, pinning my arms to my sides, while another grabs my feet so that I'm swinging in the air like a broken doll. I bite, I kick, I do every escape maneuver that I've been taught, but there are more than twenty soldiers surrounding me.

I fight them anyway.

My fist meets flesh. My foot slams into a groin. A soldier cries out, and he aims his rifle butt at my head, but then there's a shout from the back of the room.

"Stop!" a voice says in German. "She's not to be harmed!"

"Sir—"

"Those are your orders! Put down that weapon. Now, detain the girl and use the tranquilizer."

A syringe looms in my vision. "No!" I manage to cry out, but it's useless. The needle sinks into my leg, and a horrible burning climbs through me, singeing every cell it touches until a scream is knocked loose out of my throat. Spots dance in my vision, and I almost welcome the exhaustion that soon overtakes me. But before I lose consciousness, a face hovers over mine. Bearded and smiling.

"Hello, Fräulein," the man says.

It has been so long since I've heard English that I think I must be hallucinating. My head bobs up and I blink at him—and he looks oddly familiar—but my eyes go blurry and my arms go heavy and it's all I can do to stay awake.

"There, there." The man brushes a hand through my hair, gentle as my mother's, but his words curdle my insides. "I'm so pleased that you're here. Sleep now, but soon we'll get very well acquainted. I can promise you that."

December 1, 1942

Dear Luce,

I finally got the letter you sent back in August. I was beginning to think you'd forgotten about me and were hoarding all of Maman's galettes for yourself. You greedy little thief. All ribbing aside, thank you for writing and for visiting Ruthie for me. I'm already plotting the adventures we'll have when I'm home. Uncle Sam might not be paying me much, but it'll be enough to get us out West.

Our transports have finally come, so we're heading out tomorrow. Everyone's getting packed up and writing letters home since it might be a little while before we'll be able to write again. So I figured I should tell you something, but I don't want you to get mad. Promise you won't blow a fuse on me?

Ruthie and I got married right before I shipped out. She wanted to wait until I got back from the war, but I had to make it official before I left. You know I love her and I wanted her to know that. I wish you were there at the courthouse with us, but I didn't want you in trouble if Papa found out. I swear we're going to have a proper wedding when I get home, with a cake and champagne and everything. Ruthie also said that you should be her maid of honor. What do you say? Is it a deal? Just don't tell any of this to Maman or Papa. I haven't let them know yet, and I don't plan on saying anything until I see them face-to-face.

I feel real awful for not telling you sooner, but I'll make it up to you somehow. How about I take you to a fancy restaurant in California? Or what if I bought you every Nancy Drew book ever published? Whatever you want. Just don't be mad. Please, Luce.

Miss you.

Theo

SEVENTEEN

When I wake up, I taste blood. I cough but the taste lingers, so I try to roll over to get a sip of water. I usually keep a glass on my nightstand, but my arm refuses to move. If Tilly is playing a joke on me, she doesn't know what she's getting herself into . . .

"Tilly?"

No answer. I attempt to sit up, but my arm still won't budge and neither will my legs. My eyes jerk open to near darkness. Dim light filters in from the gap underneath the door, and there's just enough of it for me to see the leather straps wrapped around my wrists and ankles. The straps are fastened to the metal cot that I'm lying on and tightened over the gray hospital gown that I'm wearing. A ceiling fan blows stale air against my forehead.

Where in the world am I?

The memories come back to me in photographic bursts: our attack on the laboratory, the soldiers all around me, the terrible words I saw scrawled on the chalkboard before everything went numb and black.

Panic pounds at my chest, but panicking won't get me out of these straps or out of this room. I breathe in and breathe out until I can gather enough wits to take in my surroundings. I see four plain walls around me, and across from me, there's a cabinet tucked against the wall. There's also a chair next to my cot, but that's it. A simple room. Knowing the Nazis, though, their plans for me will be far more complicated. If they've kept me alive this long, then they've done it for a very specific reason—a reason I'm not too keen on discovering.

Wherever they've taken me, whatever they've put in me, I need to find a way out. I heave my body against the restraints, but the straps don't even groan. Searching for another option, I look for something to cut me free—a scalpel or scissors—but the Germans aren't stupid enough to leave those things lying around.

The doorknob turns slowly, and my heart spins. I wait for the soldiers to pour inside, but none come. Instead, an old man shuffles in, and he doesn't bother turning on the light.

I shut my eyes and feign sleep. The man's footsteps near the bed, and he hums as if he's strolling through a candy shop. He ventures so close that I could reach up and crush his throat—if it weren't for these restraints. While he continues his humming, I hear the scritch and scratch of a pen moving across a clipboard.

"I have an inkling that you're awake, Fräulein," he says suddenly.

I don't move a muscle.

"There's no need to be afraid," he continues in French. "Aren't you the least bit curious about me and why you're here?"

His words tug like a lure at all of my questions. I don't want to open my eyes for him, but at the same time I know that it's useless for me to keep pretending that I'm asleep. At some point I'll have to face him, and I might as well get it over with.

I open my eyes a sliver and take him in. The dark room cloaks him in shadow, but I see the sharp edges of his clipboard and the crisp lines of his doctor's coat. Exactly what sort of doctor he may be, I don't know.

"How was your rest?" he asks. When I don't answer, he switches languages with ease. "Do you prefer that we speak in English? Forgive me if mine is rusted. Is that what you Americans say?"

A shiver tickles over my skin. How does he know that I'm American? Had I been talking in my sleep?

He chuckles. "Where are my manners? Let me make the proper introductions." He flips on the light switch and I finally get a good look at him—and an alarm screeches inside of me.

"You," I whisper.

"It seems that you recognize me."

I jerk my arms against the straps again. Suddenly the room feels far too hot. I need to get away from this man. I know him—and I know what he's capable of.

"Calm down, Fräulein." He scoots his chair next to me, and I scramble as far away as I can.

"Get away from me, Reinhard!"

He smiles, showing a bright gold tooth shining from the corner of his mouth. "You believe that I'm Elias Reinhard?"

I don't know why he's playing dumb. I'm absolutely sure that he's Reinhard. He looks just like the photograph that Dorner showed to me, despite the fact that his beard has turned snow-white since the photo was taken. I hadn't expected his smile, though. It's friendly and warm, in spite of the yellowed teeth—the sort of grin that makes you want to trust him. For that reason alone, I know that I can't.

"What have you done with my friends?" I ask.

"They're both well, just as you are."

I tug at my shackles. "I wouldn't describe this as 'well.'"

"Those bindings are for your safety, Fräulein Blaise. We wouldn't want you rolling off your cot in your sleep, now, would we?"

"How do you know my name?"

"You'll quickly come to see that I know a good bit about you, Lucienne. Or Lucie, as you prefer. Perhaps you can think of me as an admirer of yours."

Nausea slinks into my stomach and settles there. "Where are we?"

"In your room."

I don't like the way he says that it's *my* room, like I'm never getting out of it. "What are you planning on doing to me?"

"Ah. Wonderful question." He leaves my side for a moment to retrieve a syringe from the cabinet. He fills it with an amber liquid and carries the syringe toward my bed, cradling it as if it's made from the finest crystal. "My plan for you is contained inside this very glass." He holds the syringe up, allowing the amber to catch in the light. "Let me explain . . ."

Everything inside of me recoils because I know what he's holding. "Don't touch me with that!"

"Why are you afraid?"

"I know what's in there. It's Zerfall!"

He smiles wide enough to fill the entire room. "Nothing could be further from the truth."

"Don't lie to me, Reinhard."

He pats my hand even after I wrench my fingers away from his. "My name isn't Reinhard. It's Dr. Nacht." He tips the syringe back and forth in his hands. "And this serum isn't Zerfall. In fact, it's not a virus at all."

It's such a bald-faced lie that I nearly laugh. "I saw the schematics myself."

"What schematics? These?" He returns to the cabinet and removes a thick folder from a drawer, which he then places on my lap. He flips it open and spreads the paperwork onto the cot: numbers and graphs, maps of the laboratory, and black-and-white photographs. Just like Dorner's.

I don't say a word. I won't betray Dorner's identity, although I'm sure Reinhard—or Nacht, as he insists on being called—has figured out his mole.

"Who showed you these schematics?" he goes on.

I shake my head.

He digs through the photos to pull out one that I've never seen. "Is this him?"

I squint at the picture. It's Dorner, all right, but his mussed hair has been combed back and he isn't wearing his glasses. That isn't the only thing that has changed about him, either—he's wearing a uniform. A *Nazi* one.

Is this a trick?

"You look confused, poor thing." The man named Nacht continues. "That isn't your fault. Despite your intelligence, you've played so well into our deception." He taps a finger on the photo that looks so much like Dorner. "He told you quite the story, I'm sure. Let me see if I can recall the details . . . A carefully researched virus, a plan to launch the disease against the Allies, and a cure to protect the Germans from it. He called it Operation Zerfall. Didn't he?"

Lies. All lies. I rub my nails against my palms, tuning in to the pain I'm causing myself rather than what he's telling me. I should trust Dorner . . . shouldn't I?

The man leans back into his chair. "The documents he showed you were forgeries. Granted, we put months upon months of work into them to ensure that they looked accurate, even to a scientist's eyes, but in the end they were all meaningless."

"You're lying."

"It's the truth." His hand strokes mine, and his fingers are soft as pudding. I shudder. "You see, there is no virus. No terrible disease. Simply put, there is no Operation Zerfall."

My mind springs back to the little girl crying tears. "The photos—"

"Yes, the photos." He returns his attention to the folder and fans a few out onto my cot. He stubs his finger against one that shows a balding man. "Patient Nine. He lived quite a while, much to my surprise. And here. Patient Thirty-Two." He pulls out a photo hidden beneath the others, and my heart jerks to a stop. The little girl. "She lasted longer than the subjects before her. It was a pity when she finally succumbed." He gives a little shake of his head. "But what a gift she left to the *Wunderwaffe* project. The things we learned from her . . . I see that I'm getting ahead of myself, though. You see, these photographs are indeed authentic, but these subjects—my patients—didn't die from a virus. They gave their lives for a purpose much greater."

Now he's talking nonsense. "Stop it, Reinhard—"

"My name is Dr. Nacht." His hand curls around my fingers, his attempt at comforting me. "You have, however, met Elias Reinhard." He shows me the photo of Dorner again. "It's *this* man, the one you know as Alexander Dorner."

A chill sears through me, and he keeps talking.

"Hauptsturmführer Reinhard is one of the most promising young officers in the Nazi military. He was the one who concocted the Dorner alias, and he was quite meticulous about it—studying pathology terms and perfecting Dorner's quiet demeanor. I wouldn't have expected any less, considering that he's my nephew."

My chest feels flayed open, and he isn't finished.

"I thank you for what you've done," he goes on. "Reinhard has infiltrated London because of your work. I learned last night that he has already sent his first message to his superiors in Berlin, and they hope to receive many more soon—once he has unturned the Allies' strategies and next missions."

It hurts to breathe. Everything Dorner told me was a carefully crafted lie. This was all a trap, and I fell right into it. Not only that,

I'm the reason why the Allies have taken him in. If Dorner—or Reinhard, whichever his name is—gains the SOE's trust, then who knows what secrets he'll pass on to the Nazis?

What have I done?

"But now we must get to work," says Dr. Nacht.

"Where are we? If this isn't a laboratory—" My voice stops cold because something new dawns upon me. If Dorner has been successfully smuggled into Britain, then why am I still alive? What does Dr. Nacht intend to do with me?

"Oh, this is indeed a laboratory, but its purpose doesn't include studying diseases or engineering a plague, although I'm sure the Führer wouldn't mind if such a thing were possible. He does, however, approve of the work that we *are* doing. For what I hold in my hand"—he waves the syringe at me—"may bring your Allies to their knees. And you shall assist me in it."

My mind immediately jumps to the photos he showed me. Am I next in line?

He reaches for my arm, the needle careening toward my skin, and I come alive. I bite, thrash, kick, and curse, but it doesn't stop him. His grip is surprisingly strong as he takes my ankle.

"I'd relax if I were you," he tells me. "Your attempts at escape, while noble, will increase your stress levels, and that may cause the serum to bring you greater discomfort."

Despite everything I throw at him, he plunges the needle through my skin. I scream as the serum enters my body, burning its way into my veins.

"Quiet, now. Focus on my voice. Don't fight it. Breathe."

The serum knifes its way through me, its blade hot and sharp. I cry out, "Why don't you put a bullet in me and be done with it?"

"Kill you? No, no. That's not my intention at all. Although, yes, death can be an unfortunate side effect of my serum regimen, but I have faith that you'll survive. This is a risk we must take in the name of the Führer, and in the name of science in particular."

I whimper because I've no idea what he means by that—or what it will mean for me. But all of that is soon forgotten as the fire rages through me, clawing paths into all of my senses. I teeter on the collapse of unconsciousness—or death, I don't know—when Dr. Nacht draws his lips next to my ear and whispers:

"You, Fräulein, shall be my masterpiece."

EIGHTEEN

The next time I open my eyes, a gray-haired nurse with a puffy mole on her cheek stands ready to greet me. In her hand she holds a metal spoon that she pushes into my mouth. A grainy paste hits my lips.

"*Iß doch!*" she barks. *Eat up.*

I cough out what she has fed me and blink furiously around the room. I'm still lying on the same cot and wearing the same gown as before. My limbs remain strapped, too, although now I feel a light-headedness that I didn't before, a gray haze that dampens my thoughts. Is it an effect of the serum? I'm not sure. There's no sign of Dr. Nacht, although his last words stay fresh in my ears.

My masterpiece. A cringe curls inside of me. I don't know what he means by that, but I know that I'll soon find out.

I struggle to recall what he revealed to me. There is no Zerfall. There is no virus. It was all a story that Dorner fed me—even the name he gave me wasn't real. But that's the one piece of the puzzle that I don't understand. If Zerfall is nothing but lies on paper, then what was the purpose of luring me in and strapping me to the cot? What was in that serum that Dr. Nacht injected into me?

The nurse sighs noisily and shoves another bite into my mouth, but I spit it out and the food splatters over the both of us.

"Where are my friends?" I demand.

"*Iß doch!*"

"What did you do to them?" Each word comes out faster. "What are you doing to me?"

She looks furious enough that I wouldn't be surprised if steam billowed out of her nose. When she sets the bowl down hard on the floor, triumph flares inside of me, but it's short-lived. The nurse reaches for a syringe that's filled with the same glittering liquid that Dr. Nacht used on me. She turns the needle toward my arm, and I go ballistic.

"No!" I thrash against my restraints, twisting my body until the leather rubs my skin raw. None of it does any good. The nurse merely moves to the end of the cot, takes a good hold of my foot, and sinks the needle into my sole.

Again, the burning, the pain. I scream.

"Hauptsturmführer Reinhard gives his regards," the nurse tells me in halting English. To rub it in, she smiles, and her teeth are yellower than Dr. Nacht's.

Reinhard. Dorner. Whatever his name is, I'm going to cut off every one of his fingers and toes if our paths ever cross again. If I ever make it out of this prison.

Minutes pass by. Every time I get close to blacking out, the nurse slaps me back awake. We repeat this three times until my screams dim into whimpers and the pain recedes, leaving in its place the thickening mist that continues to dull my thoughts, like static over your favorite song on the radio.

The nurse dips the spoon back into the bowl. "Open your mouth," she says slowly.

I begin pursing my lips.

"You're hungry. You wish to eat," she says. "Listen to me."

Confusion clouds my mind. I don't want to listen to her. Do I? Then my stomach groans, and I think about how empty it feels. Would a small bite be so terrible?

Yes.

That one word kicks through the haze, and I keep my mouth shut.

"Fräulein, open up," the nurse says. She hovers the spoon an inch from my lips, and the static grows louder in my mind, pushing out any other thoughts.

What was in that serum she gave me?

At that moment, Dr. Nacht steps into the room, clipboard at the ready, humming the same cheerful tune as the last time we talked. He notes the spoon in the nurse's hand, and he smiles.

"Ah, Fräulein! Eating you breakfast?"

"She's fighting me, Herr Doktor. I had to administer another serum injection."

"Small steps, Nurse Keser, small steps. This is all expected. These American patients are most strong-willed, but my serum should win out in the end." He nods at her and says, "Take her to the restroom, then you're dismissed."

After Nurse Keser helps me to the bathroom and chains me to my cot again, Dr. Nacht clasps his hands behind his back. "It will take some time for the serum to take full effect. A few weeks at the soonest. A few months at the latest. If all goes well, you'll think of me quite differently once the regimen is finished. You'll come to see me as your ally. Your friend, even."

I fight through the thought-fog, punching a hole straight through it. His friend? "I'd rather die than let that happen," I spit out before the haze sets back in.

His smile reaches his eyes. "You might feel differently soon. That's the power of the serum. It harnesses the mind. It molds it. It sculpts it."

Is that why I can't think straight? Is he molding me as we speak? The very thought makes me jerk my wrists against the straps, but it isn't long before Dr. Nacht shushes me.

"Eventually you will become the clay on my potter's wheel: soft, pliable, and easily manipulated," he continues, "and once the treatment is complete, it shall be a remarkable transformation—the first of the sort in the history of humankind. A true masterpiece of science."

A puppet at his bidding. He tries to pat my hair like I'm a prized doll, but I knit together all of the willpower I can muster and lurch my head away.

"So stubborn! But as I said, we'll take everything one day at a time. I call this first phase of injections 'the softening.' You might experience fatigue. Some of my former patients described a cloud or a fog in their thoughts. This is the serum suppressing—or *softening*—your will so that it will become moldable for scientific purposes.

"When the softening is well underway, we'll continue on to your reeducation. I'll show you photos and tell you stories that will help build your allegiance to the Third Reich. Many of my former patients found this phase to be fun."

Somehow I doubt that his photos or stories will be any fun. And I wonder why he keeps referring to his *former* patients. Are they all now dead?

"Finally we'll enter the third phase. Reintroduction. Granted, this is a far-off goal for now, but eventually I hope that the reeducation will hold and that you'll be ready to travel home."

"Home?" I whisper.

"To America." He hums a snippet of "The Star-Spangled Banner." "I thought you would like that."

Is he tricking me? The confusion multiplies inside of me, and no matter how hard I shake my head it won't dissipate. Dr. Nacht touches my hair.

"Try not to fight the serum, Lucie. It'll be useless in the end."

My treatments begin like clockwork. I start with two injections a day, along with constant monitoring by Dr. Nacht and his henchwomen nurses. Every couple of hours, the nurses swoop into my room to check my pulse and breathing rate and then to stick me with a needle for a sample of blood. In spite of Dr. Nacht's warning, I fight them each time. I won't make this easy for them. I thrash against the leather straps; I make them drop their needles. Once I manage to bite a nurse's finger.

In the end, though, they always win. They muzzle me. They sedate me. They remove small bits of me—my blood, my skin, and slowly, my mind.

I lose count of the days. Maybe a week has passed since we left headquarters in flames, or is it two? A month even? The fog has stretched its fingers into every corner of my mind.

Dr. Nacht eagerly scribbles notes on my progress, and we've started playing a little game to see how far I've come. He'll hold up a photograph of Adolf Hitler and spout a string of sentences: *This is the Führer. Do you support him, Lucie? Yes, you do. Do you agree with the tenets of the Third Reich? Yes, very much so.* Over and over he repeats these words, and over and over he waits for me to recite them back to him. I've been able to say nothing each time, but there are days now when the fog gets too dense and I can't remember what I'm supposed to say. Whenever that happens Dr. Nacht gets this little smile on his face, like it's nearly Christmas.

But I've concocted a strategy of my own to keep that smile from spreading.

Theo.

I keep my brother at the forefront of my mind every time Dr. Nacht approaches me. I focus on Theo, and I use him as my anchor each time my tongue tries to betray me.

Do you support the Führer, Fräulein?

I grit my teeth and say no.

Do you support the Third Reich?

I remember what Theo died for and refuse to answer.

Eventually Dr. Nacht's smile grows flat and he greets me at every session with a sigh instead of a grin.

"I'd hoped we would've made more progress by now. How disappointing," he tells me. "You've left me with no choice but to increase your dosage. To the highest possible levels."

When he reaches for a fresh syringe, I don't struggle this time. Let the serum kill me. Let this all be over. At least I'll see Theo again, if he's waiting for me somewhere. I'll be able to tell him how sorry I am for how things ended between us. But if there's only blackness ahead of me, it'll be better than what I'm living now. The needle sinks into my arm, and I'm ready to go.

But Dr. Nacht won't let his masterpiece die that easily.

I'm not sure how much time has passed when I wake up again. All I know is that I'm still in the same room with my arms and legs strapped like before, and I want to weep because I was so sure the serum would've killed me. How much more can my body take before it gives in?

"Lucienne."

I go still. Hope blasts through my heart when I see her at the foot of my cot. "S-Sabine?" I croak out.

"It's me." She steps toward me, and I think I must be hallucinating. Is that an effect of the serum? Dr. Nacht hadn't said so.

"Are you . . . real?"

She nods, and proves it by placing her hand over mine. Her skin is ice-cold, but it's her skin that I'm touching. Not an illusion. My fingers cling around hers.

"How . . . ?" I clear my parched throat, which hasn't tasted water for hours, maybe even for a day. "How did you get out of your room?"

She doesn't answer me straightaway, but that doesn't matter. She's alive. Together we'll find Tilly and escape. I try to move, but I'm still shackled. "Can you release me?"

She doesn't touch the leather straps. "I didn't come here for that."

I struggle to sit up. "We don't have much time! The guards are going to find out that you're gone and come looking for you any second!"

"The guards already know that I'm here. They let me in to speak with you."

My head falls back hard against the pillow. The realization strikes me like a bullet to the chest. The serum. Of course. "Did Dr. Nacht get to you already?" A cry chokes out of me. "You have to fight him! Don't stop fighting, Sabine. This isn't who you are. It's the serum controlling you!"

Her tone goes flat and she says, "No, it isn't."

"It's forcing you to say that!"

"I'm here of my own accord."

"This is all part of their plan!" I have to talk some sense into her. If we wait much longer, I might succumb to the effects of the serum, too. "Your name is Sabine Chevalier. You're an agent for Covert Ops. You hate the Nazis and Germany and Adolf Hitler." I rattle off bits and pieces of her old life, but none of it takes hold.

Sabine's gaze remains on the floor. "I wasn't given the serum. They didn't need to."

"Don't believe anything they've told you! They've locked you up for days and pumped your body full of poison and . . . and . . ." My words dry up because I finally get a long look at her. Her eyes are clear and her hair is carefully combed. She's wearing a simple dress instead of a hospital gown. She doesn't look like she's suffering from any effects of the serum. She doesn't look like she has taken any of it at all. If that's the case . . .

Sabine says quietly, "I chose to work for them."

"That's . . . impossible."

"They asked me to come see you. Dr. Nacht told me that you're not responding well to the serum."

She might as well have gutted me. Sabine, working with the Nazis? My vision blurs, and I know it's not from the serum. I could take Dorner's betrayal but not this. Please, not this.

"Lucienne," she says.

I can't even look at her, so I snap my head away—but I can't escape her voice.

"Lucienne," she tries again. "The Nazis will get their way in the end whether you fight them or not."

"Oh? Like *you* fought them, Sabine?"

She flushes, whether from anger or embarrassment I don't know. Maybe both.

"How long have you been a double agent?" I snarl at her. "How long have you been deceiving Tilly and me?"

She crosses her arms but says nothing. There's nothing to say, really, not after what she has done to us, but I thought she'd be gloating and lording this fact over me. But her mouth simply tightens into a grim line.

"It doesn't matter." She sniffs. "I came here to help you, not for a lecture."

"Help me? You *killed* Major Harken, and you turned Tilly and me over to the Nazis—and now you say that you're helping me?"

"This serum could be the death of you. Dr. Nacht will continue with his regimen until you're deemed 'changed,' or until you die. You can choose to live."

"Choose to live?" I parrot her. "Choose to become his little puppet? Like you have?" She tries so hard to turn her face to stone—a trick I always thought she had learned from Major Harken—but there's a furrow in her brow. "What did they pay you to turn? Was it money?"

"I didn't come here to talk about that."

"A hundred thousand francs? A million? Name your price, Sabine. You apparently had one."

Her wince morphs into a scowl, but her voice stays steady. "Don't be a martyr. Save yourself from the pain."

"I'll keep fighting until it kills me," I say through a clenched jaw. "I'm not a traitor like you are. Did you tell them about Covert Operations?"

"No. They've suspected our existence for months, since before you arrived in France. All of the people we've killed haven't gone unnoticed. That's why they concocted Operation Zerfall in the first place: to draw out Covert Ops."

"I'm sure you helped them with that."

"No," she says again. "That was months in the making. They dropped hints of Zerfall to their collaborators, like that fellow you killed—Monsieur Travert. They knew we'd be lured in sooner or later."

And we were, like hooked fish. I remember meeting with Dorner for the first time—how I played right into his hands. I should've strangled the life out of him right there in Madame Rochette's attic.

I'd like to do the same to Sabine, too, for her part in all of this. Betrayal spears my heart again, fresh and white-hot.

"What about Major Harken?" I remember the message I heard on the radio, the one the Germans sent to him. Supposedly. "He was innocent, wasn't he?"

There's the slightest waver in her voice when she says, "Yes, the radio message was faked."

A chill runs over my skin. Harken's last words pound in my head like a hammer on my coffin: *Don't trust her.* I should have listened to him. I should have trusted him over her. "Why did you kill him?"

"The Nazis ordered me to. They made it clear that they wanted female subjects. Dr. Nacht . . . prefers them. They also believe that you and Tilly will draw less suspicion back within the OSS."

A dark laugh rips out from me. Of course. We used the same philosophy on the Nazis—that they would hardly suspect a young woman of being an agent. Who would've thought that they'd take a trick right out of our own playbook? I ask her, "If the Nazis knew about Covert Ops' existence, then why didn't they arrest us in Paris?"

Sabine gathers a breath before continuing. "Dr. Nacht knew about the L pills after the Germans caught one of Covert Ops' agents. He knew that you and Tilly would be ready to kill yourselves, too, if it came to that. That's one of the reasons why he insisted that you come to the laboratory of your own free will."

He didn't want damaged goods. Or dead ones. "What were his other reasons?"

She turns away. "They wanted to see what Covert Ops was capable of."

A bitter taste enters my mouth. We were lab mice, Tilly and me. Dr. Nacht dangled a little piece of cheese for us, and we came running. We thought we were going to save the Allies; we were willing to die for it, too, if it came to that. But instead, we threw ourselves right into their sticky web.

"Go ahead and laugh," I say hoarsely, but Sabine merely shakes her head, her eyes filled with pity. I wish I could tear out the both of them. "Pop open some champagne. Pat yourself on the back. Go spend the money the Nazis bought you with!"

Her cheeks flame. "Lucienne—"

"Harken's little pet! I wonder how Jean-Luc would feel if he knew what you've done. Have you thought about that?"

Fury roars onto her face at last. "You know nothing," she whispers.

"How much did they pay you?" I shout after her. "A million?"

She stalks toward the door.

"What did they give you to murder Harken? How much did his life cost?"

She stops and turns back until I see her profile. "A life for a life," she murmurs. "Wouldn't you do the same for your precious Theo?"

Then she exits the room, leaving me alone with her revelation.

NINETEEN

A week has ticked by since Sabine's visit. I've pulled apart and put back together her words again and again, but it doesn't take away the sting of them. *A life for a life.* The Nazis must have her brother, then, and that's why she climbed into bed with them. But that doesn't erase Sabine's betrayal. We were supposed to be allies. Sisters, even. That's what Covert Operations stood for. Yet she handed us over to Dr. Nacht, knowing what he would do to us.

There's a question that floats through my mind, though, darting in and out when I'm lucid enough. If our positions had been switched, if it had been Theo's life on the line, what would I have done? No doubt I'd want my brother back, but when I think about the price I'd have to pay—about trading Tilly to the Germans—it makes me want to throw up the porridge that Nurse Keser fed me for lunch. Any sympathy I had for Sabine shrivels to nothing.

Soon, however, I forget about Sabine. I forget about nearly everything. I've been pumped so full of doses that I'm left exhausted. Each time the syringe hits my skin, I search for my memories of Theo to fight off the haze, but my memories of him have blurred, covered in a fog I can't break through—and why should I want to break through it?

What a silly thing to do.

I'm beginning to wonder why I joined the OSS in the first place. Dr. Nacht tells me that it's a corrupt organization that used me as a pawn. *Do you enjoy being a pawn, Fräulein?* He asks me that every time I see him, and I shake my head for him. He pats my hand and tells me, *We'd never treat you that way.* I'm starting to believe him, too. The Germans would care for me and watch over me, unlike Major Harken and my papa. And all they'd ask for in return is a little favor—to go back to the States and ask for a reassignment within the OSS. A desk job. I'd have access to the office's most secret intelligence and, when the time was right, I'd pass along a few of those secrets to Dr. Nacht via radio. It might be dangerous work, but I'd be justly rewarded. The Führer himself would sing my praises.

Won't that be nice? Dr. Nacht says. *Wouldn't you like that?*

He repeats the question to me every day, and I'm getting closer to telling him yes. But there's this churning in my stomach that holds me back. I think it has to do with someone named Theo. Or Ruth. One or the other or maybe both.

Or are both of them lies that the OSS has told me?

When Dr. Nacht returns to my room one afternoon, he holds his usual clipboard in one hand and balances a small cardboard box in the other. I smile at the sight of him, but a quiet alarm bell whispers to me that I shouldn't be happy to see him at all. Soon, though, Dr. Nacht administers a new syringe of serum and I sink back into my cot with a sigh.

"How are you today?" he says.

My lips twitch into another smile. "Fine, Herr Doktor."

"Wonderful. You've made some noticeable progress in the last two days. After that bumpy start, you've come very far. Not as far as my other patient but a long way nonetheless."

Disappointment hums through me. "Other patient?"

"Your colleague Matilda."

Matilda. Do I know a Matilda? A memory floats up. Oh, yes. "Tilly?"

"Yes, both of you were terribly manipulated by that organization you were involved in, the OSS. Don't you remember that?"

"I do," I murmur, "but you saved me from them."

"That I did. That's a good girl. For our session today, I've brought you a little something."

A honeyed feeling flows through me. I wonder if he brought a "little something" to Tilly, too. Hopefully not. "Just for me?"

"Just for you." He opens the box and allows me to peek inside. "See here?"

I take a look, wondering if it could be a chocolate bar or a strudel— I have been very good these last couple of days—but what I see inside makes me flinch.

"Now, now, don't be afraid. She's harmless." Dr. Nacht scoops my present from the box and places it into my hand.

I nearly snatch my hand back, but I know this wouldn't please him, so I push down that feeling. "A mouse, Herr Doktor?"

"A *special* mouse—one of the specimens from the animal lab across the hall. I picked her out for you."

The tiny creature, with red eyes and cream-colored fur, sniffs at my palm and digs its needle-sharp claws into my skin.

"Go on and give her a gentle stroke. She'd like that," he tells me, watching me as I pat the mouse along the spine, doing as he says because I don't want to disobey him. "What should we name her? Lulu? Jutta?"

I've never named a mouse before, but Dr. Nacht is waiting for my reply. "Jutta seems nice."

He claps his hands together. "Then Jutta it is."

Dr. Nacht lets me spend a few minutes playing with Jutta. I stroke her fur from neck to tail—which, I agree with Dr. Nacht, is quite soft—and allow her to climb over my arms. Her whiskers twitch at the new scents of my room: alcohol, bleach, the sausage on Dr. Nacht's breath. She's nothing like the brown mice that darted across my apartment floor at home, stealing our crumbs and leaving their droppings along the wall. Besides, Jutta is a present from Dr. Nacht. Because of that she's very special.

Dr. Nacht taps his pen against his clipboard. "We don't have much time left in our session."

"Must you leave so soon?"

"I'm afraid so. I've other patients to attend to. Before I go, though, I have a favor to ask of you."

I sit up. This has to be important. "Yes?"

He captures Jutta, who has been exploring the edges of my cot, and drops her into my hand again. "Careful. Do you have her?"

"Yes, Herr Doktor"

"Good, good." He finishes jotting a note down onto his clipboard. "Now I'd like you to crush Jutta's windpipe."

My hands freeze in place. "What?"

"You heard me," he says with his usual smile. "Crush the windpipe—a little pressure on her neck. It won't take long, considering how fragile she is compared to you."

I glimpse at little Jutta, her whiskers twitching. I want to ask him why he wishes for me to kill her, but he wouldn't appreciate that. So I keep my mouth closed.

"Go ahead."

I've killed mice before. Dozens of times. But not like this.

"Fräulein."

I press my thumb and pointer finger against Jutta's soft neck, but something holds me back from squeezing. A small voice rises within me, clawing from beneath the fog, begging me to stop, shouting at me to stop listening to him.

Dr. Nacht scribbles onto his clipboard again. "I believe you can do it."

I want to please him very much, so I tighten my hold on Jutta. A squeal escapes from her little mouth, and her little paws scratch at my skin. A little more pressure and it will be done. Jutta's short life, easily snipped.

And yet my hesitation keeps tugging at me.

Dr. Nacht's fingers tighten around his clipboard. When he speaks to me next, his voice has hardened like a fist, the first sign of frustration that he has shown me. "I gave you an order."

I hear the edge in his voice, and my grip loosens on Jutta. That's all the time she needs to leap out of my hand and onto his foot. Dr. Nacht curses and shakes her off his shoe, stumbling back in the process. I don't see what happens next, but I hear a terrible crunch. When he lifts his shoe, I see a slick of red.

He shakes his head at me, disappointed, which makes my chest hurt. I throw my head back against the pillow and chastise myself for my stupidity. Why didn't I kill the mouse when he asked me to?

"I'm sorry, Dr. Nacht," I say swiftly. Guilt punches my heart for disobeying him. He has treated me so well and has given me so much, but now I've lost my chance to earn his smile this session. "I don't know what came over me."

"I know exactly what has come over you." He releases a sigh and wipes his shoe on the floor. I take a small comfort that he doesn't sound frustrated with me anymore, but what he tells me next makes me dizzy. "I'm afraid you're still fighting the serum."

"I'll try harder. I promise."

"I've underestimated your resolve. That's my fault, but I must remedy it." He slides open the drawer and takes out not one but two syringes, both filled to capacity with serum.

"Dr. Nacht," I say through the haze that has settled around me. "If you'll give me one more chance—"

"We're running out of time," he says. "I've promised the Führer results and he'll have nothing less than that." He approaches my cot.

Both syringes sink into me, and I'm soon lost in a thick shroud. The extra dosage makes me sleepy and my eyelids soon begin wilting; but before the blackness takes me under, I grasp onto one stray thought. I can't let Dr. Nacht win. I have to stay alive—for Tilly, for Maman, and for Ruth.

Somehow, some way, I need to escape.

TWENTY

In my lucid moments, I sew together my last shreds of sanity and come up with an escape plan. I'm sure Harken would never approve of it. He'd call it weak on a good day and desperate on any other, with a survival chance of about zero; but it's the only plan that I've got.

So I wait.

Dinner is served—a plate of corn mush and some sort of meat that has been cooked until it has lost all flavor, but I swallow every bite of it. I can't cause a scene. When the plate is empty and my stomach full, I wait for Dr. Nacht to arrive for my morning session, but it's Nurse Keser who strides into my room instead, ready to administer my next dosage. My heart sinks. I spent hours waiting, but Dr. Nacht doesn't even show up. But I decide to launch my escape plan anyway. Once that needle hits my arm again, I might fall completely under the Nazis' clutches.

It takes all of my willpower to pull back an edge of the serum's haze. "Good day, Nurse Keser."

She ignores me and gets about her work: checking my pulse, shining a light in my pupils, taking a peek down my throat. She rubs my forearm with alcohol before she readies the syringe. It's now or never . . . but what was my escape plan? It has already slipped through my fingers.

"Stay still," Nurse Keser grunts as she presses the needle against my skin.

"Wait—"

"What for?"

I struggle against the straps, but Nurse Keser squeezes my arm and shoves in the needle. The serum surges through me, but I feel no pain from it. My body must have adjusted to the dosage because now a calm sigh falls out from my lips. The last scraps of my plan fade into nothing. Not that it matters. Another minute passes and I don't even remember why I told Nurse Keser to wait in the first place. I close my eyes, ready to drift off into a dreamless oblivion.

Nurse Keser's footsteps thud toward the door just as someone else comes into the room. "What are you doing here, girl?" Nurse Keser barks.

The girl answers, "Dr. Nacht sent me."

The sound of that voice forces me to open my eyes. I've heard it before. Where, though, I can't recall.

Nurse Keser snorts. "He did, did he?"

"You're welcome to check with him if you'd like."

"I certainly will. Come with me . . ."

I blink toward the door and almost choke at what I see. A girl with dark hair slams the heel of her hand into Nurse Keser's throat, fast as a snake. Nurse Keser clutches at her neck, and the sounds coming out of her mouth are gasping and terrible. She tries to call for help, but the girl swings a leg through the air and clips Nurse Keser's temple. The older woman collapses onto the floor, her head smacking the tile with a dull plunk.

The girl approaches my cot, and I notice that she's wearing a loose men's jacket over plain trousers. Whoever she is, I'm sure I'm her next victim. I want to scream for Dr. Nacht, but the serum is ready to take me under.

"Don't be afraid," the girl says softly. From her pocket, she pulls out a syringe that's filled with a silver liquid rather than the usual gold.

I wrench my wrists against the restraints. "Dr. Nacht!" I say, only it's nothing but a whisper.

She jabs the needle into my calf, and my back arches up so fast that it might snap in two. Then my body crashes back onto the cot, and I start shivering all over. I have no idea what this girl has injected into me. Poison? Whatever it is, it's the exact opposite of Dr. Nacht's serum, ice instead of fire.

The girl's face hovers over mine. "You'll get warmer. Give it a few minutes."

"What . . ." My teeth chatter so violently that I can hardly get a word out. "What was in that . . ." I point a shivering finger at the empty syringe.

"I gave you something to clear your head."

Or something to kill me, more likely. This girl broke into my room and knocked out Nurse Keser, but if she wanted me dead, she should've strangled me by now. Another minute sweeps by, and my blood begins to thaw. Along with it my mind starts clearing, too, as if a giant hand has brushed away the fog that Dr. Nacht lovingly planted there. I blink up at the girl with new eyes.

Not just any girl.

Sabine.

"We don't have much time," she tells me. "I'll undo your restraints, but don't move too quickly. I'm sure your legs aren't used to walking, and the antidote may make you nauseous."

"Antidote?"

"The injection I gave you. Nacht keeps a few vials of it in his office. You'll likely need another dose at some point, but too much of it at once could stop your heart."

My teeth stop chattering, and the goose bumps that had sprouted over my skin disappear. As my mind continues clearing, a memory returns of Sabine and me in this room. Of her confessing that she chose to work for the Nazis. My eyes narrow at her. Is this one of Dr. Nacht's tests?

I wait for Sabine to finish loosening the straps around my arms before I grab her by the neck and squeeze. "Did Dr. Nacht put you up to this? Did he?"

"Are you mad?" she rasps. Her fingernails scrape across my skin, but I refuse to let go until I get answers from this traitor.

I tighten my grip, fueled by the fury that has been locked away tight from the serum. But now the anger runs fresh through me, and I dig my fingers deeper into her neck. "Let's see if your beloved Dr. Nacht comes to your rescue now. Do you even feel guilty for what you've done? Murdering Major Harken." Desperate sounds come out of her throat, but I don't care. "You might as well have killed Tilly and me, too."

"I—I had no choice."

"You always had a choice!"

"My brother—"

"I'm sure you've made him proud by what you've done."

"Jean-Luc—"

A cramp travels up my arms. I'm out of breath after being strapped to my cot for who knows how long, but I won't release her. Although that doesn't silence Sabine.

"Jean-Luc"—a vein bulges on her forehead, and her entire face has turned red—"is dead."

My grip weakens, and she uses that to wrench away from me. She doubles over at the foot of the cot, coughing until her throat grows hoarse. "He's dead?"

"The Germans let him die," she says between gasps.

She's lying. That's my first thought. But as I watch Sabine struggle for breath, I don't know what to think. Her eyes are rimmed red, like she has been crying all night.

"How?" I say.

"Pneumonia."

"When?"

She looks away. "I don't know when it happened. Weeks ago, maybe. I found the telegram after I snuck into Nacht's office. He kept promising he'd give me proof that Jean-Luc was alive and well." Her eyes brim with new tears, which she swipes away with the back of a hand. "He lied to me."

"Is that why you've come here? Now that Jean-Luc is dead, you think I'll forgive you?"

"No."

"Then what do you want?"

"I came here to help you escape."

"Just like that? Jean-Luc is gone and now we're friends again?"

"I did what I did for my brother. I never said I thought it was right." Her brows cross, and somehow she wipes clean the anguish from her face. "We don't have much time. Are you coming or not?"

I look at her, then at the door. She killed Harken in cold blood. She betrayed Tilly and me. And I remind myself that this could all be an elaborate ruse for Dr. Nacht to test my loyalties. I don't trust her or him one bit, but if she's truly trying to help me escape, how can I turn her offer down?

"Tell me when you turned against us," I say.

"Why does it matter?"

"You know why."

She releases a tense breath through her nostrils. "After we parted ways en route to Dorner's drop-off. I didn't know it at the time, but the Nazis had been following me since my arrest in Cherbourg. They recognized me as a potential agent, but they decided to let me go to see where I'd lead them."

"Recognized you how?"

"When they captured Jean-Luc a month ago, they interrogated him and eventually . . . he broke." Her features cloud over. "He confessed to them what little I'd told him about Covert Ops, and then the Germans discovered the photo of him and me that he kept in his pocket. They circulated my picture across France."

"Why didn't they capture both of us together?"

"Because we were with Dorner, and they needed one of us to shepherd him to the boat so that he could infiltrate the SOE. And they knew . . . they knew that if they arrested me first, they had leverage to get me to turn on Covert Ops."

A life for a life. The Nazis held Jean-Luc hostage and used him to get to Sabine.

"But now Jean-Luc is gone," I say hollowly.

She sends me a look as sharp as the daggers she polished in the weaponry. "You would have done the same for Theo. Don't deny it."

"Betray my country? My friends?"

"I didn't have much of a choice." Her cheeks heat. "Are you satisfied, or do you wish to keep chatting?"

"The latter. Why didn't Dr. Nacht give you the serum?"

"I'm not American or British, and those are the countries that the Nazis want to infiltrate with double agents."

"Because you already are one."

Her mouth shrivels. "Make your choice. Stay here if you want. Dr. Nacht has plenty more of that serum set aside for you. But if you want a chance at escape, then you'll need to come with a traitor like myself."

I measure what she has told me against the doubt lodged in my heart. If this is one of Dr. Nacht's little schemes, he'll be sure to punish me for listening to Sabine. More syringes, more serum, more straps to hold me down—but all of that will be coming for me anyway if I stay. Dr. Nacht will stop at nothing until I become his obedient pet. I may not like putting my life in Sabine's hands, but I see no other way out.

The decision made, I undo the restraints that choke my ankles and rub the feeling back into them. "I'll go, but we can't leave without Tilly."

Sabine doesn't even blink. "Follow me. I know where she's being held."

TWENTY-ONE

We tie up Nurse Keser's hands with one of my leather straps and drag her body beneath my cot. When we're finished gagging her, Sabine takes hold of another one of my straps and points it at my wrists.

"I'll need to bind your hands," she says.

"Why?" It comes out harshly. I'm finally free from those restraints. There's no way I want to feel one next to my skin again.

"We have to keep up appearances in case one of the scientists or soldiers stops us in the hallway. I'll tell them I'm taking you to see Dr. Nacht."

I glance at the door. "How many of them will be out there?"

"Not many. It's a little past nine in the evening. Most of the staff has gone to bed, and the soldiers should soon change shifts. If someone bothers us, though, I'll take care of it."

"The Nazis let you roam around the laboratory that freely?" Could they be that stupid?

"Not freely, but Dr. Nacht has granted me a couple liberties."

"For turning in Tilly and me?"

Her face sours, but she nods. Despite my reluctance, she proceeds to wrap my wrists, and I let her for Tilly's sake. "There's something you should know."

"I'm not in the mood for your advice."

"It isn't that." Now her face looks like she has tasted curdled milk. "Matilda . . . Matilda will be different when you see her."

"Different how?"

"She has responded well to the serum."

"Dr. Nacht told me that."

"Yes, but—" She thrusts her hands against her sides and shakes her head. "There isn't time to explain, but she'll need a good dose of the antidote. Likely two or more." Before I can ask what she means by that, she opens the door. "Follow my lead and say nothing."

We enter the hallway, and Sabine transforms in mere seconds. She lifts her chin and sheds any trace of apprehension, dragging me behind her as if I'm not worth the dirt underneath her fingernails. Sabine yanks at my elbow to keep up with her, but the scent of the ammonia-wiped floors makes me queasy. It also doesn't help that traces of Dr. Nacht's serum remain lodged in the crevices of my mind, blurring my vision and causing me to sway. I may need another dose of that antidote sooner rather than later.

"Deep breaths," Sabine whispers to me. I do as she says, and my senses begin to rouse. My eyes adjust to the bare bulbs hanging over my head, and my ears tune in to the hushed sounds of the laboratory—the smack of footsteps, the hum of a fan, and, from somewhere far off, a woman wailing. Could it be Tilly?

Soldiers march through the sterile hallway, a black pistol on each hip. As we pass one of them, I can see the sharp questions ready to jump out of him, but Sabine is quick to quell them.

"I'm on Dr. Nacht's orders," she tells him in halting German. He frowns a little but lets us go.

Sabine stops in front of a door that appears no different from the dozens we've passed. She shoves it open without knocking. Once we're inside, I see that the room looks identical to mine. There's a cabinet in one corner stocked full of syringes, and there's a cot pushed up against the far wall. Tilly lies on top of it, and I don't think my heart has ever jumped so high.

Tilly sits up at our entrance, perplexed. "Where's Dr. Nacht?"

"Tilly—" I start, but Sabine holds me back.

"I do the talking," she says, quietly undoing the strap on my wrists.

I'm not sure if I like her giving orders, but with the serum chewing at the edges of my mind I decide not to protest. *Deep breaths.* The best thing I can do for Tilly is to regain as much of myself as I can get.

Tilly, however, looks much better for the wear. Her hair is brushed and her skin is a healthy pink. This is the Tilly that I've gotten to know at headquarters—but it's clear that she doesn't recognize me. She plants her feet on the floor tiles, and I notice that her arms and legs haven't been strapped to her cot.

"Dr. Nacht is busy at the moment, but he sent us here to administer a new dosage," Sabine tells her.

Tilly pulls back. "Where's Nurse Keser?"

"She's unavailable, too." As she nears the bed, Sabine tucks her hand slowly into her pocket for the antidote.

Tilly scoots onto her cot again. "I'd like to speak to Dr. Nacht. Please don't come any closer."

"He'll arrive very soon. In the meantime . . ." Sabine springs on Tilly and stabs the needle deep into her thigh. I rush in to clamp my hand over Tilly's shouts for help, but it doesn't matter much because the antidote is quick to set in. Tilly's back arches, just like mine did, and her teeth clatter like a jackhammer as the chemicals race their icy fingers through her bloodstream.

"Where do we go from here?" I ask.

"Above ground. There's an emergency staircase not far from this room. We'll run for it."

"*Run* for it? That's the plan?"

"It's our only choice," huffs Sabine. "I didn't have many resources down here. We won't be completely defenseless, either." She lifts her jacket to reveal two pistols she has tucked into her belt loop.

"Two pistols?" I say. Against the entirety of the laboratory's forces?

"These were hard enough to come by as it is. And I have a few more ideas up my sleeve." She doesn't elaborate on what these ideas are, though. "Don't worry. I'll get us to the stairwell. Now help me with Matilda. We've waited too long already."

Tilly shivers on her sheets and murmurs nonsense about how she can't disappoint Dr. Nacht. She's in no condition to go anywhere, much less make our escape, and I tell that to Sabine.

"Take her left arm and I'll take her right," Sabine replies. She hoists Tilly's arm around her neck. "Hurry, Lucienne—"

The door opens, and Dr. Nacht stands in its frame. His mouth is open, ready to greet his favorite patient, but he almost drops his clipboard at the sight of us.

"What is the meaning of this?" he demands, sweeping into the room. His gaze narrows upon Sabine, but it's Tilly who responds.

"Dr. Nacht?" She can barely get the words out because her teeth are clacking together so loudly. "They put a needle in me. I'm cold."

The shock on Dr. Nacht's face swiftly shifts to horror, then fury. "What have you done?" he hisses at Sabine. "Dear God, what have you done?" He whips around, probably to call for the soldiers. Sabine tries to chase him down, but she stumbles against Tilly's added weight. She gapes at me.

"Stop him!" she cries.

My legs stumble into motion before I realize what I'm doing. My feet aren't used to running yet, but Dr. Nacht is old and slow and I yank him down by his collar. He struggles to shake me off, and we go tumbling next to the medical cabinet. Before he can scramble away from me, I pin down his arms.

"Fräulein, listen to me!" he says, wriggling under my weight. "You're confused. I'm here to help you."

His words tug like a lure at me. It's the serum, I know. Or what's left of it. But I push past its remaining effects. "Helping me by turning me into your puppet?" I spit at him.

He blanches when he sees that his plea has no effect on me and cranes his neck toward Tilly. "These women are trying to hurt you, Matilda! We have no choice but to exterminate them."

Tilly's head whips from him to Sabine and then to me. She's trying to fight the serum, but it still has a stranglehold on her. "I don't . . . I don't know . . ."

"Help me!" Dr. Nacht cries.

Tilly's face goes slack. She tries to break from Sabine's grip, but to Sabine's credit she doesn't let go.

"Matilda!" Dr. Nacht says again. He begins screeching for help, and it won't be long until someone hears him. While I silence him with one hand, I reach into the cabinet with the other, wrapping my fingers around a syringe stored inside. Moving fast, I jam the needle into his neck and inject every drop of the serum into his blood. Dr. Nacht goes rigid and gasps as the fire sears through him. A literal taste of his own medicine. It's not enough, though. I have to finish the deed.

I take out another syringe and swat away Dr. Nacht's outstretched fingers that are attempting to block me. The whites of his eyes are showing as he realizes what I plan to do. "Please!" he begs.

A tremor shakes through my hand, just like with Schuster and Travert, but this time I don't hesitate. I bring the needle down, straight into his heart. He gasps and lurches up. The pain must be excruciating, yet his gaze searches for mine still.

"What have you done?" he whispers.

I make sure that those words are the last he'll ever utter.

When his chest stops moving, Sabine breaks the silence. "Is he dead?"

I nod once. Slowly I get to my feet. A memory swims up in my mind, something that Sabine told me weeks ago—one of her pieces of advice. But she was right that time. The killing does get easier.

Tilly wails at the sight of Dr. Nacht gone limp, but Sabine quiets her with another dose of the antidote. I run toward them.

"Stop!" I say to Sabine. "You said that another dose could kill her!"

"What other choice did we have?" she retorts. "She was going to fight us tooth and nail to the stairwell." While Tilly shivers and tucks into a ball to keep warm, Sabine heaves her back onto her feet. "*Merde.* Matilda, move your feet!"

"Don't talk to her like that!" I say.

"We're wasting time. Let's go," Sabine replies.

Like a lumbering ox, Tilly sways and staggers but stays upright with our help. Sabine hands me one of her hard-won pistols, but I know we'll be facing Goliath once we leave this room. A well-armed and well-trained Goliath.

"The soldiers will shoot to maim," Sabine murmurs. "For you and Tilly, at least. You're too prized to kill."

"What about you?"

"That's my concern, not yours." She checks her ammunition and tilts her head at the door. "The stairwell is tucked away around the corner. Make sure that Matilda keeps up with us."

That's the extent of our planning. We sneak into the hallway, and Sabine grasps onto the chain that sets off the sprinkler system, giving it a hard yank. Water drenches our clothes, but I don't ask what she has in mind. This must be one of her ideas that she mentioned before.

As the water puddles at our feet, Sabine waves to us to follow her. We soon find the laboratory in chaos. Nurses scramble to protect paperwork while the few patrols on duty bark orders that get swallowed in the downpour. No wonder Sabine decided to pull that chain. I hurry after her with Tilly in tow and my pistol at the ready, but I don't get to fire off a single shot. Sabine takes care of the three soldiers who shout at us to halt, taking them down with a neat bullet to each of their foreheads. I'm about to tell her *good shot*, but the words die on my tongue. She used that same aim to kill Major Harken. I remember his warm blood on my hands, but I have no choice except to continue my alliance with Sabine until we reach safe ground again. She'll need to pay for what she did. Harken deserves that much, and I have to make sure of it.

We're breathing hard and sopping wet by the time we reach the steps. Thankfully there are no sprinklers in the stairwell, which gives me a few seconds to sweep the hair from my eyes. I direct Tilly up the first flight of stairs and look up to find ten more stories to climb. We need to hurry, and I turn around to say that to Sabine; but I notice then that she hasn't followed us.

"What are you waiting for?" I say to her.

In answer, she lifts up her shirt to reveal four slim packs of white powder that she has tucked into her waistband. She places each one gently on the floor, and I stare at the powder, agape. It's Aunt Jemima.

Explosives. I don't know where or how she got it, but she has enough to blow a significant hole in the laboratory.

"Take Tilly and go. I need to destroy the facility," she says.

"Are you mad?" I tell Tilly to wait while I track back to Sabine. I've already gathered what she has planned. "You set off that much powder and you'll go down with it!"

"Not necessarily. I've learned from the best." She nods at Tilly, and her lip twitches into a half smile. "And not if I'm fast enough."

She's lying and we both know it. "No one's that fast."

"We'll see."

"Sabine—"

"The Germans won't be long now. Go!"

She's right, and yet I hesitate. Despite what she has done, despite her betrayal, I don't want to leave her behind.

"Go or stay, it's up to you," Sabine says stubbornly, "but I've made my choice." She rips open a powder pack and reaches into her pocket for a blasting cap. She's going to blow this entire building to high heaven—and us with it if we linger any longer.

The Nazis draw closer. I can hear their shouts. I urge Tilly to start climbing again, but my own feet remain rooted on the steps. I want Sabine to pay for her crimes, but not like this. Let her spend the next decade in a jail cell, not buried with the Germans here.

Sabine pours out the Aunt Jemima onto a dry patch of the concrete floor. "I'll give you one minute to get up those steps and not a second more."

"There must be another way!"

"Sixty seconds. Fifty-nine."

"Stop—"

"Fifty-eight." She peers behind her, and our gazes clash. Hers dares me to remain where I'm standing, even though she knows that she'll win. She nods upward to Tilly. "Take care of each other."

"You still have time to come with us!"

"A word of advice? Run. Fifty-seven, fifty-six." She keeps counting, and I know it's useless for me to wait a second longer. I feel mashed up and pulled apart, but I urge my shaky legs up the stairs until I no longer feel them. All the while, I glance back, hoping to find Sabine has changed her mind, but no one's there. So I take her advice. I run.

By the time I've reached the top step I hear the *pop pop pop* of gunfire, followed by the sound of Sabine's voice. The sound travels up the stairwell and lodges into my ears, where it travels into my heart and breaks it to pieces.

"Au nom de mon frère!" she cries. *"Pour Jean-Luc!"*

I shove Tilly through the door and into the open air just as the ground beneath us begins to quake. Outside, two soldiers spot us and reach for the rifles, but the explosion overtakes all of us. A plume of fire bursts through the door, and we're launched into the air and tossed to the ground again. The blast shakes me to my bones, but I pick myself up and lug Tilly toward the fence that surrounds the compound.

Hand over hand we climb the fence, and once our feet are planted on the other side I finally look back at the laboratory. The lone building above ground is shrouded in fire and smoke, and the soldiers who were stationed up here are running and shouting in disarray. But what can they do? There's no fire hose big enough or close enough to douse those flames. There should be no survivors, but that doesn't stop me from looking for her anyway. If anyone could've made it, it would've been Sabine.

"Lucie?" Tilly comes up behind me, her voice as fragile as a child's. "Where are we?"

I clutch her hand and lead her away from the fire and the serum and these last nightmarish weeks. We flee into the darkness until I hear nothing but the whir of the wind and the hoot of a bird—and the echo of Sabine's last cry before she sacrificed her life to save us.

For Jean-Luc.

December 23, 1942

Dear Luce,

I'm beat tired, but I wanted to write you before I hit the sack.

I've got bad news. Gordo is gone. One second he was asking me if I had an extra chocolate ration while we were out on patrol, but in the next second he wasn't saying anything at all. Palmetto, our medic, said that Gordo didn't suffer. Funny thing is, I don't have a scratch on me. It doesn't seem fair.

There is a little bit of good news. I got promoted yesterday to Private First Class. Merry Christmas to me, though I don't feel much like celebrating. I'd be happy to trade in my new mosquito wings if it meant having Gordo back, but I'm going to keep fighting and showing Hitler what we're made of. Gordo's death won't be for nothing.

There has been talk around camp that we'll push up into ▓▓ once we've taken care of the Germans here. Wonder if the ▓▓▓ ices there are as good as Mr. Benedetti's. After that, maybe we'll head into ▓▓▓▓. Remember those bottles we used to throw into the harbor when we were kids? I always hoped that one of them would make it to ▓▓▓▓, and now there's a real chance that I might see ▓▓ and even ▓▓▓▓▓. I think that would make Maman proud if I made it to her hometown. I think of you both every day.

I hope you've forgiven me about getting married. I haven't heard from you, so I'm betting you're still mad at me. I get it, but I miss reading your letters, Luce. Maybe that could be your belated Christmas present to me—one letter to tell me that we're square again.

I wish I could come home to spend the holidays with you all, but give Maman a kiss for me and look in on Ruth if you don't mind. I've asked her to watch your back for me. She's your sister now. I figure if I can't be there to scare away Phil Frakes, then she can do it for me.

Say a Hail Mary for me before bed tonight. You promised, remember?

Take care of yourself.

Theo

TWENTY-TWO

I flee from the laboratory as fast as my tired legs will go, all the while hauling Tilly along behind me. As we stumble over leaves and stones, I try to remember Laurent's parting words, reaching for them like a life raft. We have to find our way to his cousin's home in Stenay. There's no other place for us to go. It's too much of a risk to hide at Laurent's, not to mention the fact that he lives hours away by car, and there's nothing left of headquarters to return to.

We won't be safe anywhere in France, I realize. Even if we reach Stenay without getting arrested, we can't stay there for long. Not without papers. Not with Tilly so broken. Somehow we need to find our way to London. There's an OSS office in the city where we can stay and recover. How exactly we'll get there . . . well, I'll figure that out. *One step at a time*, I tell myself.

It takes us three full days to reach the tiny village of Stenay, even though it's only a dozen miles from the laboratory. To avoid the Nazis and their search dogs, we travel solely at night. We hide whenever a truck rolls past. We scrape by on stolen food and sips of rainwater. We don't sleep. At least *I* don't sleep. Tilly manages to sneak in a few naps, but I can't risk letting her out of my sight, so I have to do without.

With her mind still muddled by the serum, she has already tried twice to run back to the laboratory. I had to pull her into a ditch and put her in a chokehold until she fell unconscious, which I hated myself for doing, but I didn't have another choice. Dr. Nacht was so close in turning her into his "masterpiece." If Sabine hadn't broken us out in time . . .

Sabine's last words ring in my ears, but I need to silence them for now. I have to get Tilly and myself to safety first—everything else can come later.

Tired and hungry, we reach Stenay as a summer storm swoops in over our heads. The rain falls in great pellets, so heavy that we might as well be walking through water, leaving us soaked and clammy. Tilly clutches on to me like a child, muttering how we'd be dry if we were back at the lab, and for a second I almost agree with her and turn us around. A question floats up into my mind: *Why did we leave the laboratory in the first place?* We were well taken care of by Dr. Nacht and Nurse Keser. They only wanted to help us.

No. I blink and shove those thoughts away. Despite the antidote Sabine gave me, there are times when I can feel the remnants of the serum whispering to me. I wonder if Dr. Nacht's voice will always haunt me, and that makes me shiver all over. I remind myself that he's dead and Sabine blew up his laboratory. Even if Tilly and I wanted to turn around, there'd be nothing left for us there.

Although Stenay is within our sights, I skirt around the humble village rather than cut straight through it. There'd be too many eyes to avoid if we entered the town limits, and looking the way we do—

dirty and dressed in rags—we'd be sure to attract the wrong sort of attention. So I take Tilly past the narrow canal that flows around the village and hurry under the shadows of the stone watermill, pressing onward until I locate a two-story farmhouse that should belong to Laurent's cousin.

Tilly's teeth chatter. "I'm freezing," she whispers.

"We'll be warm before you know it. We're almost there." I hope my voice doesn't reflect the uneasiness swimming through me. My sights zero in on the house, and I wonder if this is the right place. The blue paint has long flaked off the exterior, leaving the wood beneath it exposed like tired bones, and a jungle of vines has climbed over the front façade. But my eyes detect a faint trail of smoke puffing out of the chimney, which means someone must be home.

The thought of dry clothes and a roof over my head finally forces me to step forward, but a warning goes off in my head, telling me to wait. Harken taught us to be cautious to a fault, but remaining in the open is another risk entirely.

Ignoring my training, I help Tilly up the front steps and unsure how I'm going to explain us. Before I can think of something to say, the door opens a crack and a woman peers out at us. She's younger than Laurent, about forty, but she has the same smooth skin and prominent cheekbones. Their resemblance aside, I know better than to fall into her arms.

"Madame?" I say. It comes out a whisper, and I clear my throat. "Your cousin told us that you might help my friend and me. Monsieur Laurent Bordelon."

Upon hearing his name, she opens the door a little more. "Laurent mentioned you might come by, but that was weeks ago. Where were you?"

"We . . ." I don't know how to answer her without getting into the details, and I can't relive those memories now, just as I can't think about Sabine. I tell her, "We were detained by the Germans."

She surveys the front of the house, a look of suspicion plain on her face. "Laurent said there would be three of you."

A lump forms in my throat. "There's only two of us now."

We stare at each other, and I don't know if she'll let us in or not. There wasn't time for Laurent and me to come up with a passcode to give her. She'll have to take our word that we're not a pair of German collaborators.

A desperate thought takes shape in my head. I have just enough strength left to knock this woman out. Tilly and I need food and shelter, and if she won't give it to us willingly, then we'll have no choice but to take it. We're not going back to the Nazis.

That's the thought running through my mind when Tilly sneezes. It's a thin and pitiful sound, and there's a shift on the woman's features. Her wariness melts, just slightly, and she beckons us inside.

"If you're friends of Laurent, then you'll be friends of mine. Let's get you out of those wet clothes. I'll heat some water for a bath." She motions for me to follow her and delivers us into her washroom, where she tells us to dry ourselves off. Once the tub has been filled, I help Tilly undress.

"I'm Anaïs," the woman says after Tilly has climbed into the bath. Without batting an eye, she helps me sponge Tilly down and does the same thing for me when it's my turn. After we've both been bathed, Tilly and I get dressed in Anaïs's extra clothes and tuck into a meal of roast rabbit and carrots. She apologizes for not having any bread or potatoes to offer, but I tell her that this is the very best food that we've eaten all month—and that's the truth. This makes her smile, but it doesn't last long.

"I'm afraid I must leave you two for a little while. I have to speak to the Resistance about how to return you safely to Paris," she says, clearing our plates and saving the bones to make a soup stock. "Unless there's somewhere else you have to go?"

I nod. "We need to get out of the country altogether. To London, preferably." Not only will we be safe in England, I need to speak with the SOE as soon as possible. They're under the assumption that Covert Ops has vouched for Dorner, and who knows how many lives have been lost already because I trusted Dorner's intel. I'm sure he's very pleased at how readily I believed his lies. A piping-hot anger slices through me, and I wish I was in England at this very instant, ready to rip the smirk off Dorner's face.

Anaïs doesn't appear surprised at what I've told her. "It's a dangerous route to London, but feasible. We've helped a few Allied airmen into Spain, though we've never smuggled women."

"We can handle the journey," I tell her. "Will you help us? Please?"

"I'll see what I can do. Until I return, you two should go into the cellar. The Germans have been patrolling the village regularly."

I'm sure that's because of Tilly and me, but I say nothing about that because I don't want to alarm Anaïs any more than I already have. While she pulls on her boots to leave the house, Tilly and I head into her cellar, where we settle behind a crate of onions and limp carrots. Evening sets in, leaving us in darkness. At some point I nod off, but I spring awake when I hear a truck puttering somewhere down the road. I gather Tilly farther back into the shadows until we can no longer hear the noisy engine. I release a tight breath, relieved that they didn't bother stopping, but it isn't long until they return again.

An hour later, there's a pounding at the door, followed by a flurry of furious German. *"Tür auf!"* When no one answers, there's a crash. Footsteps storm into the house, and my heart beats so fast that I go light-headed. I tug Tilly beneath the staircase and cover her mouth in case she has an outburst. One peep out of her and we'll be done for. I don't have a rifle or a pistol pen or even one of our daggers on me, just a simple kitchen knife that Anaïs gave me for protection.

The cellar door swings open, and the stairs creak loudly as a lone soldier sweeps down the steps. I feel strangely awake, although I've hardly slept in days. *Calm and collected*, I remember. I've escaped a whole facility of Nazis. I can handle one more, if I can get a clear shot.

I hope that the soldier will take a cursory glance around him and depart, but he shuffles deeper into the cellar, kicking aside a box and knocking over a lamp. His boots draw closer to where we're hiding, and I mouth at Tilly to stay silent. Thankfully she's in one of her more lucid moments.

Now the soldier is mere feet away. I can hear him sniffing the dusty air, and I can smell the ripe scent of his uniform. I grip the knife handle tight. It's either him or us, and I promised Sabine that I'd take care of Tilly.

But the cellar betrays my plans. My shoe crunches over an old onion skin, and the soldier spins around, his rifle arcing toward me and his hands fumbling for the trigger. Before he can reach it, I slash the blade at his chest and cut through the gray fabric of his uniform. He falls back, startled, and I kick the rifle barrel away from where he has aimed it—my heart. Swiftly I lunge and drive the knife into his neck. He makes a gurgling sound and grapples at my hands, but I already feel the strength leaking out of him. He coughs out blood that sprays onto my arms, and he crumbles to the floor, twitching.

A shout comes from upstairs. Another Nazi. *Merde.* A few seconds later, a new set of boots hammers down the steps, but I'm ready for him. Channeling every ounce of hatred I have toward Dr. Nacht, I grab the fallen rifle and shoot. The bullet strikes his cheek and he falls into the cellar, his limbs flailing wildly before he lands by my feet, unmoving.

"Lucie," Tilly breathes, coming up behind me. She blinks at the two bodies.

"I'm . . . all right. Are you?" I pant.

She nods. "Your hands."

I look down to find them covered in blood. Tilly tries searching for a cloth or rag to clean them, but I don't move to help her. I just stare at my dirtied hands. They're the same ones that killed Travert and Schuster and even Dr. Nacht, but they no longer tremble and shake like they once did. When did I become the hardened agent that

Covert Ops trained me to be? Would my brother recognize this new Lucie? Would I want him to?

But Theo would've wanted me to survive, and I've done just that. I might not be the girl that he once knew, but I'm still his sister. Even if this war has forever changed me.

"Girls?" I hear Anaïs calling from upstairs. Soon, she looks down in the cellar and her face turns chalk white at what she finds. *"Nom de Dieu!* What happened?"

"The Nazis came." My voice sounds tired, dulled at the edges. "I'm very sorry, but we had no other choice."

"It's no matter now. Are you hurt?" She waits for me to shake my head before she urges us to come upstairs. "We should go."

"What about the bodies?"

"Leave that to me. First, we need to get away from the house."

A punch of guilt strikes me in the chest. Anaïs took us in like Madame Rochette did, and now she'll have to abandon her home, too, because of us. Exhaustion falls over me at that thought, and I don't think I can take another step, but Anaïs pulls at my arm and says to please hurry. She gathers some money and wipes the blood from my hands with a cloth. Within twenty minutes we're on the run again.

We steal away to Verdun. A feeble moon lights our path as we wind across a quiet cemetery filled with crosses from the Great War, and we slip down a road to the humble home of the local Resistance leader. The man must've been expecting us because he takes us immediately to his barn and presents us with our options for reaching London. Not too surprisingly we don't have many—the Nazis have made sure of that. The Germans have bulked up their forces along the coast, meaning we can't take a submarine like Dorner did. That leaves us with the alternate route of crossing into Spain and smuggling ourselves in a fishing vessel bound for England. It won't be an easy trip, but I agree to it immediately, and not only for Tilly's sake. Dorner will be in London, too.

That night, I lie awake in the barn and think about locating Dorner and shooting him in the stomach, where it'd take hours for him to bleed out. A fitting end to a Nazi like him. Come the morning, I brush my hair and put on a floral-patterned dress that the Resistance has given me, all the while imagining my hands wringing Dorner's skinny neck. I'll choke him until he blacks out, and then I'll wake him up to do it again. And again.

Once I'm ready, Anaïs hands me a folder that contains Tilly's and my new identities. From here on out we'll be known as cousins Élise and Élodie Coupe, two farm girls on our way to visit friends in Perpignan, a town in southeastern France that isn't far from the Spanish border. Once we've arrived in Perpignan, we'll cross over the Pyrenees range by foot and sneak into Spain, which has decided to stay neutral in the war. Still, neutral or not, I'm sure we'll face a new batch of dangers there. For one thing, I don't speak a word of Spanish.

Anaïs accompanies us to the station and insists on escorting us to the platform herself. We weave through a packed crowd, passing three Nazi guards along the way who are inspecting the contents of a young Frenchwoman's carryall. She trembles and bites her nails as they rifle through her things, but her bad luck is our good fortune, because the

Germans don't give our papers a second glance. It's just as well, because Tilly isn't having a good day. She's jittery and jumpy, and she might start yelling in German at any moment. We need to get on our train car fast.

After we find our platform, I embrace Anaïs and she whispers into my ear, "We'll arrange for a friend to find you at the Perpignan station. He'll say to you, *The irises will soon be in bloom.* Your reply will be, *What a sight they'll be to behold.*" As I memorize both code phrases, she tucks a slim bottle into my palm and nods at Tilly. "For your cousin."

I look down at the bottle. It's sleeping syrup for illnesses, often given to sick children, and I'm sure the Resistance bought it off the black market. When I glance up to thank her, I see that Anaïs has already vanished. There's not a trace of her in front of me, and my thank-you dies on my lips.

We board the train and it begins a slow chug down the tracks, and I can't help but recall the last ride that I took—with Sabine. If I shut my eyes, I can see her clearly, dressed in her Fifine alias and flirting with Lieutenant Schuster. A knife twists inside me at the memory, and I wonder if I'll always feel so double-sided about her—anger at her betrayal yet anguish at her sacrifice, hating her and missing her all the same. How can the girl who saved my life over and over be the same one who fed me to the wolves?

Focus on the mission ahead, I tell myself. I can't let Sabine muddle my thoughts now, and so I settle Tilly into an open seat by the window and ask her to take a sip of the syrup.

"What's this for?" she asks.

"It'll help you sleep."

"Why do you want me to sleep, Lucie?" Tilly asks this a little too loudly, and I wince because she has used my real name instead of my alias. Across the aisle, a red-haired woman peers at us from behind her newspaper, a curious spark in her beady eyes. She reminds me of the gossips at my family's parish back home who'd sigh at Theo's long hair and who'd whisper at the bruises on Maman's arms. This woman, however, might not be as harmless as those church ladies. She could be a collaborator, for all I know, ready to turn in anyone who has raised her hackles—and her sights have already prowled upon Tilly and me.

I lean into Tilly. "Please drink a little of the medicine," I whisper, hoping that she won't bark out a *Heil Hitler* now that we're confined to this train car. "It's what the doctor would want."

Her eyes alight. "Dr. Nacht?" she whispers back. That's all it takes for her to knock back a swig of the syrup, and she's out in no time. I breathe a little sigh of relief, but I see that the red-haired woman is still peeking at me. I challenge her with a glare. If she even thinks about pointing us out to the Germans, I'll kill her.

An hour passes and then another, until an entire day has come and gone aboard the train. Twice we're delayed by track work, but at last I catch a glittering glimpse of the Mediterranean. Before long the engines sigh as we pull into Perpignan, and the passengers begin gathering their valises. I wait for everyone to disembark ahead of us, including the nosy redhead, who waddles down the aisle and out of view. Only then do I nudge Tilly awake.

"We have to get off now," I say into her ear.

She blinks at me sleepily. "Where are we, Lu—"

"We're playing a game, remember? My name is Élodie and yours is Élise. We're cousins."

Tilly yawns. "Do we have to play?"

"Come on, lazy bones. Everyone else is already gone." I help her to her feet, just in time to see a young French policeman approaching our car and pointing a bony finger at me. He might not be a Nazi, but he's nearly as bad—a German puppet in French dressing. A chill wriggles down my back, but there's nowhere to run off to. I'll have to see what he wants.

"Your papers?" he asks.

I flash a friendly smile. "Certainly, sir." As I reach for my false papers, I give the station a quick once-over. The swooping peaks of the Pyrenees loom above the train station, pretty as a painting. The platform has mostly thinned out around us, but I do notice four more policemen standing by the ticket counter, their arms crossed and their clubs in plain view.

The man in front of us finishes looking over my papers but doesn't return them to me. In fact, he tucks them away in his pocket. "You best come with me, mademoiselle."

Tilly scoots to my side. "Did we do something wrong?"

"Not at all. Don't you worry." I pat her hand to reassure her despite the rush of blood to my head. This can't be good. I ask the policeman, "Is there a problem, sir?"

"Follow me." He gives me a little push, and my thoughts scatter at what we should do. I could take him down easily. He's thin as a haricot vert, but his friends are a different story. With Tilly out of commission I couldn't take on all of them at once.

The policeman escorts us through the station, and I expect him to lead us into an office for interrogation. I'm about ready to grab Tilly's hand and throw an elbow into the policeman's neck, but for some reason he strides straight out of the station and points us to a parked car. He dips his head toward mine.

"The irises will soon be in bloom, don't you think?" he whispers.

The code phrase! I blurt out, "What a sight they'll be to behold," but a spot of hesitation lodges in my voice. It's hard to overlook the uniform he's wearing.

"We must go quickly." He opens the back door and gestures for us to get in. "I'll explain everything when we're on the road."

My hesitation grows threefold. I have to decide now if we should trust him or not. After what Tilly and I've been through, I know this could be another Nazi ruse. This policeman could've captured Anaïs's real friend and wheedled the code phrases out of him. But what else can I do? We don't know another soul in Perpignan and we can't exactly turn around. We have no weapons and no money, aside from a few francs in my pocket. I may not like it, but we'll have to take our chances with this man until he gives us a reason not to.

Tilly climbs into the backseat, and I get into the front, making sure to rest my fingers on the door handle just in case. The policeman tips his hat to us and steps on the gas. "I'm Maurice, by the way." He glances at me, and he must sense my nerves. "Didn't Anaïs tell you to expect me at the station?"

"She did but she didn't mention you'd be dressed like . . . that."

"I see. No wonder."

"How do you know Anaïs, might I ask?"

"My family lived next to her when I was a boy, and we've kept in close contact since I came to Perpignan. Last year, she recruited me herself into the"—he swallows awkwardly—"the underground." Even inside the car he doesn't want to name the Resistance, and I can't blame him for that. Though his admission does put me at ease a little. I let my hand slip off the door handle.

I'm about to ask Maurice where he's taking us when Tilly taps his shoulder from the backseat. "Are we going to see Dr. Nacht, sir?"

"I beg your pardon?" he says, startled.

I shake my head at him. The last thing I need is for Tilly to say something odd, which would cause Maurice to drop us off as quickly as he picked us up. To Tilly I say, "We have to be patient. We'll see the doctor soon enough."

Maurice makes a turn and we're no longer in view of the station. "I'm unaware of any doctor—"

"Just play along," I whisper.

"Is your friend unwell?"

"We were held by the Nazis for some time. Her mind was affected."

That's all I'll say about the matter, and it seems to placate Maurice. Or maybe the Resistance is paying him well enough that he doesn't mind. We continue on in silence, and I watch the view shift beyond my window, from the quaint red-roofed buildings to the calm waters of the sea. In more peaceful times, I can imagine tourists sipping strong coffee and strolling by the sea, hand in hand; but now the roads are quiet and the residents have all hunkered into their homes, getting ready for the looming curfew. There's hardly a corner in Europe that hasn't been touched by this war. Everywhere I go, the shadow of the swastika stretches over me.

As the car nears the outskirts of town, I lean toward Maurice. "Will we be stopping soon?"

In answer, he points straight ahead. "No, we're going to the mountains, mademoiselle."

So soon? I thought we might be able to rest the night before we start our trek through the Pyrenees.

Tilly yawns and leans her head against the window. "I'm sleepy," she says to no one in particular.

"Try to rest. I'll be here when you wake up," I reply. I watch her curl up in her seat and drift off in a matter of minutes. I wish I could do the same, but I can't stop staring at the steep mountains ahead. Some of the taller summits are capped in snow, even in the middle of the summer, and I shiver at the sight. Spain may be close, but first we'll have to survive the climb.

"Are you all right?" says Maurice.

"I'm fine," I lie.

All I know is that we're a long way from home.

TWENTY-THREE

We drive from Perpignan straight through a tree-filled valley, where we're sandwiched between lush green mountains and sleepy stone villages. It's an entire world apart from the clogged sidewalks of Paris. We make a brief stop at yet another safe house, but this time in the quaint ski town of Ax-Les-Thermes, where Maurice collects our supplies for the long hike ahead: warm clothes, hardy boots, and a rucksack for each of us that's packed with enough food for our trip. We'll have to carry all of our necessities on our backs. There won't be any street markets along the way to buy a crepe; and neither will there be any hospitals if we get frostbite. It'll be a cold and exhausting trip, the Resistance warns us, but the thought of tracking down Dorner drives me forward.

Night has fallen when we arrive at our drop-off point east of town. We're surrounded by nothing except for a brisk wind that bites at my cheeks and the jagged crests of the Pyrenees, lit by starlight. The Resistance provided me with a wool sweater and long jacket to wear, but I shiver and blow warm air into my hands, knowing that the temperatures will only get colder as we start our ascent.

While Maurice checks our packs, I help Tilly lace up her boots, but I notice a sheen of tears in her eyes.

"What's wrong?" I say, alarmed.

She traces a finger along her temple. "What did Dr. Nacht do to me, Lucie? Sometimes I can hear him." Her finger points at the middle of her forehead. "In here."

I drop the laces and hug her close. "We're going to sort this out soon enough. There'll be an entire hospital of doctors in London to help you get better."

"I don't know if that's possible anymore," she says, clutching on to me.

"Of course it's possible." I touch my forehead to hers. "You're going to be your old self in no time." Silently I cling to this hope. Because if the doctors can't fix Tilly, then, in some way, Dr. Nacht has won.

Tilly and I don our mittens, and Maurice comes up behind us. He'll be acting as our guide to cross the mountains. "Ready?" he asks. "We better get moving."

The three of us form a line, with Maurice up front and myself in the back, just in case Tilly decides to wander off. As we start the climb, Maurice warns us to stay silent. We're not to sneeze or cough or utter a word under any circumstances because we'll soon enter the *zone interdite*, the forbidden region between the two countries that's frequently patrolled by customs officials from France, Spain, *and* Germany. They'll be hunting for fugitives like us, their ears tuned for any human sounds. One sentence, one word, could spell our doom.

The mountain air grows brisk, then chilly, then numbingly cold, but Maurice never stops. Far below, the little ski towns disappear from view. and soon all signs of civilization vanish. Our only company is our labored breath and the howling wind that chaps our skin. To keep my mind off my freezing fingertips, I make a list of everything I'll do when we reach London. I'll take a hot bath, first of all. I'll drink a whole pot of tea. *Real* tea. And I'll talk to the SOE and blow Dorner's cover sky-high. He must be so smug, thinking that he has wormed his way into the Brits' good graces, and the thought of seeing him in handcuffs keeps me fighting through the cold.

I'm thinking about hot tea and Dorner in chains when Maurice yanks both Tilly and me to the ground. My face smacks against the dirt and a rock cuts into my cheek, but Maurice presses a finger against my lips to keep me quiet. It's for good measure, too, because when I lift my head slowly I glimpse a man leaning on a ledge not far below us. He's wearing a white hooded parka, and he must've dozed off because he should have spotted us coming. I'm not sure if this man is German or French or Spanish, but judging by the size of Maurice's eyes he isn't a friendly.

Maurice nudges Tilly. "Keep climbing," he mouths to her. Then he gestures for me to hold still. It seems like he wants us to continue upward, but more slowly, one-by-one to minimize any noise we might make. Giving Tilly a nod, I watch her crawl up the rise, holding my breath with every inch that she moves. She has almost reached the top of the nearest ridge when her foot slips, loosening a rock that tumbles down the mountainside. I flatten myself against the ground even more, but the damage is done.

"Verdammt!" the guard says, bolting awake from his perch. He lunges for his rifle when he spots us. "You there! Halt!"

"Run!" I shout at Tilly. I jump to my feet and am about to push Maurice forward when I see that he's reaching for something strapped to his ankle. A gun. He jerks it free and aims, but the guard shoots off a round first. The shot echoes across the peaks.

"Merde!" cries Maurice. He's so flustered that he drops the gun, but before he can retrieve it I snatch it up.

"Go! I'll handle this," I say, hitting the ground again before he can answer. While he scurries up the rise, I wedge myself behind a boulder and locate the guard. He's shouting at us and scrambling over the rocks to reach us, and a hot panic rises inside me.

Pushing the air from my lungs, I steady my hands before another thought can cross my mind. I pull the trigger and a sharp cry stabs through the bitter air, followed by silence. The guard crumples out of my view, and I start to reposition myself, but Maurice has crawled back to me and pulls at my arm.

"I have to finish him off!" I tell him.

"He's dead."

"How do you know for sure?"

Maurice only tugs harder. "No man can survive the amount of blood he'll lose. Please, you need to trust me. If any of his comrades are nearby, they're bound to find us if we don't move."

I hate the idea of leaving behind unfinished business, but the thought of facing more Nazis is an idea I hate even more. So I tuck the gun in my waistband and hustle after Maurice and Tilly, and I don't think about the body that we've left on a chilly mountainside.

———

Hours later, Maurice finally announces that we should be in the clear. We've seen no other trace of the patrols, and he leads us toward a battered hunting cabin that overlooks a moonlit lake. Reflected starlight glitters on the dark waters, pretty as Christmas candles, but I hardly notice the view. I'm too busy staggering inside and stumbling to find wood to light the fireplace, but Maurice won't hear of it. Too dangerous, he says. He tells us to get a little rest, and he gets no protest from Tilly and me about that. We fall onto the near-frozen cots, too exhausted to unlace our boots, but it isn't long until Maurice prods us awake again. By then I'm shivering all over, but I don't get any pity from him. He merely hands me my pack and swings open the door, allowing the stinging wind to sneak inside and wrap around our ankles.

It takes every last scrap of my strength to propel me back outside. Maurice strikes a fast pace up the peak, but I struggle to keep up. I've lost all feeling in my hands, and I'm not sure how my legs are still moving. It's nearly impossible to breathe, let alone move, and it's all too much. I collapse onto my knees, gasping, and not even the thought of strangling Dorner is enough to make me get up.

"You must keep going, mademoiselle!" Maurice says, backtracking to my side. He pulls me up, but I'm deadweight in his hands. He curses, but I don't care. Let him leave me here. At least I can close my eyes and get some rest.

"Let me try," I hear Tilly say. She hooks her hands beneath my arms and hoists me onto my feet, and then she holds me against her so that I won't topple over. "Here we go. One foot in front of the other, Lucie."

"I can't—"

"Yes, you can. One step. Do it for your brother."

I blink at her slowly. She sounds so much like the old Tilly that I've come to know at headquarters, but the moment doesn't last for long.

Tilly adds, "And do it for Dr. Nacht. He'll be so pleased to see us, won't he?"

My heart crumbles, but there's so much hope on her face that I shape my lips into a smile. She continues to urge me forth and I comply, one foot in front of the other, but I don't do it for Dr. Nacht. I do it for Theo. I can almost hear him next to my ear, nagging at me for giving up so easily and telling me to move faster. I need to keep going for Maman and for Ruthie, he'd say. So I do. I've let him down before, but I won't let him down now.

We scale one peak after another, and I lose all sense of time. Eventually Maurice locates a stream and we follow along its banks. Gradually, the waters turn from trickling to gushing, and the stream widens into a fast-flowing river that bends around a small town. I'm about to ask Maurice how much farther we need to go when he stops and points at the village. "You did it, girls," he says with a grin. "We've made it."

I nearly collapse again. "We're in Spain?" I whisper.

"That we are." He claps me on the back. "I hope your Spanish is adequate."

Tilly cries, and relief floods through me. We've crossed the border and left France behind us, but I only give myself a few seconds of celebrating before I round my limp shoulders and think about what will come next. We can't breathe easy yet. We're in an unknown country and we have no weapons. Until we set foot on English soil, I can't let my guard down.

Maurice escorts us to the edges of the village, which doesn't look much different from the French ones we passed yesterday, aside from a few signs written in Spanish. We sneak into a safe house owned by a friend of Maurice, where we change our clothes and feast on a fresh loaf of bread that the owner left for us before heading off to his job. I glance longingly at the soft mattress in the bedroom, but Maurice polishes off the bread and tells us to gather our things.

To me he says, "We can't stay. It's best for you to go to the train station in San Juan de las Abadesas as soon as possible." He hands me a soft leather pouch filled with bronze peseta coins. "That should be plenty to get you a ride there."

I stare at him. "Won't you be coming with us?"

"I'm sorry, but I can't miss another shift at work. This is where I must leave you, but you'll be in safe hands. A Resistance contact will meet you at the station. I've worked with him twice personally. His name is Emilio, though he's better known as Little Emilio around these parts." He gives me a code phrase to use and what to listen for in return, but I cut him off.

"You're leaving us in the hands of 'Little Emilio'?" I glance helplessly at him, then at Tilly. I'm not sure I have it in me to get both of us out alive.

"I've already escorted four airmen who went on to London, and you two girls are tougher than them all." He gives us each another hearty pat on the back and that's that. "Safe travels."

There's nothing I can say to change his mind, so I murmur a thanks. He put his neck on the line to get us into Spain—and the OSS will pay him handsomely for that—and I can't ask any more from him. This is what I agreed to, after all. To reach England, Tilly and I will be passed from Resistance member to Resistance member, like a dangerous game of hot potato. It's a tried-and-true system, and I'm grateful for it, but I can't help but feel weary and wary anyway. With each new Resistance contact we meet, I have to place my trust and my life in their hands. And that's not easy, because the last time I trusted someone, Tilly and I ended up in a Nazi lab.

My heart is clattering fast once Tilly and I arrive at the train station. I did my best to spruce us up by combing our hair with my fingers, but there's only so much I can do to hide our haggardness, even with a new change of clothes. A man with a dark mustache sniffs at us when we walk past him, and I guide Tilly toward the schedule board to escape his searching eyes. He's wearing plain trousers and a button-down shirt, a far cry from a soldier's uniform, but Maurice warned us that there might be undercover German agents searching for refugees. I sweep my eyes over the station. Where is our contact?

I pretend to look at the schedules, hoping that Emilio is merely running late and didn't lose his nerve in retrieving us. The mustached man keeps watching us, though, and that makes me anxious. From the corner of my eye, I see him folding his newspaper under one arm and walking toward us, his broad shoulders as wide as an icebox. I reach for Tilly's hand, ready to tell her to run.

"Bonjour," he says quietly, in a heavy accent. "I'm Emilio."

I think I must've heard him wrong. This enormous man is "Little Emilio"?

"Little Emilio is a nickname," he's quick to add. "You're the 'cousins,' I presume?" Then he recites the code phrase that Maurice told me, and I tell him the response word for word. It appears that this giant of a Spaniard, who looks like he could kill me with one blow of his fist, will be our next escort.

"The train should be leaving on the hour. I've already purchased the tickets." He motions for us to start moving. "Shall we?"

I hand him a few coins to repay him for our tickets and follow right after him, because I'm too tired to ask anything else. Emilio cuts through the throng like a blunt butcher knife and finds a row of seats at the back of one train car. Once on board, he waits for the train to start moving before he fills me in on the details of our journey, his voice muffled from the rumble of the tracks below. That's how I find out that we're making our way to Spain's northern coast, where a fisherman awaits to take us across the sea. Usually the Resistance prefers to smuggle refugees down to Gibraltar or into Portugal, since Spanish ports are carefully monitored, but they've made an exception for Tilly and me. The sooner we reach Allied soil, the better.

The ride to Barcelona is thankfully uneventful, and Tilly and I spend most of that leg curled up fast asleep. From there, we switch trains to Zaragoza, with our destination set for the coastal city of Bilbao, the last major town on our route. Along the way we see more than a dozen Spanish civil guards with their snug gray-green uniforms, but they shuffle past us without much trouble. That's the benefit of having Emilio as our escort.

When we disembark in Bilbao, a quick-moving breeze greets us and tells me we're nearing the ocean. Emilio deposits Tilly and me on a wooden bench while he uses some ration tickets to purchase food. Spain might be neutral, but it has had to enforce rations because of the war, too.

While we wait for Emilio to return, Tilly and I stretch our legs and rub the cricks from our necks. We've been in Spain for over thirty hours, almost all of it spent on trains or waiting in steaming-hot stations. But we're nearly there. We only have to take one more train to a little port town before we can climb aboard the fishing boat that's bound for England. For the first time since we left the laboratory, I'm tempted to think that we're truly going to make it.

And as soon as that thought takes form in my head, trouble finds us again.

Beside me, Tilly's back goes as straight as a broomstick. "Lucie," she whispers.

The hairs on the back of my neck prick up. I've told her too many times to use my false name. "What is it? Do you see Emilio?"

"No, look!" She points toward a flock of passengers who've recently disembarked from Pamplona. They shuffle by in a tired line, some carrying heavy valises and others carrying children. I try to shush Tilly, but she's insistent. She juts a finger at a bearded old man struggling with a suitcase in each hand.

"Please sit down," I whisper to her. I clamp a firm hand around her arm, but she jerks away, her eyes glowing bright.

"It's him!"

"Who? We don't know that man."

"He's found us!" She waves at him with both arms. "Dr. Nacht!"

Merde. Aside from his white beard, that man is a far cry from the doctor. Not that Tilly notices or cares. She barrels toward the old Spaniard, babbling in a mixture of French and German, and the entire station stops to stare at her. Murmurs erupt. Whispers pummel my ears. It isn't long before a Spanish civil guard takes notice of the fracas. He was leaning against the ticket counter just a second ago, but now he's making a beeline toward Tilly. I search wildly for Emilio but he's nowhere to be seen.

With no other options, I wrench Tilly to my side and give the guard an apologetic smile before I bury us in the next wave of passengers. I search for an exit and pretend not to hear the guard shouting from behind in alarmed Spanish. I spot a pair of doors and quicken our pace to reach them, but as I grasp the handle I bump into Emilio, literally. He almost drops the paper bag he carries, which smells strongly of fried fish.

"What's the matter?" he asks me, a cross look on his face. "I told you I'd be back—"

"Behind us!" I whisper.

Finally Emilio sees the guard hollering at us, and he blanches. "What happened? Never mind, never mind." He tosses aside the food and shoves us outside. "Run!"

Tilly has gone frantic. She claws at my arms and asks to see Dr. Nacht immediately, but Emilio and I wrestle her into the street, where we take off sprinting. Emilio spots an idling taxi and shoves us into the backseat, at which point the driver starts yelping and flapping his hands for us to get out. But he's silenced once Emilio reaches into his pocket and tosses a pile of cash at him.

"*Conduzca*," Emilio barks, and the car peels onto the road. Struggling to catch my breath, I glance out the back window but see no sign of the civil guard. Though that doesn't mean we're safe—not by a long shot.

We bump along the road for a few miles, bypassing a handful of horses and wagons, until Emilio insists that we stop and take the bus to cover our tracks. This doesn't prove very easy, because there's a gas shortage in Spain, and the bus schedules have grown as unreliable as the water pipes in Paris. But through sheer force of will and a little bribe money, Emilio locates the correct route that we need and delivers us to the port.

By the time we reach the dock we're already two hours late, but we find the fishing boat still anchored. At the sight of us, the fisherman merely takes a puff of his pipe and sticks out a hand toward Emilio, ready for his payment. Emilio empties the rest of our money into the man's tanned palm.

"Get on board, you two," says Emilio, breathing hard.

"I don't know how to thank you," I say, but he waves me off and gives Tilly and me a gruff good-bye before motioning for us to get on the boat.

I climb aboard, and the scent of blood and fish almost knocks me over. The fisherman throws his head back and laughs at that, revealing a mouthful of brown teeth, and practically pushes us belowdecks. We settle onto a pile of old yet surprisingly clean blankets. Tilly falls asleep in minutes, but I can't stop peeking above deck, waiting for the Spanish police to flag us down and escort us back over the border— this time in handcuffs. But no boats follow us. It isn't long before dry land vanishes and we're surrounded by endless water.

Finally I lay down beside Tilly to rest, but as soon as my head touches the blanket the tears come pouring out. I can't help but think of everything we've lost along the way, from headquarters to my brother's letters, blown into a thousand little pieces. In the last letter he wrote to me, he said it wasn't fair that he was alive while so many of his friends were dead. Now, at last, I understand the burden of his words. I've never felt this alone.

Theo's gone. So are Delphine and Harken and Sabine. Even my parents are an entire ocean away—not that I'm eager to return home to Papa's drinking. I left Baltimore without looking back, and a part of me wouldn't care if I ever set foot there again . . . except I'd like to hug Maman and I'd like to see Ruthie. Theo asked me to watch out for her. She's my sister, he said.

That thought warms me for the rest of the night.

***

At daybreak the fisherman jolts me awake with a garbled shout, and I scramble up the ladder to see land ahead. A fishing village pops into our sights, surrounded by a stone retaining wall to protect the town from high tide—and maybe from intruders like us. While he smokes a pipe, the fisherman hoists a white flag onto the sail. A signal, perhaps?

I don't give the flag much thought because I'm overcome. How long has it been since we escaped the laboratory? Or headquarters before that? I'm already thinking about sleeping in a soft bed and taking a bath, a long one with plenty of bubbles and soap.

The boat approaches a dock, and I leap onto it before we come to a full stop, more than ready to be back in Allied territory. Tears prick my eyes when I see that we aren't alone. There are ten soldiers at the end of the pier, each of them wearing the brown uniform of the British army. I sure wasn't expecting a reception like this, but the Resistance must have alerted the SOE that we'd be coming.

I wobble toward the Brits on my shaky sea legs, and one of them steps forward to meet me. He looks about Major Harken's age, and his wheat-blond hair is brushed neatly under his brown cap. I assume he's in charge by the way he tilts his chin upward like Sabine used to do.

"I wasn't expecting a welcoming committee, but you sure are a sight for sore eyes, sir," I say. I jut out a hand toward him, and he stares at it quizzically before giving it a tepid shake.

"My name is Colonel James," he says in a proper English accent, just like out of the movies.

"Lucie Blaise." It's odd saying my real name, and even odder speaking in English. I haven't used it in months, and it feels foreign on my tongue. "I'm not sure if you were told, but I'm with—"

"OSS, yes. We were informed by the French Resistance." He says this matter-of-factly, almost coldly. Well, I guess I shouldn't have thought that he'd clap me on the back and call me *old chap*, but it might've been nice after what we've been through. "We were told to expect two of you."

"My colleague Matilda Fairbanks is right behind me." I wave for Tilly to come forward, and she staggers off the boat with the fisherman's help. "She needs medical attention straightaway."

"Yes, we'll see to that. If you'll follow me, then—"

"Do you happen to know Alexander Dorner's whereabouts?" I interject. It's rude of me, but this can't wait a second longer. "It's urgent."

His pale eyes meet mine at the mention of Dorner, but he says nothing of it. "It's best if you come with me first. We shouldn't discuss such matters out in the open."

Fair enough, but that doesn't stop me from wanting to hop in the nearest vehicle and go searching for Dorner on my own. "Very well. Where are we headed? To the American embassy?"

"To a facility where you'll be debriefed and given time to recover." He smiles politely, but there's no warmth behind it. A chill shivers down my spine, and I wonder why he's treating me so coolly. The Brits and Americans are allies, yet he's acting like I'm an unwelcome houseguest.

"I don't need time to recover. I need to find Dorner, *sir*."

"Again, we shan't discuss such matters here, Miss Blaise." His smile has vanished, and he nods at the soldiers surrounding Tilly and me. "Now, if you will, my men and I will escort you to our facilities, where you'll receive medical care and where we may talk more freely."

His tone doesn't brook any argument, and his soldiers herd Tilly and me toward a row of parked vehicles not far from the pier. We have no choice but to climb in, and no matter how many questions I ask—*Where are we going? What's going to happen to us? Where is Dorner?*—Colonel James remains as silent as Queen Elizabeth's tomb.

We drive all the way to London. At the sight of the city, my gaze glues to the window. It's in worse shape than Paris, with rubble littering the sidewalks and entire buildings left smashed, courtesy of the German Luftwaffe. We zigzag around the debris until the car turns onto Baker Street, depositing us in front of a building with a brown-brick façade that resembles a nice hotel. But a hotel it is certainly not.

Colonel James accompanies Tilly and me to an awaiting team of doctors and nurses who pepper us with questions of the biological sort and poke at us for hours on end. They deem me malnourished and slightly anemic but otherwise physically fit, and so they pass me back to Colonel James, who hands me a fresh set of clothes and leaves me in a third-floor bedroom that smells faintly of ammonia.

"What about Tilly?" I say when I see that the room only holds one cot. "Where are you putting her?"

"The doctors hope to run a few more tests. We'll update you shortly. Until then, please wait here for further instructions." He exits the room before I can reply.

Hours pass before Colonel James returns. When he comes back again, this time with a folder tucked underneath his arm, I'm in a foul mood.

"Where have you been?" I demand, leaping to my feet to meet him halfway. "I'm a Covert Ops agent! I'm an American citizen! Why've you locked me up in this cell?"

He simply clears his throat at my outburst. I doubt he'd flinch if a grenade exploded ten feet away from him. "This isn't a cell, Miss Blaise. You were free to step out at any time, were you not?"

"That's beside the point," I say darkly. "I didn't risk my neck a dozen times getting out of France to be put in this cage."

"My apologies, but the processing of your arrival required certain protocols. We needed to look into your background. Surely you can understand why we needed to take precautions."

I scowl, because that's easy for him to say. "What have you done with Tilly?"

"She remains under the care of our physicians. As you mentioned, she has required significant medical attention."

"I want to see her."

"You may see her at any time, but I prefer that you wait until you've answered my questions."

I frown. "What questions?"

"Earlier today, you spoke of an Alexander Dorner."

"Where is he? Is he in London?" The questions shoot out of me, and I can't stop them. "How much have you told him about the SOE and the OSS?"

Colonel James puts up his hands to slow me down. "One at a time, please. First, let's sit." He takes a seat on the lone metal chair in the room and gestures for me to sit on the bed. Reluctantly I do so. "Let's start a bit further back." He opens the folder and scribbles a note on the papers inside. "We learned a couple weeks ago that Covert Ops' headquarters in Paris was compromised and destroyed. It was assumed that all of the agents there had perished."

I swallow the bitter memory of that night. "Yes. The Nazis discovered us, so we set the fire to protect our operation. Major Harken was killed, but three of us survived."

"You, Miss Fairbanks, and . . . ?"

"Sabine Chevalier." My throat cinches. "She was killed in the line of duty later on."

He flips through a few pages in his folder. "We do have a record for Sabine Nassima Chevalier. Daughter of François and Amina?"

I nod, though I never knew the names of Sabine's parents or even her middle name. Even in death, I'm learning more about her than I knew in life.

"My condolences," says Colonel James softly before he returns to his usual clipped tone. "Where did the three of you go after your headquarters was compromised?"

The weight of his question threatens to smother me. I don't want to relive the memories of the laboratory, nor do I wish to reveal everything to the SOE, even if they are our allies. Don't I owe the intelligence to the OSS first? But until I can see an OSS agent, Colonel James is my best bet in hunting down Dorner. So I take in a long breath.

"We followed a lead given to us by Alexander Dorner. We went to Verdun searching for a *Wunderwaffe* facility . . . but it turned out to be a lie."

He sits forward, his interest heightened. "There was no facility?"

I sidestep the question and throw out an accusation instead. "Dorner isn't who he claims to be."

"So, you see, that's where this discrepancy lies. It wasn't long ago that Covert Operations vouched for this very same gentleman."

"Well, he completely fooled us." My blood simmers as the explanation tumbles out of me. "His real name is Elias Reinhard. Hauptsturmführer Reinhard to his colleagues. He's the mastermind behind a massive Nazi operation to infiltrate England and get into the SOE's good graces." Shame causes my cheeks to burn scarlet, because I was part of that, but I will make things right. "I'm sure Dorner—or Reinhard, rather—told you about Operation Zerfall and how it'll change the entire course of the war." By the way Colonel James's eyes flare wide, I know I've hit my mark.

Colonel James sits back in the chair, studying me. "What of the coordinates and photographs he brought with him?"

"The coordinates were accurate, but everything else was a forgery. The whole lot of them."

He goes quiet before springing to his feet. "Thank you, Miss Blaise. If you'll excuse me."

"Will you arrest Reinhard?" I'm quick to follow after him.

"I must speak with the others."

"What others?"

"My superiors. If this man is indeed Elias Reinhard instead of Alexander Dorner, then we'll need to question him at once."

"Will you bring him here, to this facility?"

"That has yet to be determined."

"I want to speak with him. One-on-one."

A wan smile stretches over his dry lips. "Let's not get ahead of ourselves, Miss Blaise."

"I can get him to talk like no one else can. I've spent days with him. I've studied him." I watch the gears spinning in Colonel James's head as he considers my proposition. "After you bring him in and have interrogated him yourselves, I want to see him."

His eyes focus on me, shrewd and calculating. "Might I ask why?"

"He and I have unfinished business." That's all I'll say about that.

"Like I said, I'll answer every question you throw at me about him. I'll talk to your superiors if they'd like. Just get me a meeting with Dorner."

Colonel James tilts his head to one side and, after considering my offer, tells me, "I'll see what I can do. And you best come with me."

I don't even have shoes on, but I follow him out the door in my bare feet. For the first time in weeks, there's a bounce in my step and a zippy jolt in my veins.

Poor Dorner will never see this coming.

TWENTY-FOUR

Four days later, Colonel James returns to my room at our appointed meeting time. I'm sitting at the edge of my bed, dressed in a pressed blouse and a black skirt that the SOE has supplied for me. I take a sip of hot water, wishing that it were tea or coffee, but the war rations haven't been exempted for the SOE. I barely slept the night before. I was too busy counting down the hours and then the minutes to this meeting.

"Ready, Miss Blaise?" says Colonel James at my door.

"Ready," I reply, and follow him out.

He takes me down the stairwell. We leave behind the sunny corridors of the upper stories and exchange them for the swinging overhead lamps of the building's basement, which cast a harsh glow upon our faces. My heels strike against the dusty floor, and I tuck my hands behind my back to keep them from fidgeting. This will likely be the only chance I get with Dorner face-to-face. I have to make it count. Only one of us will leave this meeting alive today.

"How long will I have with him?" I ask.

"Five minutes."

"Only five?"

"It's all they'd agree to. Most of my superiors didn't think it was a good idea for you to see him at all."

"But you convinced them otherwise?"

"We had a deal, did we not?"

That's something I've learned about Colonel James—he's a man who keeps his promises. I told him all he wanted to learn about Dorner, and in return he has arranged for this little rendezvous, despite what our higher-ups at the SOE and the OSS have had to say. Both agencies have been in upheaval these last few days. First, the SOE interrogated me for hours about my dealings with Dorner. Then they dragged in Dorner himself—who had apparently burrowed himself within the British intelligence community quite well since his arrival—and questioned him separately. The interrogations lasted for days, with the OSS joining in, but both agencies kept me at arm's length. They told me to rest; they thanked me for my service. But I saw the wariness in their eyes, the same look they gave Tilly. I knew they weren't sure what to do with me, not after what I'd been through with Dr. Nacht. Would I start yelling *Heil Hitler* like Tilly sometimes did? Or worse?

A small part of me couldn't blame them for thinking what they did, but the rest of me wanted to kick some sense into them. I'd put my life on the line countless times for the Allies, and yet my own agency thinks I might be some Nazi marionette. That stings, to be honest. The only person who doesn't seem to look at me that way is Colonel James.

We walk through two sets of iron-barred doors and past a pair of uniformed guards who've been tasked with making sure no one enters or leaves the basement without permission. At the sight of Colonel James, however, they step aside at once.

We stop as we approach the last room along the dank hallway. There's a small square window inset on the door, and Colonel James motions for me to look through it. When I do, I see the inside of a cell with concrete floors and a metal toilet. There's a man sitting on a cement bench that's bolted to the floor, positioned in a way that I can see only his profile. But it's enough.

It's Dorner, that's for sure.

"He can't see us," Colonel James murmurs.

"How long has he been kept here?"

"Since you made us believe we should."

"Will there be a trial?"

"Yes, though the date is to be determined. Until then he'll remain here."

I relish the thought and reach for the doorknob, but it's locked, of course. "Where's the key?"

"One moment." He purses his lips. "I'm to remind you of the parameters set by both the SOE and the OSS concerning this visit. Five minutes. Not a second more. You're not to lay a finger on him, either."

"He's a spy."

"Miss Blaise." A blade sharpens in his voice. A warning.

"Very well," I lie.

He unlocks the door, but before I head in he has one more word of caution for me. "Remember," he says, "not a finger. I'll be watching."

"Duly noted, sir," I say, and step inside.

My pulse hums. I spent all night plotting what I'd do in this moment. What I'd say to Reinhard. What he'd reply. And how I'd kill him. Colonel James might be watching me, but I know I can get the deed done before he can stop me. Dorner should be a simple kill, too, since he has been incapacitated. His left ankle is chained to the wall, and his wrists have been handcuffed. As Harken would say, easy prey.

If Dorner is shocked to see me, he doesn't show it. He greets me with his usual polite smile, and I wonder how long he has practiced it in front of the mirror. Was that part of his Nazi training?

"What an unexpected surprise," he says. His hair is dirty, and he's wearing a poor-fitting white shirt and trousers, like a boy who decided to play dress-up in his father's closet. He also looks plumper since the last time I saw him. Maybe he was taking full advantage of whatever the Brits were feeding him before they took my accusations seriously and threw him into this cell.

"Hello, *Reinhard*," I reply, even though he'll always be Dorner to me.

"Dearest Marie-Louise." He stands to welcome me, never once flinching at the sound of the chain rattling behind him. He isn't wearing his glasses anymore. I'm guessing he never needed them in the first place. "You know, you never told me *your* real name."

"Call me Blaise," I say.

"Blaise." He tests out the sound of it. "Do I have you to thank for my new quarters? Not even a week ago I was sitting down to a fine quail dinner with my new English friends, but then"—he lifts up his cuffed wrists—"this."

I pace around him and take in his living conditions. Mold gathers in the corners of the cramped space, and something foul-smelling drips from the ceiling and puddles on the floor. Lovely. "You are very welcome."

"I assume once you set foot in England, my cover was blown."

It wasn't that easy, but I say nothing about it. "How astute of you, Reinhard."

His grins. "Now that I know your name, it's only fair that you know mine."

"Your uncle was the one who told me. He also told me all about your little plans."

"I wouldn't call them 'little,'" he says. *That pompous weasel*, I think. "I hope you enjoyed your time with my uncle Alfred." He taps a finger against his forehead. "Are you feeling well? Any memory loss, or some other side effect of his experiments?"

Just for that, I'm ready to send my shoe into his teeth, but I know that Colonel James's eyes are on my back. If I plan on hurting Dorner, I'll have one chance and once chance only. I'll have to kick him with my words until then. "I'm feeling much better now that I've blown up your uncle's laboratory."

At my revelation Dorner proceeds to pick at a thread on his shirt, but I see a hairline crack in his smile. "It's no matter. There are other laboratories to carry on his work."

"Perhaps, but I doubt it will be easy to carry on your uncle's work now that he's dead." I watch his hands freeze, and I wish he'd look up so that I could see his face at what I say next. "I killed him, you know."

His chest rises and falls, and slowly he looks up at me. His blue eyes have grown dark and menacing. Calculating how to hurt me. *There you are*, I think. The real Elias Reinhard. But like a true chameleon, he shifts and wipes his face clean.

"Have you come to kill me as well?" He opens his arms to me, allowing full access to his chest. "Will you put a bullet in my heart with one of your pen contraptions?"

"Alas, I don't have one with me."

"Then what's your preferred method? A beating? Strangulation?"

That would take too long, I think. I'd barely get Dorner unconscious before Colonel James came barreling through the door. I take one step closer to him, but he doesn't move.

"Or a knife to the stomach?" he continues. "I'm sure you'd relish seeing the blood drip out of me."

"You're right. I wouldn't mind that," I say softly. What I wouldn't give for a knife right now—the sharper the better.

He laughs. "I see. By killing me, you could avenge your fallen OSS colleagues. Major Harken, for instance. Oh yes, the Nazis learned his identity months ago. I also overheard from the SOE that he died in a fire."

I stop myself from wincing, not wanting him to see that he has hit a soft spot. Harken didn't die because of the fire. Sabine killed him. But in the end, Dorner has the blood of both on his hands.

"What about your friend Odette?" he continues. "Is she alive?" His lips arch upward, sharp as scythes. "If she is still breathing, I wouldn't mind introducing her to my friends in Berlin. A pretty thing like that."

My fingers twitch, but I keep them at my sides.

"Have you lost your nerve?" Dorner teases. "I can see it in your eyes. You'd like nothing more than to kill me."

Be done with it, Lucie, a voice whispers inside me.

"Did my uncle get to you after all? Did his serum make you sympathize a little for me, Fräulein?"

I see red. Hearing him call me that—how Dr. Nacht used to address me—sends me hurtling to the edge, and I don't care one bit that Colonel James is watching from the window. I could snap Dorner's neck before the SOE or the OSS or the entire Allied forces combined could stop me.

I'm ready to break him, but for some reason I hold back. There's something in his eye. In the edge of his laugh.

The realization smacks me right in the face.

He's *baiting* me.

Dorner wants to die. He sees the writing on the wall, and he isn't stupid. He'll be tried and executed months from now. With that bleak of a future ahead of him, he must view me as the easy way out. Until the very end, he'll use me.

I turn my face away from his in order to steady my breath, to stop myself from killing him now. Because nothing would make me happier. Then an idea comes to a boil in my mind, and I let it bubble over. One side of my mouth kicks up. I won't give him what he wants, but I will give him what he deserves.

"You've grown too soft-hearted, Blaise," Dorner says.

I ignore that and say, "I don't believe you met my friend Tilly. She was another one of your uncle's subjects."

"Did she die?" he asks, all round-eyed.

"No, she's alive." I resist slapping him. "What a relief for her family, too. You might have heard of them—the Fairbanks? They're very well known in America. They come from money. Heaps of it."

"How nice. They will need that money to pay for her recovery, I imagine."

I'm tempted to claw his eyes out. "She'll recover, don't you worry. Her parents and uncles will make sure of it. Both of her uncles are politicians, by the way. I've been sending them updates about you." The last part is a lie, but only a partial one. I do plan on contacting Congressman Fairbanks and Governor Fairbanks, and I'm sure they'll rally to this cause.

I sharpen my own smile for Dorner. "Tilly's uncles are powerful men with powerful friends—friends who will make sure that you remain in prison for the rest of your life."

He rolls this over in his mind before he smirks. "You're bluffing."

"I could be, yes." I lean forward so that he hears every word I have to say. "But let's see who's bluffing a year from now, when you're rotting in this cage. Let's see who's bluffing in a decade, when you've forgotten the feel of the sun. And let's see who's bluffing when you're a bent old man and your brain has rotted into insanity."

A vein pulses on Dorner's forehead. His smile has disappeared. "We shall see, Fräulein. You're not the only one with powerful friends."

"You truly think the Nazis will come to your aid?" I jut my chin at the damp walls. "Hitler hasn't been able to conquer England yet—what makes you think he can get in to rescue you?" I turn away from him, and a beat passes.

"Wait."

I tilt my head back toward him.

"Listen to me. Perhaps we can make an arrangement." Somehow his voice has gone tender. He sounds like Dorner again, all soft vowels and rounded consonants.

"An arrangement?"

"Yes. I have intelligence about the *Wunderwaffe* and the Nazi high command."

"What sort of intelligence?"

His smile reappears shyly. "Important intelligence. Highly classified. We could work together, you and I."

I remain where I stand. An image of Major Harken flashes in my mind, followed by Sabine. Then Tilly comes to me, alive but so terribly broken. All because of this man. I make sure that Dorner is staring straight at me before I spit into his face. He lurches back, disgusted, and tries to attack me, but I plant a kick into his stomach. He goes down onto one knee and gasps for air.

"That's for Harken!" I say.

Another kick, this time in the ribs.

"For Sabine!"

An elbow to his nose.

"For Tilly!"

I'm about to dig my fingers into his throat when Colonel James barrels into the room and tears me off Dorner. "That's enough!" he shouts. "That's more than enough."

I don't fight him on that. I wasn't going to kill Dorner, but I didn't want to leave him without a few mementos.

"Out," says Colonel James to me. He thrusts me toward the door, but I twist around to see Dorner one more time. He's lying on the floor, blood gushing from his nostrils. He looks ready to murder me.

"Farewell, Reinhard," I say, panting. "I hope you enjoy this cell."

As Colonel James shoves me into the corridor, Dorner screams a list of expletives behind me, but I hardly hear them. Let him scream. Let him beg. I'll make sure that no one will come to help him.

"I thought I made myself clear," Colonel James says, obviously not pleased with my behavior.

"He's alive."

"Only because I interceded."

"I wasn't planning on killing him."

"I beg to differ."

I stop in the middle of the hall and remove my arm from his grasp. "If I'd wanted him dead, he'd be dead."

"He'll need medical attention, you know," Colonel James says with a sigh.

"Then give it to him. But I'm going to make sure that he spends the rest of his days in a jail cell. No trial. Just those four cement walls. You can count on that."

I stride away quickly before the colonel can answer me. I'm not arguing with him about this matter. Dorner will never take another breath as a free man again.

As I climb up the stairwell, I can still hear him shouting from his cell. He's calling for me. He's cursing my name. His fury is a song to my heart.

"Good-bye, Herr Reinhard," I whisper.

TWENTY-FIVE

When the Nazis stop me at a checkpoint these days, I'm ready for them with a new string of lies.

My name is Julia Bellerose. I'm eighteen years old. I reside in Brest, at the very tip of western France where the winds howl and the sea spray is frigid cold. And you'll often find me carrying a basket of brown eggs at my hip, plucked fresh this morning from my grand-père's farm.

I've been lucky so far. Since I parachuted back into France five months ago, I've had four run-ins total with German soldiers, but all of them were as harmless as mosquito bites—irritating, but nothing a sharp scratch couldn't fix. They'd search through my purse and my basket of eggs, pilfering a couple for their own stomachs, but then they'd send me away. I don't blame them for not prodding further. I'm not much to look at nowadays, just a skinny farm girl with dirt under her nails and mud beneath her shoes; and the Nazis have much more important things to worry about, like the Allies overtaking Italy or the American soldiers arriving in Europe by the week.

The war is slowly shifting, and I along with it. After eight weeks in London, I was itching to get into the field again, but the OSS was wary. They spent another eight weeks assessing me, administering physicals and mental tests and asking so many questions about Zerfall that I lost my voice answering all of them. In the end they deemed me "adequately recovered." I take that to mean that they don't think I'll turn into a Nazi. Then the agents gave me two choices: either desk duty in England or an honorable discharge and a plane ticket home. Much to their irritation, I picked a third option: returning to France.

They flat-out refused at first. They called me mad. In the end, however, I wore them down. After all, Covert Ops needs spies like me who can speak fluent French and who are trained to kill if it comes to that. That's why they finally handed me a new parachute and gave me a battle promotion to agent. Finally. I'm sure they doubted that I'd last a week, yet here I am almost a half year later.

This time around, my assignments have been simple. I sell my eggs and listen for intelligence. I collect parachute drops from Allied planes. Then I radio all my findings back to London. Rinse, repeat, and without much of a mess. I'm sure Harken would be proud. I hope he would be, anyway. Tonight, however, I've written up a different agenda for myself—one that's for me, and me only.

Under a new moon, I shoulder my leather satchel and hurry across a dirt road that carves a lonely trail toward the chilly shore. I glance around me, just to be safe. It's long past curfew and civilians aren't allowed anywhere near the beach, but I've already decided that I'll take my chances. Besides, I'm not exactly a civilian, now, am I?

The winter wind blasts me from behind while the icy mist of the ocean hits me from the front, but I press on toward the white-capped Atlantic waters. There's a good layer of fog that greets me, too, which will provide me enough cover for what I need to do.

If Major Chapman knew what I was up to he'd probably flay me alive, but he's hundreds of miles away in Paris, hidden in a tiny flat in the 4th arrondissement with just a bed and a radio to keep him company. Chapman is Harken's replacement. He was sent by Covert Ops to France three months ago, but he has inherited a very different organization than the one Harken created. There's no more headquarters. No more briefings. Covert Operations has been stripped to the basics—just Chapman and a network of field agents, each of us buried in our little corners of France, keeping our eyes open and our fingers busy and wreaking havoc however we can. I send him updates every week to keep him satisfied, and that's the extent of our correspondence. So Covert Operations has lived on, despite all the turmoil it has gone through. I just wish that Harken were here to see it.

I reach the barbed-wire fence the Nazis have erected along the coast and grab a blanket from my bag to throw across it. Once I climb to the other side, my boots plant onto the craggy rock that covers most of the Breton shoreline.

As I tiptoe over those rocks, I can't help but think about Tilly. I got a letter from her only a week ago, smuggled to me via the OSS. She told me that she has a view of the ocean from her room in Connecticut and that she takes walks on the sand every morning as part of her recovery. Her family flew her back to the States right before my return to France, and her parents have hired a hive of doctors to help her recuperate. *The nurses poke me from sunup to sun-down, and they keep giving me these tonics to drink that taste like gasoline,* she had written. She had ended the letter with: *How are things going with the new crew? Maybe one of these days I'll be able to join you all.*

Tilly might be writing in code about our new agents, but even the Nazis would be able to read the hope in her words. I know that she desperately wants to hang the title of "Agent" next to her name again, but I doubt I'll see her until the war ends. Her doctors won't let her return to France without a clean bill of health, and I'm sure Chapman wouldn't take her back even if she had one. She was still spouting *Heil Hitler* when we reached London together. As much as I want her back, she'd be seen as too much of a risk to bring back into Covert Ops' fold.

I take comfort in that, though. I'd much rather have Tilly scarred yet alive than scarred and dead. I don't want to lose another friend to this war.

An angry wave breaks over the rocks, sending cold water into my boots, and I know I better get a move on things. I reach into my bag and pull out two glass bottles from it, each one holding a slim slip of paper. I wrote both of them this morning. A letter for Theo. A letter for Sabine.

I step to the edge of the stony cliff as the frothy waves tumble ten feet below me. My right foot sinks into a puddle and more water sneaks into my boot, but I'll deal with the wet socks and cold feet later. I take Sabine's bottle into my hand, the glass cold to the touch. She has been gone for months now, and there are some days when I still don't know what to think about her. I don't know if I can let go of the anger I feel at her betrayal, but at the same time I think I finally understand why she did it. I may not agree with it—and Tilly will have to live with the consequences of Sabine's choice for the rest of her life—but she did try to make things right in the end. I've decided that has to count for something.

I launch the bottle into the air, and it disappears into the thickening fog. Soon, the current will push that bottle out to sea and toward a place where there won't be any bombs or war. It's the sort of place that I hope Sabine is in now, someplace where she can be with her brother.

"Safe travels," I whisper.

I reach for the second bottle. For Theo's. My chest twinges and I curl my fingers around the neck of it, as if it's my dead brother's hand. There are actually two letters inside of this bottle, one from me and one from Ruthie. I wrote to her when I was in London, and she had written me back before I left. She thought I had run off to California, and it wasn't until she'd received my letter that she discovered I had been on the war front all along. She told me to keep safe and that Theo would've been real proud of me, but that wasn't the part that made me tear up. No, it was the way she had signed it: *Your sister, Ruthie.*

I cork the bottle and toss it far into the waves. It's fitting, I think. My letter together with Ruth's. Theo would have liked that.

With the bottles dispersed, I know that I should sneak back into town, but I linger for a moment longer and look up at the dark clouds.

I don't know if Theo is somewhere up there watching over me, but if he is, I think I know what he'd ask from me.

"Hail Mary, full of grace," I say. Whether or not I believe in that prayer anymore, I've repeated it every night for Theo because I promised him once that I would. And here I am, ready to make him another one. "I'll take care of her, you hear?" I whisper to the clouds. "I'll watch out for Ruthie."

I pick my way back over the rocks. My little cottage is a few miles off, and there are three dozen tasks waiting for me once I return—radio messages to send, a pair of binoculars to fix, and a list of possible recruits to look over—and the thought of all that makes me bone-tired. At times like these, when I'm cold and exhausted, I wonder if I should've taken up Covert Ops' offer for a plane ticket home. I could be with Maman again. I could drink tea with Ruthie. I wouldn't wake up every night with every croak and groan of the floorboards. But there'll be time for all of that later.

I came to France for Theo, but now I stay here for myself. I don't plan on setting foot beyond these borders until this country is free from Hitler's hands and until we're all free from the Nazis' tight noose. That's my newest mission—not vengeance or punishment, but this small speck of hope that we won't always be ruled by the swastika. And I swear to that on my name—not as Sister Marchand or Fleurette Dupre or Marie-Louise or Julia Bellerose—but as me, Lucie Blaise.

AUTHOR'S NOTE

The three female agents at the heart of *The Darkest Hour* and their stories are fictional, but they were inspired by real-life World War II heroines. There were countless unsung women who helped fight against the Axis Powers, and as I researched their lives, I was awed by their bravery. There was Marie-Madeleine Fourcade, a young Frenchwoman who took command of 3,000 spies after her superior was arrested by the Nazis. Or Hannie Schaft, an auburn-haired spitfire in the Dutch Resistance who, when facing her own botched execution, shouted at the German SS officer who misfired, "I am a much better shot!" Then there was Virginia Hall, an American woman who spied for both the SOE and OSS, and whom the Nazis called the "limping lady." Little did the Germans know that the source of Hall's limp was her prosthetic leg, which she had nicknamed Cuthbert.

Virginia Hall served as a major inspiration for Lucie's character in particular. An expert in disguises, Hall helped build the French Resistance and avoided capture for years, despite Wanted posters bearing her face plastered around Vichy, France. But when the Nazis seized all of France in November 1942, she was forced to flee to Spain via the Pyrenees. I wove details of her escape into Lucie and Tilly's flight out of France, although Hall left in November, when the conditions were much harsher.

For further reading on these brave women and others, I recommend *The Wolves at the Door: The True Story of America's Greatest Female Spy* by Judith L. Pearson, a biography of Hall; *Code Name Pauline: Memoirs of a World War II Special Agent* by Pearl Witherington Cornioley, an autobiography that details the exploits of an SOE spy in France; and *Women Heroes of World War II: 26 Stories of Espionage, Sabotage, Resistance, and Rescue* by Kathryn J. Atwood, which profiles numerous daring women who fought the Nazis throughout Europe.

Both the SOE and OSS recruited, trained, and deployed female agents during WWII. The British SOE was formed in July 1940, while the American OSS followed less than two years later in June 1942 under official military order by President Franklin D. Roosevelt. The OSS was divided into several branches, including Secret Intelligence, X-2 Counter Espionage, and a Maritime Unit that specialized in sabotage-by-sea. However, the Covert Operations branch exists solely in the pages of this book.

There was another OSS branch—called Research and Development—that created many of the spy gadgets that Covert Ops employs, from silenced pistols to the L pill to the Aunt Jemima explosive. Aunt Jemima could actually be eaten and baked if necessary, although it wasn't recommended. (A military cook unknowingly ate a muffin made from the substance and nearly died.) Sodium pentothal, or "truth serum," wasn't developed by the OSS, but it was tested by its successor, the Central Intelligence Agency. The reliability of this chemical, however, is disputed.

Operation Zerfall is another fictional detail in this novel, but the *Wunderwaffe* program was very much real. The Third Reich hoped that their various "wonder weapons" would crush their enemies, such as a massive tank that towered four stories tall and a "sun gun" that would use solar rays to scorch Allied cities from space. Many of these ideas, understandably, never made it past the design stage. Additionally, while the Nazis (as well as some other Axis powers) did the unthinkable and experimented on humans during the war, Dr. Nacht's program to create sleeper agents and infiltrate the U.S. government is fiction.

The wartime French government has a unique and controversial place in the history of WWII. After the Nazi takeover in 1940, Paris remained the official French capital, but the government itself moved to the spa town of Vichy, where its leaders willingly collaborated with the Germans. On paper the Vichy regime oversaw all of France, but in reality the country was split into two halves: the southern *zone libre*, or "Free Zone," led by Vichy leaders, and the northern *zone occupée*, or "Occupied Zone," which was run by the Nazis. But after the Allies launched Operation Torch in 1942, the Germans decided to seize authority of the Free Zone as well.

Life in wartime France was very difficult for most people, which I've tried to show through Lucie's eyes. Rationing abounded and blackouts were widespread and inconsistent. Able-bodied French workers were transported to Germany and forced into hard labor, while

French "undesirables" like Jews and Communists were sent to intern-ment camps—where many awaited deportation to death camps like Auschwitz. Books that capture what life was like in Nazi-occupied France include *When Paris Went Dark: The City of Light Under German Occupation, 1940–1944* by Ronald C. Rosbottom, and *Americans in Paris: Life and Death Under Nazi Occupation* by Charles Glass. The latter introduced me to Sylvia Beach, an American expat who opened a bookstore in Paris called Shakespeare and Company. That shop was closed in 1940 and—alas—it never had a hidden basement where the OSS could set up shop. Yet the spirit of Sylvia Beach lives on. In 1964, another American expat in Paris renamed his bookstore Shakespeare and Company in honor of Beach. You can visit the shop at 37 rue de la Bûcherie.

The North African front of WWII is often overshadowed by the histories of the European and Pacific theaters, but the battles fought in these campaigns (from Egypt and Libya to Morocco, Algeria, and Tunisia) swung the war in the Allies' favor. On November 8, 1942, Allied forces launched Operation Torch, a major attack on Vichy-held French North Africa. The Allied generals expected little resistance, but the Vichy French forces initially pushed back. However, after a few days of fighting, they ultimately aligned with the Allies. After Operation Torch concluded, the North African campaign stretched into Tunisia and lasted until May 1943, ending with the surrender of 250,000 Axis troops. This final victory allowed for the Allied inva-sion of Sicily that summer, which marked the beginning of the end of the Axis Powers. Rick Atkinson's Pulitzer Prize–winning book, *An*

Army at Dawn: The War in North Africa, 1942-1943, is the seminal work on this period, and I consulted it often to understand what a soldier like Theo would've experienced.

At the close of the war, many Allied spies returned to ordinary lives. Some married and raised children. Others wrote books (like Roald Dahl, former British Security Coordination) or took up the culinary arts (like Julia Child, former OSS). Then there were others, like Virginia Hall, who continued their work in the intelligence community. The OSS may have been shuttered at the war's end, but in its place sprang the CIA, for which Hall worked as an intelligence analyst. I'd like to think that Lucie would've followed a similar path, serving her country and making Theo proud and breaking the notions of what a woman could or couldn't do.

ACKNOWLEDGMENTS

To the women of the OSS and SOE, thank you for your courage. You are heroes, plain and simple.

To the Allied veterans of WWII, especially the ones who served in North Africa, thank you for your service. Your bravery will never be forgotten.

To Jody Corbett, thank you for being the editor that every writer hopes for—smart, passionate, insightful, and kind. I feel so lucky to work with you!

To the entire Scholastic team, thank you for your hard work in turning my Word document into a real book! A special shout-out to Carol Ly for making it look so beautiful. It's such a dream come true to be a part of the Scholastic family.

To Jim McCarthy, thank you for being Mr. Agent Awesome. I'm so grateful to have you in my corner.

To Sonja Gogic, thank you for being an amazing friend and for taking such wonderful care of my little "crankopotamus." I couldn't have written this book without you.

To Amanda Fein and Allison Young, thank you for cheering me on during my entire writing journey. You are the two best friends a girl could ever wish for.

To Ellen Oh, thank you for the many lunch dates and writing sessions we've had over the years. I thank my lucky stars for our friendship.

To Robin Talley, thank you for reading an early excerpt of this manuscript and for offering your encouragement. I needed to hear it!

To Dr. Paul Kerry, Julia Cain, Monte Fairbanks, Andrew Whitlock, and Franziska Patterson, thank you for helping me with the French and German translations in this novel. All mistakes are my own.

To Kristy Tung, thank you for being the perfect sister. I look forward to our adventures eating cheese and pastries across France one day!

To Aimee Rose Richmond, thank you for sharing the first twenty months of your life with this book. It has been a true joy watching you grow, and maybe one day we will read this novel together—although first I need to teach you the alphabet.

To Justin Richmond, thank you for being you: my first reader, my other half, my best friend. I love you very much.

ABOUT THE AUTHOR

Caroline Tung Richmond is the author of *The Only Thing to Fear*, as well as a freelancer writer.

A self-proclaimed history nerd and cookie connoisseur, Caroline lives on a mountainside in Virginia with her husband, their daughter, and Otto von Bismark, the family dog—named for the German chancellor (naturally).